Love will find a way...

WOOD

CATHRYN FOX

LAUREN HAWKEYE

Dear Reader,

One summer evening as I was waiting for my husband to get home, I get a text from Lauren Hawkeye. The exchange went something like this.

Lauren: *Wanna co-write something fun.*

Lauren: *Or just ignore me, because I'm insane.*

Me: *I'm in.*

Lauren. *Sheik Prince, Billionaire, Biker...how about a logger?*

Me: *A logger....ooh.*

Lauren. *And we would call it Wood. Bwa hahaha.*

Me: *Yes on Wood...OMG, yes.*

Lauren: *I was joking. But okay LOL.*

Lauren: *I'm picturing a sweaty man, with an axe on the cover*

Ten minutes later the cover comes through

Lauren: *I think I'm in love.*

Me: *OMG, Freaking LOVE!!*

Later that night my husband got home, and I looked at him and said, Lauren and I are writing a lumberjack story. He shook his head and said, I can't leave you two alone for a second without you getting in to trouble.

And that is how this all got started.

We were originally going to write a hot erotic lumberjack story and put it out last October, but as we plotted it grew, became an epic love story, which we fondly refer to as Outlander meets Sons of Anarchy—Lumberjack style.

We're excited to introduce to London and Wood, and take you back in time where you'll get swept away by the beauty of Cape Breton Highland's, Nova Scotia, and lose yourself in a love story so epic, it spans centuries.

Cathryn

CHAPTER ONE

Archaeological Dig

L AST WEEK, UPON arriving in the Cape Breton Highlands, the quiet was what hit me first. The sounds of civilization were there, of course, but they were muffled, as though the entire island had been wrapped in a thick layer of wet wool. We'd arrived after dark, so I hadn't been able to see much of anything through the creeping fingers of fog curling through the air, and the briny scent of salt had added to the sensation that I was stepping into an entirely different world. In the morning, however, as I walked to the motel's diner, I was able to see the rolling hills upholstered in velvety green. Craggy spears of rock jutted out over the water, and the smooth mirror surface of the lake itself was so clear I could see the stones pebbling the bottom. I'd felt like Dorothy, landing in Oz.

But I wasn't Dorothy, and this wasn't Oz. No, this was another dig, in yet another part of the world, one I'd been given no choice but to attend by my two overly-enthusiastic archaeologist parents. They'd never stopped to consider that perhaps I didn't want to go to the chilly autumn dig on Cape Breton Island, a tiny spit of land on the eastern coast of Canada.

I was a bit of a slow starter because it hadn't really occurred to me until now, in my twenties, to kick back at the rules and restrictions that my parents had pressed down on me my entire life. I'd started to see, from viewing friends with their families, that I didn't need to do everything I was told anymore. I didn't have to share every detail of my life with them. It occurred to me, actually, that doing so was more than a bit weird.

Still, I hadn't pushed back against this dig. Not because I particularly wanted to go to Canada, a place I knew nothing about apart from the fact that it was supposed to be really freaking cold and that they ate weird things, like gravy and cheese curds on their French fries. Ew. No, I'd gone along with the job that I wasn't given a choice in because I wanted the money, which was slightly better than decent.

My parents were both from old money. Money wasn't an issue for me... as long as I did what they wanted.

I was no longer okay with that. I couldn't see the future, so I had no idea what was to come—maybe one day I'd decide that I wanted to be an archaeologist after all. That said, it wasn't what I wanted now. I wanted to use the money from this dig to turn my photography hobby into something more serious, which my parents would never be okay with.

Yes, if I wanted to be independent, I could have

gone and gotten a job that had nothing to do with caves and rocks and old bones. If I was honest with myself, I'd taken this job because of the professor heading up the dig.

I was going to finally get to work with Dr. Sean Alexander. The first time I'd met him, I'd been a gawky twelve-year-old with long blond braids and hips and boobs that had developed faster than the other girls in my class. He'd been twenty-two, pursuing his master's degree in—you guessed it—archaeology, under my mother's tutelage.

My parents had invited him to dinner. He'd winked at me from behind those sexy wire-rimmed glasses, and I'd been a goner. Every time I'd seen him since then, the little flickering flame of my crush would flare brightly again, even though I'd heard enough over the years to know that he never lacked for female attention.

And this time, when he'd asked for me to be the dig's photographer, and looked me over with those delicious chocolatey-brown eyes, I'd detected a decidedly flirtatious spark in them.

I was twenty-two now—definitely old enough. The notion made my skin flush all over every time I thought of it.

"London." I shook my head at myself. Yes, this dig paid well and might lead to a sexy little romance I felt I deserved after my years slogging around the world, digging up artifacts. But the biggest bonus for me was that the location had some stunning scenery that I wanted to capture on camera.

I needed a portfolio of my best work to apply to the

fine arts program, and Polaroids of ancient tibias and femurs weren't going to cut it. I'd been familiar with cameras since I was old enough to hold one. Now, though, I thought that I wanted to create art with the pictures I took, not just document bones and rock shards.

I winced at the thought as I traced a finger over the cheap laminate of the diner table. My parents… they weren't going to understand my change of heart. They were both archaeologists, and my grandfathers on both sides had been in the field, too. I was third generation, and for my entire life, the esteemed Drs. Fiona and Cody Winters had assumed that their daughter would one day be Dr. London Winters, as well.

Yeah, they weren't going to take this well.

The jingling bell over the diner door intruded on my thoughts, and I quietly slid the shots I'd taken over the past week into the file, hiding the evidence. My parents had paid for this dig, so ultimately they were the bosses of everyone here. I wouldn't put it past someone to rat me out, telling them my attention was focused more on photos of the vast, silvery lake and the craggy hills that surrounded it than on the artifacts being excavated.

When I was five or six years old—I couldn't exactly remember—we'd been on a dig in Cairo. My parents had been down in one of the deep pits, and they'd been shouting up to me at the top as they uncovered pottery shards.

Far more interested in my toy monster truck, which reminded me of some of the trucks the guys on the dig had, I hadn't displayed the appropriate attention.

Thinking that this was a good moment to impress upon me the wonders of his field, Dad had hauled himself out of the pit and pulled me over to where a rough table had been set up.

"The things we find in these places, London, they're so much more interesting than a toy from the grocery store." He'd tried to hold my attention. It hadn't worked. Frustrated, he'd picked up something that was resting on the table, something he found fascinating—a human skull someone had brought along for reference. Grabbing my truck from my hand, he'd waved the skull in front of my face. "Look! Look at the wonderful things we find!"

I'd Hulk-smashed that ancient skull with the truck, and had never lived that moment down. As I grew older, other kids who'd been dragged to the digs had teased me relentlessly. My father had expected, I think, that I'd clap my hands with wonder and delight. Instead, I'd let out an ear-splitting scream and burst into hysterical tears as I looked at those human remains.

I still had nightmares about those empty eye sockets, the way the wired jaw had jiggled.

No, I didn't think I was going to get much support when I switched my major. Assuming I got into the program, of course.

Footsteps caught my attention, and I tapped my fingers over the folder holding my secret. I was anticipating the newcomer to be Sean—I *might* have even timed my visit to the diner accordingly—but my fingers itched to sweep the folder off the table, just in case.

Sean was hot, but he was also on my parents' payroll.

When I finally tore my stare away from the folder, I found not Sean, but a stranger. My gaze landed on a burly guy who looked to have a few years on my twenty-two. Resembling nothing so much as a rugby player, he had dark auburn hair cropped close to his head and a nose crooked from being broken. His gaze slid over the packed diner, filled with tourists soaking up the last of the summer, and landed on the empty chair across from me. He moved with a grace a guy his size shouldn't have as he cut across the room, towering over me and my table.

"This chair taken?" He slid his backpack off his shoulder and let it dangle from his hand as he waited for me to answer.

"No." I shifted nervously in my seat, my early-morning serenity shattered by his presence. Up until college, I'd been homeschooled on dig sites. *Awkward* was a generous word for how I functioned around the opposite sex—yet another reason that Sean showing interest in *me* had had my stomach tying itself into tight knots of anticipation.

"Emmett Murdoch." He dropped his solid body into the chair and shoved his backpack beneath his feet. "Just got here this morning. I'm a grad student at University of Colorado, here for the dig."

"Nice to meet you." I swallowed thickly. He seemed to be waiting for me to say more, so I mimicked what he'd told me. "I'm here for the dig too. Penn State, undergrad."

"Yeah, thought so." With a nod, he gestured to the backpack at my feet. Little did he know it held the Nikon camera that felt so right in my hand, as well as the Polaroid camera and film that I used for documenting our finds.

He grabbed the small menu stuck between the salt and pepper shaker, and I noticed a slight tremble in his fingers. "I'm starving. What's good here?"

"Everything is good here." He cast me a dubious look, and I laughed, some of my nerves evaporating. I held my hand up and waved it around the establishment. "A hotel with honest-to-God beds. A place that serves hot food. Pure luxury compared to sleeping in a tent in the middle of nowhere and eating MRE's or freeze-dried broccoli, don't you think?"

I'd done both. Let me tell you, an MRE—Meal, Ready to Eat—should have been called a Meal, Rarely Edible. Yuck.

"So, what's your story?" he asked, without taking his eyes off the morning specials. His hands were definitely shaking a bit. I furrowed my brow, wondering, but I barely knew the guy—not my business.

"My story?" Distracted by his question, I reached for my coffee cup and took a small drink of the now cold brew. I shrugged and sipped anyway—I'd had worse.

"Your story." When he flicked me a glance from over the top of the greasy plastic–covered menu, I couldn't help sucking in a tiny breath. His eyes were hazel, heavy on the green, and something in the way he looked at me caught my attention. "Did you have a grandpa who gave you an arrowhead? Did you visit a dinosaur museum for a field trip and fall in love with the idea of being the one to discover bones? Did you close your eyes and stab a finger into the course catalog and just land on archaeology?"

Before I could answer, the waitress in the hideous pumpkin orange uniform with white trim stepped up to us. Refilling my coffee, she flashed a smile at Emmett, and I sure didn't miss the way her eyes lingered.

She looked him over, a flirtatious smile curving her lips. Jesus, she had to be fifty. *Cougar much?*

"Here for the dig?" she asked as she filled his coffee cup to the brim, then oh-so-helpfully handed him a fresh bowl brimming with packets of cream and sugar.

I eyed my bowl, which had one solitary packet of Splenda left in it. She didn't seem to care about that.

Emmett nodded, either oblivious to the way she was blatantly checking him out, or choosing to ignore it. "I'll have a bagel, with cream cheese and a glass of orange juice. A big one."

My stomach took that moment to grumble, a reminder that I'd been sitting here drinking coffee all morning. "I'll have a bagel, too. Toasted with butter, please."

The waitress jotted our order down, and when she disappeared, Emmett turned those bright, curious eyes back on me. "So, your story?"

I reached into my bag and pulled out the Polaroid camera Sean had given me. "Dig photographer."

Steeling myself, I waited for the *look*. The one that lumped me in with all the 'lesser' people. Only scientists had beautiful minds, after all, and I was just an undergrad, a grunt, and even worse, the daughter of the people with the money.

Not a great combo for making friends. I'd long ago adopted an attitude that said I didn't want any, but I knew how I felt inside.

The look didn't come. Instead, his mossy-colored eyes narrowed and scrutinized my face intently like he was searching the recesses of his mind. "You're London."

I nodded. "That's right."

"Your parents are funding this dig."

"Nepotism at its best," I said before he could, wincing inside. *Damn it.* When he lifted his head to meet my gaze, his cute dimples flashed in a smile, sending a little shiver of something through me. "Dr. and Dr. Winters wouldn't have it any other way."

A strange sensation hit my gut like a sucker punch when I took a moment to look at those dimples. They contrasted with his ruggedness in a super sexy way.

He cocked his head. "It's only nepotism if you're not qualified."

I couldn't help but crack a smile, and as I did, I felt the outermost layer of my shell start to crumble. "You're saying I'm qualified?"

He reached for his coffee, but the shaking of his hand had intensified, and his fingers hit the cheap ceramic, knocking the cup over.

"Shit!" he cursed, and we both jumped to our feet. I grabbed my file before the coffee spread, crying out in dismay as the pictures I'd been hiding slid from the folder, sailing to the ground.

Emmett gathered a handful of napkins and tossed them over the muddy puddle. The bitter scent of burnt coffee permeated the air. "Sorry. I need—"

His voice fell off as I dropped to my knees, scrambling to collect my photos, shoving them back into the folder before he could see them. A large hand, rough with callouses, closed over mine to stop me.

"You took these?"

CHAPTER TWO

Old Friends

M Y HEART THUDDED at the genuine intrigue in his voice. "Yes."

He picked up a picture of Sean, one of many that I'd secretly taken, where the long-time object of my affection was lost in thought, staring down at a tableful of potsherds. Those big, rough hands plucked a few more of the prints off the linoleum. Students studying on the campus grass, unobserved by anyone but me. A boy holding his mother's hand as they walked down the street.

"I don't know much about photography, but I like these." He jabbed a finger at a self-portrait, where I'd set the camera to record my slightly distorted self in the mirror. "This one. I like this one the best. Except I don't know why you're hiding back there. A picture of you should show everyone your gorgeous face."

He thinks I'm gorgeous?

Unfamiliar warmth flared inside me. "I…thank you,"

I said for lack of anything else. No one had ever complimented me on my work before.

No one had ever called me gorgeous before.

"I like to take pictures of people when they're unaware. You know, pictures that tell a story of a person, a place, a moment in time."

He gave a low, slow whistle. "This is a hobby?"

"Um," I began, hardly able to believe I was about to tell him my deepest-darkest secret, yet compelled to do just that. He blinked at me, waiting for me to continue, but the bell over the door clanged again, obnoxiously loud, capturing my attention.

Dr. Sean Alexander was dressed for the dig in a heavy sweater and a well-worn backpack, those glasses of his pushed up his nose. When his eyes met mine, and he cast me a wicked little smile, I felt an answering tug of excitement, even though I was still glowing from Emmett's compliment.

The elation dimmed a little when I noted who was behind him. Mairi McDonnaugh, a local woman descended from the people we'd come here to study, followed tight on his heels. From the way those gorgeous almond-shaped jewel-green eyes of hers watched Sean, I knew that the stunning brunette with the alabaster skin wasn't immune to his good looks and charm, either.

"London." Sean's deep voice was excited. He extended a hand to help me up, and once I was on my feet, his thumb rubbed over my palm slowly, sensuously, deliberately.

The intimate touch took me by surprise, and my body tightened as I stole a quick glance at Emmett, who was scanning the diner, searching for the waitress who had disappeared despite her almost neon uniform.

"What is it?" My attention was torn between Sean and Emmett, and that puzzled me.

"Do you have the Polaroid with you?"

I nodded quickly. "In my bag."

"Good, come on." He grabbed me by the hand and started tugging me toward the door. Just that morning I would have gone easily and with a smile, but this time I found that I didn't care to be grabbed at.

Digging my heels in, I stayed put. Sean glanced at me in surprise, and I shrugged irritably. "We've ordered."

Only then did Sean turn to the other man. Emmett was still sitting in the booth, but he was watching Sean and me far more intently than I'd expected.

"Emmett Murdoch." Finally he stood, holding out a hand.

"Dr. Sean Alexander." Did I imagine it, or did Sean give Emmett a once-over as the men exchanged handshakes? I knew he put a bit of emphasis on the title. "Glad you made it."

Surely I had imagined it. What I was pretty sure I *wasn't* imagining was that Mairi couldn't stop glaring at me.

Just like I hadn't had a ton of experience interacting with the opposite sex, I wasn't real great on deflecting girl aggression, either. I chose to smile at her as sweetly as I could and then stay the hell away.

"You two know each other?" Sean's brow was tight as his head bobbed back and forth between Emmett and me.

"No, we just met," I answered quickly, but when Emmett cast me a sidelong glance, a twinkle in his eyes like we shared an inside joke, a strange sensation whipped through me.

Had we met before? Before I could ask, the waitress showed up with our bagels, breaking the moment. "Looks like our food is here," I said to Sean, gesturing to the waitress.

"We'll take it with us," Emmett said. I looked at him sharply as he spoke. He looked kind of pale to me, but then, I'd only just met him—I couldn't say what he usually looked like.

I nodded in agreement instead of commenting on it, glancing down at my boots. Damn it, my well-worn hiking boots were back in my room, along with my warm clothes.

"We need to get a move on." Mairi touched Sean's shoulder, and he turned his attention her way. She slid her arm into his as she guided him to the door, but I was pretty sure I caught a little triumphant flicker of her gaze my way again.

I frowned at their backs. Sean didn't exactly seem upset with the beautiful woman pressed against his side.

As I stared, Emmett tossed some bills onto the table and shook his head when I offered him my share. He shoved our bagels into his bag and frowned when he caught the way I was looking between the door and my footwear. I needed boots, and these technically fit the bill, but their slender heels and lack of ankle support made them far more suitable for a stroll through the mall.

Or for looking pretty to impress a certain archaeologist. *Damn, damn, damn.*

"You need to change." Emmett scowled at my ankle booties.

"No time." Resigning myself to sore feet for the rest of the day, I rolled my feet around in the pretty shoes. "Look. It's just a small heel. I'll be fine."

"London." Emmett swung his backpack onto his back, scowling. I noticed that he was still shaking a bit. Did he have some kind of muscle tremor? Was he sick? "You're going to break an ankle in those boots."

"You're obviously starving, and you're not taking the time to eat."

He opened his mouth to reply, but the bell over the door clanged again, cool air from outside colliding with the oven-heat in.

I glanced up to see Sean and Mairi disappear through it, neither bothering to look back to see if we were coming. "We'd better hurry before we lose those two."

Emmett sighed, but he followed me to the door, reaching a long arm over my shoulder to push it open for me. This pressed him up against my back—well, really my backpack—for just a moment, but the split-second touch made me warm all over.

Sean, now Emmett. Jesus, my hormones were out of control. I guessed that was what happened when you were still a virgin at the age of twenty-two.

Shaking off my thoughts, I pushed the swinging glass door, catching the excitement in Sean's voice as he and Mairi started into the woods, up a narrow, stony footpath. As they chattered eagerly about the king they hoped to find, we hurried after them with a brisk stride, and I cursed when my heel slipped on a rock. Emmett caught me by the arm and simply hauled me back up, righting me without breaking pace. I muttered my thanks, flushing a little.

Not wanting to stumble again, I forced all my attention on putting one foot in front of the other. Right, left. Slow and steady. No more falling. No need for Emmett to wrap those strong hands around my arms again.

"You doing okay?" Emmett's voice broke through my thoughts, and I snapped back to reality. I was sliding all over the place on the loose gravel of the path, the small heel on my boots making it hard to stay steady.

"Yeah, I'm fine." I was, for the moment at least. If anything, he was the one who still looked a little shaking, but when I looked ahead of us and saw that Sean and Mairi had started climbing the massive hill that jutted out over the Bras d'Or Lake, I groaned quietly, distracted by the long hike ahead.

These boots weren't made for walking, and I could already feel a hot spot forming on my right heel, eager to turn into a painful blister. But Sean was clearly excited, and I didn't want to be the one slowing down the crew.

A light sheen of sweat appeared on Emmett's brow, which I thought was strange—we were hiking at a brisk pace, but the air had a definite bite. And I may or may not have taken a few good sidelong looks at the well-defined muscle that I could see beneath the thin fabric of his T-shirt.

Ahead of us, Sean and Mairi had reached the top of the massive hill. The low murmur of their voices traveled back down to me on the chilly breeze coming off the lake, and I realized abruptly that I only heard the sound of gravel crunching under one pair of boots—mine.

"Emmett?" Coming to an abrupt halt, I turned and craned my head around in every direction. Emmett had stopped about twenty feet back down the hill. He stood still; his shoulders slumped forward, his backpack at his feet.

What the hell is he doing?

My feet wept as I started back down the hill, the change in angle putting pressure on all the wrong spots. A glance behind me showed me Sean and Mairi still engaged in conversation, oblivious to what was happening behind them.

"Hey!" Shouting to Emmett, I slowly picked my way back over the rocks. "What's up? Did you find something?"

He raised his head as I approached, his movements sluggish. His brow furrowed slightly as he watched me close the space between us. The light sheen of sweat that I'd noted at the start of our walk was now a full slick of dampness over his forehead and in his hair. His skin was chalky, and as I skidded down the path, he sank to his knees as though swimming through molasses.

"What's wrong?" I asked in alarm, ignoring the stabbing heat left by my boots as I slipped down to my knees in front of him. "Are you sick? Do you need me to go get Sean?"

He shook his head, then looped his fingers through one of the straps of his backpack. Trying to tug it into his lap, he mumbled some words that didn't seem to have any connection when it didn't move.

"There." He tried to tug again. Adrenaline thickened my fingers as I grabbed the bag myself, tearing open the zipper. The sound rasped at the thin air. "There. In."

Forget Sean. Emmett needed help now, and it seemed I was the only one who could give it to him. Even though I wasn't sure what I was supposed to do, I upended the bag, hoping the contents would help me figure out what the hell was happening so I could help him.

Water bottles, tissues, granola bars, juice boxes, and our uneaten bagels hit the ground—his backpack was like the best-prepared mom purse I'd ever seen. He grabbed a box of apple juice, trying to detach the plastic-wrapped straw with shaking fingers.

"Here." Heart thudding, I tore off the plastic, then stabbed the straw through the foil-covered hole, shoving it into his hands. He drained it in two sips, and I opened another, ready and prepared for when he needed it. I still wasn't sure what was happening, but no way was he going back into that fog if I could help it. He sighed with relief as he finished the second with a loud slurp, his hands resting on his knees.

I watched, wide-eyed, as a hint of pink started to creep back into his face. Adrenaline rush starting to recede, I sat back on my heels, wincing as the leather of my boots scraped over the forming blisters, and dusted my hands on my jeans.

"Any better?" Cautiously, I followed his movements as he tore open a granola bar with his teeth. Only then did he look up at me, nodding with relief and a little embarrassment.

"Thanks for that." Clenching the unwrapped bar in his teeth, he haltingly unfolded his limbs and stood, offering a hand to help me back up as well. I took it gingerly since I wasn't entirely sure yet that he wasn't going to fall right back over. "That was a bad one."

"A bad one?" I echoed as I watched him sling his bag back onto his back, half wanting to offer to carry it for him.

"I'm diabetic." Working the last of his bar into his mouth, he chewed and swallowed before continuing. "That back there was a sugar crash. I should have taken the time to eat the damn bagel. Stupid of me."

I gave him a reassuring smile, not wanting him to feel stupid. "I'm the one hiking a freaking mountain in Italian leather ankle booties."

Glancing down at my feet, he snorted out a laugh. His gaze continued up, over my denim-clad legs, my curvy torso in my snug blue T-shirt.

I was pretty sure that was appreciation in his stare. Why was it lighting something inside me that Sean's actual touch back at the diner hadn't?

My gaze slid over his body as we started back up the hill. "Does Sean know? Mairi? Someone? Just in case you're digging and that happens again? I might not always be around to rescue you," I teased. Truthfully, I wasn't going to be responsible for him falling into one of the pits and leaving his bones layered on top of ancient ones.

His smile was a little abashed. "Yeah, I told Sean when I applied to the dig. But I'm usually a lot more careful—do blood sugar checks a few times a day. And I'm on a pump. I'm good, I promise."

"Okay." My ankle twisted on a rock again—possibly the same damn rock—and again Emmett caught me and hauled me upright.

"Let's just get us both to the top in one piece, eh?" His smirk was a challenge.

"You've been in Canada too long already, *eh?*" I snorted in response.

We fell silent for a moment; then Emmett broke the quiet. "London?"

"Yeah?"

"Why are you studying archaeology when you want to be a photographer?"

I laughed, but it held no humor. "It's what my parents want."

"What about what you want?"

"I want to switch to fine arts," I blurted out, immediately shaking my head. "I don't know why I just told you that."

He shrugged like it was nothing. "So, why don't you?"

"I guess I have to prove I have what it takes first."

He stopped walking, and my heart jolted in my chest. Oh, God, he wasn't going to crash again, was he? I turned to him, noted the intelligence in his eyes as his gaze moved over my face. "I think you're capable and brave enough to do anything you set your mind to." My heart missed a beat as I absorbed his words. No one had ever said anything like that to me before. "Even overcoming a childhood phobia to save a reckless boy from a poisonous snake."

As soon as the words left his mouth, it hit me. I did know Emmett. We'd met before.

"Oh my God." I stumbled for the third freaking time as Emmett's words sank in, and as I'd already come to expect, he grabbed me to keep me from face-planting into the dust. Planting my feet on the uneven ground, I blinked up at him. "The boy with the snake. That was you."

"My fourteen-year-old self would be highly insulted to be referred to as a boy," Emmett smirked at me before jerking his head toward the top of the hill. "Look, Sean and Mairi are almost at the top. We'd better get going."

I started to walk again, but my steps felt unsteady. It had been years since I'd thought about it, but those few lightning-fast moments from so long ago were nonetheless tattooed into my memory. That Emmett was *that* boy tilted my world on its axis.

We'd been in the Kalahari Desert—a vicious choice of location, at least to my worldly ten-year-old mind. By that age, I'd been so many places and seen so many things that I wasn't easily scared. Still, the safety announcement reminding everyone to keep an eye out for black mamba snakes had probed at a tender phobia I'd picked up in Greece when I was four, and my bare feet accidentally found a harmless but disgustingly squishy snake on a morning walk.

Black mamba snakes are highly venomous. Not even the news that they preferred to leave humans alone unless cornered or threatened soothed the bone-deep terror.

Because of this fear, I'd stuck close to the dig site. There had only been one other kid on that dig—a boy of fourteen, a really cute older boy with floppy, dark red hair that hung into his eyes and an ego that didn't allow him to hang out with ten-year-old girls.

His name was Emmett. And one day as I'd hovered around the perimeter of the site, I'd heard him scream.

Most of the adults were down in one of the pits and didn't hear. I did, though, and the icy terror in his voice jolted me past my fear. Running off in the direction of the sound, I found Emmett, back pressed against a camelthorn tree.

Raised up to waist level on the ground in front of him was a ten-foot long black mamba. Its obsidian eyes glittered angrily as its neck flaps fluttered, the sound like dry paper in the still afternoon air.

When it hissed and opened its inky black mouth, and Emmett's panicked stare met my own, adrenaline took over. Bending, I snatched up a fallen tree branch as thick as my arm and taller than I was. With no idea what I was doing, I threw it beside the snake, pulling his attention away from Emmett with the dry thump of its landing.

"Back away! Slowly!" The blood was pulsing through my veins so fiercely that I was sure I was going to puke. "Now! No, don't run!"

I followed my own advice, backing slowly away as the snake surveyed the branch, then me, then Emmett again. Emmett held up his hands, palms out, as he slid along the tree trunk and, finally, in my direction. When he reached me, our sweaty fingers tangled together as the snake hissed at the pair of us.

I choked out a cry of pure relief as it finally decided we weren't a threat and slithered away into the tall golden grass. Emmett and I looked at each other wide-eyed before sprinting back to camp, back to the adults, where the full force of what had happened hit me, and I vomited into one of the pits, earning me a week sorting field notes as punishment.

We hadn't ever spoken about it—at least, not until now. "Speaking of my fourteen-year-old self, I was an ass back then." He brushed his shoulder against mine companionably. The warmth that the small touch generated went a long way toward heating the chill that the bitter wind was working into my very bones.

"You weren't an ass! You were just a teenage boy," I protested. For inexplicable reasons, I needed to prove to him that that wasn't what I'd thought, so I did the unthinkable—I shared the story of my monster truck Hulk-smash on the human skull. When his lips twitched, and he finally cracked up, I couldn't help but laugh along with him. "That right there? That was being an ass."

"You were five." His voice was full of dry amusement that quickly turned to something else. "And seriously. I never thanked you."

The sincerity in his voice made me fumble again, and I growled with frustration over my idiotic choice of footwear.

"How about you thank me by getting me to the top of this damn hill in one piece?" I was tempted to just tug the offensive boots off, but then Emmett held out a hand.

"Come on. Let me help you the rest of the way." When I accepted his hand, he twined his fingers through mine the way we had that day in the African desert so long ago. "I won't let you fall."

CHAPTER THREE

Discovering the Tomb

TEN FEET FROM the entrance, the air outside the cave seemed to vibrate.

I slowed my steps as the buzz shimmered through my body, the energy in the air unlike anything I'd ever felt before.

"Wow." Beside me, Emmett stilled, untangling his fingers from mine to shade his eyes with a hand as he looked around. I did the same—the light up here was thin and blindingly bright, and the breeze that had been brisk on the lower reaches of the hill was a sharp, icy gale here at the peak. My skin felt thick and stiff, but as Sean rushed toward me, excitement in every line of his face, I forgot about my lack of warmer clothes, even as the palm that had been pressed against Emmett's tingled.

I was giving myself whiplash.

"London, I need you and the camera inside right away." He gestured wildly, and I couldn't help but grin at the slightly manic expression on his face. "Isn't this amazing? We think our group is the first to set foot in here since the tomb was intentionally sealed."

"The tomb?" Emmett and I echoed at the same time.

Sean raked a hand through his hair, something he repeatedly did when he was turning things over in his busy brain. He already looked disheveled—no doubt by the end of the day he'd look like a hedgehog.

"Mairi spoke with the rest of the remaining local clan descendants two days ago, and we just got permission this morning to clear the entry to the cave." Sean beamed.

I pinched my lips together tightly as the woman in question slipped out from the entrance to the cave and crossed to Sean, standing a little closer than I thought was appropriate.

"This has always been the most sacred of places for our people," Mairi said. "But no one in living memory has been inside since it was sealed." Her eyes beamed with as much excitement as Sean's as she looped her arm through his. "We've had a crew removing rocks, and they just finished. And what we've found inside is just… unbelievable. So important to the history of my people."

She seemed genuinely excited, but I couldn't focus on anything except her arm through Sean's—and the fact that he wasn't shaking her off. I sucked in a breath, about to… well, I don't know, but Emmett placed a hand on my shoulder, his skin warm on the ice of my own.

"Hey." He arched an eyebrow before smirking at me. "I owe you a favor. This is it. Do not Hulk-smash the ancient tomb. Got it?"

I rolled my eyes as he teased me, but his words caused my stomach to twist. Not that I cared about him poking fun—no, I'd permitted him to when I'd told him. No, what sat uncomfortably in my gut was that he was acknowledging my crush on Sean.

Is it that obvious?

And had I imagined the heat that had sparked as our fingers tangled on the last stretch of the hill?

I shivered as I turned it over in my mind. Sean mistook the reaction. He put his hand on my arm, but it didn't quite warm me the way Emmett's had.

"Jesus, London, you're going to get hypothermia." He removed his thick corduroy jacket, then his russet woolen sweater, putting the jacket back on and handing me the pile of wool. "Get inside the cave; it cuts off the wind."

"Thank you." I slid the sweater gratefully over my head, taking a moment to inhale the scent as I juggled my camera strap. Damp lambswool shouldn't have been all that pleasant but combined with the no-nonsense soap, the hint of his shaving cream that lingered, and the crisp scent of old books that seemed to follow him everywhere, I found it comforting. The wool was stiff and scratchy, but I snuggled into the voluminous folds and reveled in the warmth.

When I looked up, I met Emmett's eyes. As he eyed me in Sean's sweater, his lips pinched together, and I felt... surely that wasn't guilt?

Tearing my stare from Emmett, I tipped my head to see Sean, but his attention had strayed. I followed his gaze with my own and couldn't hold back the quiet gasp.

The entrance through which we'd ducked hadn't been that large, just high enough for a tall woman to stand in comfortably—Sean and Emmett had had to duck their heads. Immediately upon entering, though, the cavern opened up, the large room yawning open before us, its secrets only hinted at in the butter yellow light of the mining lamps that had been set up at intervals.

"Do you feel it?" Sean searched my face with those dark eyes, and for the first time in my life, I did feel the magic he'd always talked about. That my parents had sought like an addict in need of a fix.

"I do," I said, looking around with wide eyes. I didn't add that a person would have to be nothing more than the bones piled somewhere in this tomb not to feel something here, where the very air seemed thicker, enriched as it was with secrets of the past.

The section of the cave that we were standing in was roughly the size of my apartment back in Pennsylvania, though it seemed smaller since it was closed in. And there was so much to see that I didn't know where to look first.

Slender spikes punctuated the entire space, abstract fingers dangling from above and spearing mightily up from below. Around the latter, the floor was pock-marked with shallow dips and indentations, each of which held a small pool of water that reflected the artificial light back at me. The walls, uneven and worn smooth by time, were sheened with dampness as well, lending them a crystalline, almost mystical quality. They were lined with massive stone tablets, each etched with designs almost hidden by mats of green moss.

"Fascinating, aren't they?" Taking me by the elbow, Sean led me closer to one of the tablets. My fingers itched to stroke the design before me—a swirling kind of star—but knew from childhood experience that I'd get my hand slapped.

Don't touch, London. Don't touch.

I stuffed my fingers under the straps of my backpack to keep them still.

"What are they for? What is this place?" I shifted weight, my boot landing in one of the puddles of water and slipping. I caught myself, cursing under my breath—I'd have to be careful while I was here. "Did people live here?"

Sean pushed his glasses up on his nose, and I knew from the expression on his face that we were about to enter professor mode—but this time I was truly interested. "We've only just tapped the mysteries inside this cave, of course, but my initial inspection says no. No fire pits, no animal bones, no tool remnants—all things we'd expect to find at a settlement. In fact, we've already started finding those same things at the main site, as you saw earlier this week."

"So, what's the purpose of this, then?" I was interrupted by a shout, and Sean's hand dropped from my elbow as he turned and hurried toward the sound, leaving me forgotten in the thrill of discovery.

"What? What did you find?"

I followed him at a more cautious pace, mindful of my footwear. Still, something sizzled in my veins, and I found myself hurrying as well, following Sean to a narrow crack in the rock at the back of the cave.

The crack opened to a corridor, which started off slender and gradually widened into a second chamber. Sean, Mairi, Emmett and two team members I hadn't yet learned the names of, crowded together at the foot of a rock, hiding their finding from view.

"Hey, I want to see, too!" I rounded the cluster, coming up on Emmett's left side—and yelping with alarm when I saw what had everyone so excited. Mairi spared a moment to glare at me, though her attention was quickly drawn back to the find.

Bones.

A perfectly articulated skeleton reclined on one side of the wide rock. I'd seen bones before, of course, but never a full skeleton. Still, it seemed to me that every finger, every toe, every bone of the ribcage was there, in place and whole.

One of the skeleton's—the man's—hands had been laid palm down over where his heart would have been. The other was at his side, still fisted as if around the handle of a weapon.

"Is that an axe?" I couldn't help it—I leaned in to get a closer look at the shaftless blade, squawking with alarm when I almost lost my balance. Mairi glared at me again before Sean shuffled over to stand beside me, on the side where the axe head lay. Hand on the side of his glasses, he looked over the weapon with intense focus.

"It's the head of an axe, yes." He nodded and leaned even closer, though he was careful not to touch. "No sign of use on the blade. Elaborate design carved into the metal. I'd say this axe was ceremonial, made as a tribute before burial, and likely never used."

"That's a comfort," I muttered, earning me strange glances from everyone. "What? I for one am happy that this particular weapon doesn't have any blood on it."

"Only those high up in the hierarchy would be given a burial offering of this quality." He couldn't have packed more excitement into his voice if he tried. All but jumping up and down, he looked at Emmett, then Mairi, and finally at me. I blinked with surprise when I saw that his hands were shaking. "The axe he used day to day was likely passed down, to a son or a male of his choosing."

"Why not a daughter?" I started to ask and was shushed by Mairi as Sean continued to examine the remains.

"It's him. It has to be." He pointed to the lonely axe head, giving its master a weapon even in death. "*The king.*"

Sean and Mairi exchanged a glance and moved further up the slab of stone. I felt a stab of jealousy at their unconscious symmetry. Emmett caught my eye and tapped the skin right by his own—right. No Hulk-smashing the artifacts.

Sucking in a deep breath, I did my best to ignore the very obvious fact that Mairi had designs on Sean—because God, who didn't—and turned my attention back to the long-dead king. If it was him, and Sean was thorough enough that I didn't doubt his findings, even I had to admit that it was pretty cool. "So… what's with the rock?"

"Huh?" Emmett's stare followed the point of my finger.

"Well, it's a super wide rock. They clearly broke their backs hauling this massive thing in here for the king to have his eternal nap on, so why is he all the way on one side? Was someone else in here, too?"

The others blinked at me, then at each other. Sean, Mairi, and Emmett looked up at the wall above the head of the giant stone, and for the first time, I noticed the carvings there, the lines worked deeply into the stone as if to make sure they never faded.

I'd seen enough of my parents' findings to know that these pictures told a story. I was surprised to discover that I wanted to know what this one was.

"That's a very clever observation, London." Sean beamed at me before shoving those glasses up his nose again. He pointed at the uppermost carving. On it, primitive figures of a man and a woman stood side by side. "This is traditional burial symbolism, sometimes still used today. It indicates that he was married. It seems that this tomb was meant for this man and his wife."

"So, where is she?" I stared at the skeleton. The longer I was in the cave, the less grotesque the bones seemed to be. In fact, I felt a surge of righteous indignation that he'd been barred from having his love at his side for his eternal slumber. "If he was this king guy, wouldn't you think the people would have made sure to honor that?"

"Give me a minute." Mairi was too engrossed in the carvings to snap at me like she usually would. "I'll need photos and time to translate it all. But from what I can see…"

She shifted, and the bright light that one of the other

team members had brought into the small room refracted off the metal of the axe head. It seemed remarkably well preserved, which left me with another question.

"Why is he so… you know… perfect?" Again, I found my stare drawn back to the skeleton. I'd thought that people in centuries past had been shorter, smaller, and yet these bones indicated that this had been an incredibly large man, even by today's standards. And maybe it was because I knew he'd been a king, but even though only a shadow of who he had been remained, I swore that some of his power still echoed in the tiny room.

Emmett cocked his head, gesturing at me. "Hear that?"

I strained, tuning out the hushed conversation between Sean and Mairi, the footsteps of those in the chamber we'd just come from. There… there it was. The faintest lilt, the rhythmic lap of shallow waves against rock.

"How can we hear the lake in here?" Rock surrounded us—we were *in* the rock. The lake was far beneath.

"There are a couple of corridors that we haven't explored yet. I think one of them probably leads right out into the lake." Emmett pointed at the far wall of the chamber, where drops of condensation frosted the stone. "Dampness slows the rate of decomposition. That's likely why he's so well-preserved."

"Eew." Wrinkling my nose, I took an instinctive step back from the remains. Yeah, there was something unexpectedly beautiful about all of this, but still, the thought of a decomposing body was enough to make my stomach roll.

"How did you think he got like this?" Mairi took a moment to roll her eyes at me before gesturing again at the carvings. "Now if you don't mind, I think I have the gist of some of this."

"Don't let me stop you." My tone was bitchier than I intended, and Sean frowned at me. Pressing my lips together and crossing my arms over my chest, I waited for her to continue.

"I need the rock cleaned up before I can read all of it. But the carvings indicate that this man was an important leader and also an outsider." A hum of voices whipped through the room, and I looked quickly at Sean, who was grinning.

"That's confirmation." He gestured at Mairi to continue.

"His life was cut off too soon—that's what this says here, I'm sure of it. And he sacrificed himself for his people." She frowned at the carvings. "But the next part, about his love, it doesn't quite make sense."

The others were silent, waiting for her to decipher it, but after a moment, she shook her head in frustration. "He had a wife, his queen. She was a traveler from a distant land. But that's not possible. All of the lore in my family says that his love was a princess of my people, and they never married. Her death started the war."

"Maybe your family lore is wrong," I added helpfully, stiffening when she turned to glare at me. "You know what? I'm just going to start taking pictures."

"Thank you, London. Make sure you get it all, okay?"

Sean peered at me anxiously, his breath fogging his glasses. "Do you have extra film?"

I nodded before turning back to the corridor that had led us in here. I started when I reached the part where the rock started to narrow when something flickered across the corner of my vision—just a shadow, but a definite movement.

Yelping quietly, I spun around, expecting that Emmett had followed me. But no, he was still in the group clustered around the bones, intently examining the axe head. Looking up, he winked at me, and I smiled weakly in return, my heart pounding.

I was just jumpy from hanging out with a dead guy. Shaking my head, I started down the corridor again. The voices of the others grew fainter as I neared the first cavern, but Mairi's voice cut through just before I was out of earshot.

"It says that the king and queen were both lost to the people in the same battle, but it also says that she journeyed where he couldn't follow. They might be talking about heaven and hell. But there is no hell in the mythology of my people. This makes no sense." Mairi growled with frustration.

"No matter how I read it, though… she's not here."

CHAPTER FOUR

Dark Stranger

"LONDON?"

The voice cut through my concentration like an axe through the air, and I screeched, whirling around with my hand pressed to my suddenly thundering heart. Sean winced as the sound echoed off the enclosed space shrilly.

"Sorry. I thought you heard me." He gestured around the cavern, where I'd been taking photos for hours. I realized with a start that everyone else was gone. "I wasn't exactly quiet."

"Wow, I guess I was just... focused." Bending, I scooped up the teetering stack of Polaroids that I'd taken that day and held them out. "Here. I'm almost done."

"Wow. London, this is... above and beyond." He thumbed through the first few, nodding with satisfaction. "And these are great. You'd never know you had such crappy lighting in here. You've got a real eye for this."

"You think so?" I couldn't have held back the grin.

This, *this* was what I'd been searching for, the lovely glow of validation. "I got into it."

"I can tell." He tucked the stack of pictures into his backpack and checked his watch.

"You have somewhere to be?" I asked.

"Just some things to take care of."

"Go ahead. I need to get these done, anyway. You'll probably need them to work tonight, right?" He'd worked every night since we'd arrived, and I didn't expect tonight to be any different.

"Yeah, I want to look them over, but then I think I can take some time off." The flirtatious smile that curved his lips had my pulse skipping. "I thought we could go out for some dinner… the brochure in my room assures me that we can't go wrong with the glamorous local Chinese or Mexican restaurants."

Sean wants to take me to dinner.

"That sounds nice." I waited for the rush of elation. I'd crushed on him for years.

"Bring your camera." There was a wicked glint in his eyes.

"A working dinner?"

That smile again—more like a mischievous grin— and then he lightly brushed his lips over my own, but that was all it was, just the slightest brush. He hooked a finger in the strap of the camera. "Come here. Let's try something."

Anticipation whipped through me as he snuggled into my side. Not quite the ecstatic rush I'd been expecting at the culmination of so many years of wanting, but I couldn't deny the excitement gathering tightly in my belly. I ran my tongue over suddenly dry lips as he turned the camera around and fumbled to get a grip on it backward. It was clearly awkward, but he seemed so determined that I finally had to ask.

"*What* are you doing?"

The snap of the flash made me blink. The picture that the camera spat out featured Sean's eyes and my forehead.

"You're trying to take a selfie with this thing?" I arched an eyebrow, amused. "That's what cell phones are for. Just get yours out."

"Left it in the room." Stubbornly, he adjusted the camera. I rolled my eyes. Of course, he'd left it there— for a younger professor, he avoided technology like the plague. I blinked when the flash went off again. This time, the picture was half decent, if a little close-up.

"That's not bad. Let's see if we can improve on it." I gasped when he placed his hand on the curve of my hip, half on the globe of my butt. Warmth sizzled through the thick denim, right through to my skin.

The next photo showed the surprise on my face and a wicked intent that I'd never known him to have on Sean's.

His hand moved to my waist.

The picture showed the need in my eyes.

His hand slid across my belly.

The picture showed the heat on both of our faces.

And then he pulled me into a kiss, an actual kiss, the kind of kiss I'd never had before. My hand tangled in his hair, and I was only dimly aware of the camera flash as he pulled me so firmly against him that I could feel just how fully I had his attention.

After a long moment, we broke apart, both of us gasping. A shaky moan whispered from my mouth as I brushed my fingers over my lips.

"What do you think?" He grinned down at me, dipping his head for one more brush of the lips. "Do we have a date?"

"Yeah, we do." I just wanted to take a few more pictures. I had my Nikon in my bag, and my fingers itched to use it. "Go… wrap your things. I'll be back soon."

"Wrap my things?" He smirked, and I choked on my voice when I realized how dirty that sounded. I opened my mouth to protest, but he pressed a finger to my lips to stop me.

"Okay," he glanced at his watch again. "See you in about two hours?"

Two hours. In two hours, I'd be on a date with Sean. An actual date.

I'd wanted this for so long.

So why was I suddenly so unsure about everything?

Sean left, and I turned my attention back to my work, quickly finishing with my documentation before moving on to what I wanted to do, which was to capture the magic of the cave with my Nikon. I clicked away, thrilled to have my sleek camera back in my hands after hours of lugging around the dead-weight of the old Polaroid that technophobe Sean insisted on using even though it was ridiculously outdated.

The realization that I was no longer alone jerked me out of my deep concentration, raising the tiny hairs on the back of my neck.

Had Sean come back?

I turned, and my boot scuffed against one of the photos that Sean had taken, the ones that had fluttered to the ground. I stopped to gather them up, tucking them into my back pocket with the other ones before they could be seen.

"Hey."

A sense of relief washed over me at Emmett's voice.

"Hey yourself," I said. There was that tug, that sense of being pulled in two directions. With Sean's kiss still warm on my lips, I really shouldn't have had so many warm fuzzies over the fact that Emmett was here.

He closed the distance between us, his warm, spicy scent filling the small space. "What are you still doing here?"

I showed him my camera. It was a relief not to have to hide it. "Taking pictures. What are you doing here?"

"Checking on you." My heart wobbled a little. Had Emmett climbed back up here to check on me? The muscles along his jaw clenched as he frowned at me. "You shouldn't be in this cave alone."

I squared my shoulders. "I'm a big girl."

"I know. Brave, too. I always loved that about you."

He loved that about me?

I swallowed against the tightness in my throat. "Sorry I didn't remember who you were earlier."

He shrugged like it was nothing. "I've changed."

"So have I."

"Not so much." He glances at my camera. "Did you get some good shots?"

"Lots."

"Show me later?"

I nodded eagerly. "I would love to," I said, but then remembered my date with Sean. "Maybe tomorrow, I…uh…have to go over the Polaroids with Sean tonight."

"Sure, I get it."

"I do want to show them to you though."

He pushed off the wall, and I wasn't quite ready to break the connection between us, so I blurted out the next thing that came into my mind. "You said you owed me one thing, but you were wrong."

He arched a brow, the cute dimples widening. "Oh?"

"Yeah, you see, I believe I've saved your life twice now." He leaned against the wall, and bent one knee, looking like he had all the time in the world.

He scrubbed his chin, and the sound rasped over me. "I believe you're right. You saved me from a sugar crash and a snake. I guess I do owe you another."

"Actually, in some cultures, it means you're now my protector for life," I teased. I couldn't quite believe that my normally tongue-tied self was able to poke fun at him. Maybe because of those times I'd saved his life, I was at ease.

Those mossy-colored eyes met mine, and butterflies fluttered in my stomach. Okay. *Not at ease, then.* Not at ease at all.

"So that's how we're going to play it, is it?"

Peeking up at him from beneath my lashes, I crooked my lips into a smile.

"Fine, from now on, consider me your protector.

The first thing I'm going to do is get you down off this mountain safely." He pushed off the wall, standing over me. Energy arced between us, and air evacuated my lungs in a whoosh. He touched my camera, running his finger over the strap in a manner that had me thinking about his fingers on my body.

Hormones. I had too many hormones.

"Get your things gathered up and wait for me at the mouth of the cave." We stood there, lingering a moment longer, like neither of us was ready to move. He dipped his head slightly, and I listened to his throat as he swallowed. For a brief minute, I thought he was going to kiss me, and my mind whirled with all the reasons that I couldn't possibly do that when my lips had just been on Sean's.

But a non-kiss with Emmett had my pulse pounding faster than the steamy embrace with Sean, and when his gaze strayed to the tender skin beneath the line of my jaw where that same pulse throbbed, I swore he could see it, could tell just from that how I felt about this inexplicable intensity between us.

He didn't kiss me. Instead, his quiet words echoed softly off the cavern walls. "We'd better get a move on it before it gets too dark."

Nodding, I bent to gather my supplies while Emmett started flicking off the artificial lights that were illuminating the cave.

Under his breath, he muttered something unsavory about Sean for leaving me alone, which both surprised and pleased me, but the sound of his voice fell off as he stepped into the other chamber.

With Emmett taking care of the lights inside, I emerged from the rock enclosure, blinking like a groundhog in the spring.

It wasn't dark, not yet, but a misty purple twilight had settled over the lake, bringing with it dense cotton clouds of fog that wound through the trees, the soft gray pierced by the stalwart height of the pines.

It would be night soon, and we needed to get going.

Pausing on the last stone step, I took one last glance back at the cave, pulling Sean's sweater around me, grateful for the warmth. It was all in my head; I knew that, and yet I found it hurt to walk away.

When I turned back, a man stood five feet in front of me, a man who hadn't been there before. I screamed, jolting backward, stumbling and falling back against one of the ancient rocks that had guarded the entrance to the tomb for centuries.

"Jesus!" My body tensed as I assessed the situation. This wasn't anyone I knew, and a stranger suddenly appearing when I was alone should have had my nerves twanging. Instead, I found myself pissed off, planting my hands on my hips and glaring.

"What the hell?"

The man was large, probably six and a half feet, reminding me inexplicably of the bones that lay behind me in the cave. The lost king would have been roughly the same size. He had shiny dark hair pulled into a tail at the base of his neck, and eyes the color of the lake blazed from beneath a scowling brow.

He was also, bizarrely, dressed in a tartan that wound around his waist and shoulders in some complicated way that I'd never have been able to replicate. An axe was tucked into a wide leather belt on his hips, and his face was painted blue.

"Okay, then." I eyed the man and slowly skirted around him, waiting for Emmett to emerge. "My friend is in the cave. He'll be out in a minute. So… you just do whatever it is you're doing here. Night."

The man snorted with derision, and if I hadn't known better, I would have sworn he rolled his eyes. Planting his feet shoulder width apart, he crossed his arms over an impressive chest and stared right into my eyes.

Our people will fall.

An' I canna believe

The two are the rocks

Ye think the one canna be true

They will sacrifice all

Is a lie

We canna do what needs to be done

Our children will tell their children

Our path is clear:

The key

Will be

The traitor's son

The elders tell us

In days past

Blood is thicker than water

For the children this shall change:

Though they canna be seen

The spirits know truth

We canna be saved

Ye canna believe

We each will hold

For though hope might be false

We shall fall one by one

Ye canna think

Together we are greater than apart

Ye shall see

We are broken from within

Ye canna say that

We will hold.

When he stopped speaking, he waited, as though looking for a certain reaction from me. I stared back, somewhat incredulous.

Holy depressing.

He waited. I shook my head with exasperation.

"What do you want from me?" I cried out, the words half swallowed by the wind. "Just go away. Leave me alone."

Where the hell was Emmett?

Again, the stranger seemed to be a bit disgusted. Then without warning, he turned on his heel and marched away toward the forest. I had started after him before I realized what I was doing.

He cast me a look over his shoulder, and I could have sworn he smiled.

I blinked.

And he was gone. At the edge of the trees, a lone creature remained—a deer, a magnificent white stag.

The stag regarded me for a moment, its chin lifting haughtily in the air. One impressive leap from its muscular hind legs and it too was gone.

CHAPTER FIVE

The Betrayal

THE FLAMES OF the fire were visible from halfway down the hill, the tongues of scarlet and apricot and sapphire licking at the now velvety-dark sky. I could smell the smoke, the woodsy musk clinging to my hair, my clothing despite the clear crispness of the early night air.

The dig crew had a bonfire most nights, in the pit behind the motel. It wasn't a fancy setup, a circle of concrete blocks on the edge of the parking lot, but we'd made the best of it, dragging thrift store lawn chairs, cushions, even logs around the flickering flames. As I neared, the yeasty tang of beer, the sweet, earthy smell of pot that some of the more liberal members of the team smoked grounded me, slowed my racing pulse.

I didn't believe in ghosts. No… it was more that I'd never had cause to think on the subject. My parents, on the other hand, were fascinated, always exploring local myths as we traveled from site to site, devouring the tales of ancient spirits that haunted Egyptian tombs and sacred Native American burial grounds. I'd never paid much attention to their stories.

The man had vanished, right in front of me. More than that? I'd replayed the strange encounter over and over in my mind as Emmett held onto me, guiding me down the hill, wincing as my boots scraped over the raw flesh of my heels, ears straining for sounds of movement behind me.

He'd been waiting for me—the giant man in the kilt. The notion was absurd, but I was certain.

Sucking in the familiar smells of the bonfire as I approached the group from the wooded side of the lot, I shook my head to clear it. I'd been spooked and on edge from spending the day with a dead guy.

Ghosts didn't exist, except in the imagination. The far more likely explanation was that the man was someone from town, maybe one of Mairi's relatives—a clansman with his undies in a twist over the digging up of his ancestors, one intent on scaring whichever members of the team that he found up by the sacred tomb.

Yes, that was it. He'd been out to scare us away, and since I was the only one still up there—he must not have known Emmett was inside—I'd been the lucky lady. Relief was as warm as the heat radiating out from the fire, even though a nagging little voice in the back of my head reminded me that he hadn't seemed like he was out to scare anyone. He hadn't touched me, hadn't done anything besides recite that horribly depressing poem.

I'd ask Sean about it. If there were going to be any

locals opposed to the dig, he should know about it.

The baritone roll of thunder mixed with the rumble of the voices around the fire pit. Reflexively, I looked above me—the crystalline explosion of stars visible all week was completely obscured by clouds. A storm was closing in, and I thought instantly of the newly opened cave. Hopefully, the relics would be all right through a storm.

Emmett slid his arm out from around my waist when we reached the foot of the hill, and the loss of his warmth and strength hadn't gone unnoticed by me. "Join us?"

"I…" Even with the feel of Sean's lips on mine still tingling, I was tempted to join the group around the fire for a bit, especially since Emmett was going to be there.

Sean was taking me for dinner.

I should have been thrilled, but I wasn't sure I wanted to go.

"Just for a few minutes." I'd hang by the fire for a bit, then see Sean. I was early, but I didn't think he'd mind. "Let me get out of these boots first."

He grinned. "Take your time. I'll save you a seat."

"And a beer," I called out as I hurried to my room, more anxious than ever about seeing Sean. I'd wanted him forever, but now…I just wasn't so sure.

Changing quickly, I tossed my backpack over my shoulder, the weight of the two cameras jostling around inside, which made me frown. I could understand him wanting me to bring the Polaroids, but why the camera?

Shrugging it off, I hurried from my room and back outside.

As I crossed the parking lot, I saw the crew seated on logs, bottles of beer dangling from their fingers. At the beginning of the week, I would have been way too intimidated to approach them without Sean, but today, knowing Emmett was there, I felt differently.

"…London."

I paused halfway across the lot, cocking my head as my name emerged from the rumble of voices.

"She's completely clueless." A girl who had been up in the cave with us today sniffed. "She's prancing around like she's some big shot with that camera. What the hell does she know about photography anyway?"

Something thick and oily settled in the depths of my stomach.

"Well, at least she has nice tits because there isn't much between the ears." This was a guy, one I'd barely even spoken to. "Dr. Alexander always has a girl at these digs. He always makes them the photographer, just to keep them busy while he works. The pictures she takes means nothing. He always hires a real photographer in the end. But then at night, he invites them to his room to use the camera for *other* purposes."

A series of snickers moved through the group like a wave, the sensation like a series of slaps in the face.

He always hires a real photographer? Did all of the photos I'd taken on all of those digs throughout the years mean nothing?

Were my photos that amateurish? The excitement that had buzzed through my veins over the shots I'd gotten in the cave turned to lead.

"Unless Sean's been taking dirty pictures of you, I

don't know how you could know this." A male voice. I watched, stunned into motionlessness, as Emmett hurled a handful of twigs into the fire with furious force. "Is that what you're saying?"

The guy choked on his beer in outrage before silence fell, rippling through the air before the first speaker, the girl, spoke again. "No, but we all know Dr. Alexander is a player, and clueless London is his new toy." The girl's voice was belligerent, and I wondered faintly when Sean had snubbed her.

"You don't know her." Emmett sounded like he wanted to punch someone. Right this moment, I hoped he'd do it.

"Dude. Didn't you just get here this morning?" The guy snorted. "You don't know her either. Unless… wow. She works fast."

"You want to shut your fucking mouth." Emmett's voice was cold. "Now."

"Or what?" The girl sneered. "Poor little rich girl. Why is she even here if it's not to keep Dr. Alexander's bed warm? Not like she needs the money."

"Why are *you* here? The study of archaeology requires thoughtful analysis of findings. You're missing the thoughtful part." Emmett snorted with derision. "If you'd bothered to look before making up a bunch of crap just to entertain yourselves, yeah, London is the daughter of two archaeologists who funded this dig—the archaeologists signing your check, if I'm not missing something. Because of that, she's already got more experience than you'll have when you retire. So give it a rest."

The girl gaped at him, then laughed, a low, mean sound. "Aw, are you going to be the one to console her when she finds out that Dr. Alexander is banging that Mairi chick too?"

"Spreading shit when you have nothing to back it up isn't attractive." Emmett's words were mild, but I could hear the frost rippling over them. "Maybe that's why Sean got bored of you?"

I wanted to laugh—Emmett had come to the same conclusion that I had, that this chick was running her mouth because she'd been rebuffed.

I couldn't. Even his defense didn't stop that icky feeling from roiling, then spilling over. My limbs were heavy, weighing me down, urging me to stay, to shout out against these horrible accusations.

What if they were right?

I thought of our kisses earlier in the cave. Sean had never, in all the years we'd known each other, made a move on me until now. Was I just his bed bunny of choice for this dig?

He'd told me that he'd personally requested me for the dig because I was good at what I did.

Was that a lie?

No longer bothering to be quiet, I ran for the back door of the motel. I heard a shout from the fire—from Emmett—but ignored it, not stopping until I'd stumbled my way through the hallways, all the way to Sean's room, the stupid camera he'd given me flopping around in my backpack as I awkwardly ran.

I couldn't believe it. I didn't want to believe it. But I had to find out for sure.

Tucked in my left hip pocket was my key card, and behind it was Sean's, the one he'd given me our first night here. I had yet to use it—I'd thought it was weird, actually—but now I couldn't have been stopped.

I tapped it against the lock, and when the light turned green, I leaned on the handle, all but falling into the room.

"London!" Sean was just emerging from the shower. One of the worn cotton towels provided by the motel was wrapped around his lean hips. Droplets of water slid down a torso that was pretty impressive for an academic—probably the result of all of that digging—and his glasses looked like he'd shoved them on quickly, crooked and covered with steam. "What are you doing here? I mean… aah… you're earlier than I expected."

"What am I doing here?" I stared at him with confusion. Just days ago, I would have been a little too excited to be in the same room as a nearly naked Sean. Right now, though? It just felt… *off.* "You asked me to stop by, remember?"

"Right." He raked a hand through wet hair, and my eyes tracked the movement narrowly. "Yeah, I'm, ah, just running behind. Why don't you hang by the bonfire for a bit and I'll get you when I'm ready? We'll walk to dinner."

What the hell was going on?

"I thought you wanted to look at the pictures." Sliding my backpack to one shoulder, I rattled it at him. "And to bring the camera?"

"Yeah." His cheeks flushed a bit, and that was when I caught it—the flash of movement visible even through the steam that clung to the bathroom mirror. "Uh—"

I looked from the mirror to Sean, then back to the mirror. I was pretty sure I knew who was in there with him.

"You just kissed me. Like two hours ago!" I waited for the scalding burst of pain. It didn't come. Instead, outrage colored my voice. "*Two hours!*"

He shrugged. I wanted to punch him in the nuts.

No, it didn't hurt that he'd betrayed me like this—my heart wasn't shattering or anything. But the fact that I was completely replaceable in his eyes coming so close on the heels of what I'd just discovered the rest of the crew thought of me?

Yeah, that stung.

"Everything they said was true," I whispered as I backed up, my hand gripping the doorknob.

"London—"

My vision blurred as I turned and ran out the door. God, I was so stupid.

Bursting through the front doors of the motel, this time, I braced my hands on my knees, sucking in the cold, crisp air as though I hadn't breathed for days. A choking sob escaped my throat, and, mortified, I looked around wildly to make sure that no one was around to witness my humiliation.

Alone. I needed to be alone. With that one thought at the front of my mind, I ran.

CHAPTER SIX

Electrical Storm

THE TEXT ALERT of my cell phone repeatedly buzzed against my hip as I started to hike back up the hill. I guessed it was Sean, but I truly had nothing to say to him, at least right now. And how could I face the others? None of them had any respect for me.

The fury that that thought awakened quickened my footsteps, but it wasn't long before the pain of my blisters rubbing against the heels of my flats slowed my frenzied stride. I hadn't set out in any one direction when I'd run out of the motel, unless *away* was a direction, but I realized that I'd followed a familiar path and that I'd gone farther than I'd realized.

I was almost all the way back up the path to the cave.

My pulse skittered as I quickly scanned the area, searching for any sign of the kilted man I'd seen earlier. But there was nothing, nothing but the dense forest to one side, the icy Bras d'Or Lake to the other, the shadowed entrance to the cave…

And the crackle of lightning in the pitch-dark sky overhead.

A deafening crack of thunder seemed to vibrate the ground beneath my feet. A shriek tore from my throat as the heavens opened and rain poured down in icy sheets, the frigid water flooding my eyes and making it hard to breathe.

The sweater Sean had given me grew heavy, weighing down on me until I wanted to sink to my knees. The flashes of lightning increased in frequency, illuminating my surroundings even as the rolling waves of thunder felt like an assault.

The sweater, my jeans—I could barely move under their sodden weight. Stupid, it was so stupid to get caught in this storm, but that didn't change the fact that I needed to find shelter.

In the next flash of lightning, I eyed the trees. They were whipping back and forth in the wind—they wouldn't offer much protection.

That left the cave. With my feet slipping in my flats, I pushed forward through the torrential sheets. Fighting my way up the steps left me breathless—slicked with moss, I almost fell and cracked my head on the stone twice.

Finally, finally, I reached the entrance to the cave that I'd left less than an hour before. I reached for the lamp, the artificial glow lighting the path as I ducked through the entrance, water streaming from my clothes, my hair, to slosh around my flats that were utterly ruined.

"Shit." My breath came in pants, and I braced myself

against a wall to still my racing heart, springing away in horror when I realized that I'd just put my weight on one of the carved stone tablets that I'd been photographing earlier.

Hysterical laughter burbled out of my mouth, echoing off the ancient stone walls. Jesus, I was batting a thousand tonight. Stepping back, I eyed one of the tablets—the one that Sean had kissed me in front of, actually—and the laughter rolled out of me once again.

I was such an idiot. I'd been proud of what I'd done today—had been fascinated by what I was documenting. For all I knew, Sean had just complimented me because he wanted to get into my bed.

Sick of standing in flooded shoes, I toed them off and wrung the excess water from my hair at the same time, the cold stream splashing on the floor loudly. Rolling up the hem of the sweater, I wrung that out too, then slid my backpack off my shoulders. My Nikon was in a waterproof case inside, so I knew it was fine, but I pulled the Polaroid out. An older camera, I didn't want to risk it sitting in a wet bag, though the fact that it was Sean's camera made me want to drop it the rock underfoot and stomp it into pieces.

Instead, I strapped it around my neck, a voice in my head trying to speak over the hysteria.

I felt betrayed on every possible level—not just by Sean, but by the people I'd thought my friends, by my parents, by the whole freaking world.

My phone vibrated again. I almost missed because it happened at the same time as a crack of thunder that shook the cave. Lightning speared the rock just outside the cave entrance, illuminating the corridor that led to the dead king's final resting place.

Right. I'd taken shelter in the sacred cave with the dead guy.

London, you're an idiot.

Part of me wanted to rage and burn this cave to the ground, just to free myself of some of the horrible feelings that were rolling around inside of me. There were too many of them, too many to be contained inside.

Instead, I found myself crossing the space between myself and the tomb. Slipping through the crack, I stood just inside the chamber. The lamps had been turned off in here, but the light from the front of the cave spilled through, much like my feelings would do if I didn't use everything I had to reinforce the fissure in my heart.

That overflow allowed me to make out the stone slab where the remains of a legend lay. The space at his side bothered me, a tongue probing a sore tooth.

Even through my concentration, I'd absorbed the talk happening around me today as the team prepped different parts of the site for removal and study. History told two tales—according to Mairi's people, this man had been a king, someone who had sacrificed himself for her people. Which meant, of course, that to the other party, he'd been a traitor.

King or traitor, there was no denying that he'd been an important man, at least on this small island in the frigid Atlantic sea. It didn't seem right that, in his eternal rest, he didn't have his queen by his side.

"I'm sorry," I whispered into the semi-dark. For what, I wasn't exactly sure—the lack of the woman at his side, the opening and study of his tomb. Maybe for being here right now? No matter what, as I stood there in his resting place, the silence broken by nothing but my breath and the storm still raging outside, a sense of sorrow and compassion that I'd never experienced before scraped painfully over my skin.

He deserved better than he'd gotten.

The chamber suddenly seemed too small; the air sucked out into the storm outside. Hastily I traced my steps back, stumbling back into the main room. A whip-sharp crack of thunder directly overhead sent me jolting forward, and I slipped into one of the other narrow crevices in the rock, as though the stone that had held for centuries would be able to protect me.

The cushion of air inside that crack was warm. So warm that it made me aware of just how cold I was. My fingers were stiff and cold as ice. My soaking wet jeans continued to drip, rainwater pooling on the rock beneath my toes, which were turning blue.

The warmth. I needed it.

This corridor hadn't yet been explored, and for a long moment, I thought of black bats, swooping and screeching overhead, and of snakes slithering around my toes, though I didn't think there were any reptiles in Nova Scotia.

I could be creeped out but warm… or slightly less creeped out, and get hypothermia. At that moment, there wasn't even a choice.

My fingers didn't want to cooperate, but I forced them into my side pocket, digging the rectangle of my phone out. I winced when I touched the power button—

I was so wet I was afraid that it might be toast. But it hummed to life, though the screen seemed dimmer than usual. Still, I brought up the flashlight, the weak beam of light revealing nothing but rock—no bats, no snakes.

It also showed fifteen text messages from Emmett, not Sean. The latest still flashed at the top of the screen.

London, where are you??? I'm coming to get you.

As I listened to the wind screech past the entrance to the cave, desperation set in.

I tried to text back, but the phone slipped from my hands, falling. I caught it an inch above the floor of the cave, where it would have shattered. Grinding my teeth together, I tightened my grip on it and texted back with numb fingers.

Cave.

Feeling a sense of relief to know Emmett was coming—he was taking the role of my protector seriously—I shone the flashlight into the darkness, following tentatively behind the weak beam of light.

Halfway down the corridor, which, unlike the one in the king's chamber that remained narrow, I realized that water was pooling around my feet, then my ankles, and I seemed to be on a downward slope.

Remembering Emmett's words earlier that day, I determined that this corridor was open to the lake at some point. The water lapping at my feet, though—it was warm, nothing like the sharp cold of the main body of the Bras d'Or Lake. Not as warm as a bath or anything, but a sharp enough contrast to my icy skin that I whimpered at the idea of leaving.

Just a couple of minutes. I'd stay here for just a couple of minutes, then I'd check the level of rain outside, though, by the sounds of it, it was only getting worse. Shivering, I wondered if storms like this were normal on the eastern coast of Canada, and if so, why the hell anyone chose to live here.

Guided by the pale bluish-white light of my phone, I waded a bit further into the corridor. The pool licked at my calves, then my knees and the tiny hint of warmth made me crave more.

A few more steps. I could hear the lake now, and the storm, and I clutched at Sean's sweater. The need to get back to camp was an underlying irritation, never allowing me to settle fully, but the rest of me wanted to stay right here with Emmett when he came, away from the rain, away from the humiliation of the other members of the team, of Mairi, of Sean.

I didn't want to cry—I hated crying. Still, I found my eyes stinging with salt, my sinuses thickening, and though I fought against it, a tear slipped out to scald my frozen cheek.

Shaking it off, I took several vicious steps forward, my movements chopping through water that now licked at my mid-thighs. Not wanting to drop my phone, I flicked the light off and worked the device back into my pocket.

"Shit!" The next step I took had my foot slipping on a moss-covered rock. I shrieked as I lost my footing, landing in the water with enough noise to wake the dead.

I gulped in a mouthful of water, choking as the stagnant liquid filled my mouth, my throat, tugged at my hair.

I stumbled to my feet, only to pinwheel my arms and fall again. The stone beneath me jolted, shuddered. My pulse accelerated until the muscle of my heart felt like it was going to stop as the rock shifted and slid.

The scream tore from my throat, swallowed by the water as a slide of rock carried me down a steep slope. Flinging my arms over my head, I curled into a ball and gasped for breath as I tried not to be crushed.

I knew I was falling. Shards of rock rained around me, swam through water so dark that I couldn't see, could only feel. My arms and legs moved of their own accord, trying to get me to air, but I had no way of knowing if I needed to go up or down.

My lungs burned, and stars danced in the velvety dark of my vision. My movement slowed, and soon I was doing no more than floating. I needed air—my body burned for it.

My lips parted. I wasn't providing oxygen, so my body was going to try to get it for me. Water slid into my mouth, down my throat.

Cold snapped against my skin, teeth biting into my flesh. I gasped, but when I choked, only half of it was water.

Air. Air was rushing into my lungs, searing my insides. I gasped, ducking my head under as I tried to gain my bearings, then again as my feet finally found purchase, sharp stones digging into the tender soles of my feet.

The warmth from the cave was gone. Like a full-body slap, water so thin and bitter and cold hit me with enough force to hurt, the pain icy and scalding and sliding into the very marrow of my bones like a knife.

The cold. I had to get out of the cold. My arms pushed through water fruitlessly, as though I was shoving against stone, but then the raw soles of my feet scraped against something hard, the message jolting through my sluggish reflexes to my brain.

Rock. Sand. There was ground beneath my feet. Moving on instinct, I dug my toes into the bottom of the lake and stood.

The lake. I was no longer in the cave—I was in the lake. Water lapped at my thighs, sucked at the soaking wet denim of my jeans as I gasped for air, shaking the dripping ropes of my hair out of my face.

What the hell is happening?

CHAPTER SEVEN

Lost

I GLANCED UP to see thick black, velvety clouds bleed into the once blue afternoon sky. Darkness settled, and lightning followed, zigzagging a drunken path to the forest floor. A nearby tree went up in flames as thunder rumbled like an angry grizzly. As another flash exploded overhead, I realized that a wild animal was the last of my problems.

I was standing thigh-deep in water with bolts of electricity sizzling all around me. I needed to get the bloody hell out of the lake before I became fish food.

Shouts reached my ears as I worked my way toward shore, my lungs heaving, muscles aching. My pulse stuttered, then began to beat double time.

Voices. People. Had Emmett gathered the team?

He must have, but I sure as hell didn't want to see them right now.

What the ever-loving hell had I been thinking, running out into the dark like that? Especially when I'd had such a scare with that strange kilt-wearing dude outside the cave earlier?

Beat yourself up later, London. Just get the hell out of the water before lightning strikes and you're sizzling like bacon.

Hair plastered to my face, I sloshed out of the lake, almost crying with relief when I was clear of the water. My body ached, and I was tired, so tired, but the storm was still raging overhead.

Logs were lined up on the shore, stacks of massive trunks. Where had those come from?

At the moment, I didn't care. I pushed past the need to sink to my knees and collapse, instead forcing my screaming calves to take me to the tree line, where the shouts had come from. Thunder cracked, whip-like, as I pushed my way through the brush. There—the massive pine ten feet ahead of me had a thick canopy of evergreen needles. Wrapping my arms around my chest, trying to hug in the hint of warmth that the saturated wool sweater had left to offer, I soldiered on toward the shelter. I'd be able to search for Emmett and the team better without streams of water in my eyes.

Huddled under the bough of branches, I worked on wringing water out of the long tangles of my hair, out of my sweater.

Was that a voice? Cocking my head, I strained to hear.

A shout broke through the rain, and relief surged. Shoving out from beneath my shelter, I shielded my eyes from the rain with one hand, crying out in return.

"Emmett?" Trying to shout above the noise of the storm, I spun in a circle, searching in every direction.

"Hey! Hello?"

A flash of movement caught the corner of my eye, and my heart leaped into my throat.

I whirled, shrieking with alarm when I discovered that there was someone right behind me—someone I didn't know. The stranger grabbed me by my upper arms, fingers curling into my flesh and suddenly the cold of the lake was nothing compared to the ice filling my veins.

Words flew back and forth in a language that I couldn't understand, guttural voices shouting with confusion and glee. The gleam of metal made me stumble, falling to my knees.

"*Qu'est-ce c'est?*" The man was dressed in dark-colored trousers, and a long coat made of the same rough fabric. The scent of sawdust emanated from the cloth. His hair was dark, as dark as the eyes narrowed at me with surprise.

"Please!" Since I didn't know any French—*was* that French?—I spoke in English and hoped like hell they understood. Instinct made me throw my hands up over my face, but common sense had me dropping them back down. I was just on edge from everything that had just happened. Instead of the team, Emmett had obviously alerted the nearby village that I'd gone running out into the storm like an idiot, and they were out searching for me. "I'm here! God, I'm so sorry. I can't believe so many of you got dragged out in the rain. I feel like such an idiot."

The man... he just stared at me. The corners of his lips, nearly hidden beneath a thick mustache that matched his hair, were quirked up with what seemed to be amusement.

It wasn't a pleasant kind of delight. Unease cast a feeler out in my stomach, seeking to grab hold.

"So, what's the plan?" My tongue flicked out to run over my lips; the stranger's eyes tracked the movement. "Is your car close? Can I catch a ride back to the motel? Is it even safe to be in a car during a storm like this?"

The man's eyes narrowed with confusion, and he cocked his head to one side. He stared at me like I was an alien whose ship had landed right at his feet, and I opened my mouth to explain further.

A beefy hand on my shoulder cut me off, and I cried out with a surge of panic as I was roughly forced to my knees. I barely had time to suck in a breath, the men speaking to each other with swift, musical words that I didn't understand. The hand on my shoulder slid up, tangling in my dripping hair and pulling hard enough to make me yelp, forcing my face up. The rain felt like blows on the tender skin of my face, and claustrophobia clawed at me when the streams of water slid up my nose and parted my lips.

When the hand released me, I sagged, choking as I tried to swipe water and hair out of my face.

When I could again see, my pulse stuttered in my chest.

This wasn't real. This couldn't be real. My heart was in my throat, choking me as I realized that it wasn't just one man. I was surrounded, strange eyes and lips and teeth and tongues and voices battering at me, shouting, pressing in close. Instinct was screaming at me to stand, to somehow push through the circle, to run.

That gleam again caught my attention, and rather than running, I froze in place when I realized what it was.

The man in front of me had a knife. A wicked-looking thing, his hand fisted around the hilt, the razor-like blade shining despite the water streaming off it.

The other men—they had knives, too. Some were palming them, like the first man who'd stopped me. Some wore them strapped to their hips. One man had speared an apple on the end of his that he bit into, again and again, the crunch audible even over the storm and the voices of the men.

The sky rumbled louder as I swiped fat raindrops from my eyelashes. I was surrounded—and the men didn't look friendly.

My mind still desperately tried to force the scene into something that made sense. I couldn't fathom what this was, but I reacted the way I would if I were back home in Philadelphia.

"Let me through!" My bare feet were so cold they ached as I pushed off the wet, leaf-carpeted forest floor and looked up at the towering trees. I launched myself at the thin sliver of space between the two closest to me, trying to batter my way through, but it was as effective as trying to break a board with my pinky finger. The men responded with laughter and taunting, and adrenaline shot through my veins like the lightning still streaking overhead. "Move! Get the hell out of my way!"

What the hell *was* this? I struggled to fill my constricted lungs. Dread was a lead weight, settling in the pit of my stomach.

I didn't know who these men were. Remembering the kilted man at the cave, I wondered if the locals were more pissed at us for disturbing their sacred cave than Mairi had let on.

Was this their way of protesting? Were they pissed enough to attack one of the members of the dig in the woods? Were they just going to scare me, or did they have something… else planned?

These men weren't going to budge—in fact, they seemed more amused by my order than anything. Rough arms shoved me back into the center of the ring. I landed on my tailbone, pain ricocheting up my spine as I used my arms to get to my knees, then my feet.

Turning slowly in a circle, I did a quick count, my pulse pounding faster with each head that I tallied.

Ten. There were ten men surrounding me, men with cords of muscle on broad shoulders, burly chests, tree trunk legs. Huge men, far larger than the average. Men armed with blades that were guaranteed to make me do whatever they said. Predators hunting their prey.

I struggled to think, to strategize my next move, but fight or flight instincts kicked in.

Blinded by the rain and my fear, I bolted, pushing between two of the men and out of the tight ring. They shouted, but clearly hadn't been expecting me to run, so I had a head start. Branches slapped my face, and my bare feet slipped on the wet ground. I fell and winced when I landed on a broken branch. Instinct had me wrapping my fingers around it, testing the weight, before climbing to my feet again. Using what was essentially a giant stick against ten gigantic men with lethal blades would be like holding off an eighteen-wheeler with a stick.

It was better than nothing.

Weapon in hand, I ran again. Above me, birds squawked and rustled through the thick canopy of leaves, disgruntled at being dislodged from their shelter. Every flutter of their wings and *caw* from their beaks was a tattle, betraying my whereabouts.

The pounding of feet on the ground, the slick sound of sucking mud, the crisp snapping of tree branches intensified behind me, and panic surged. I was winded, my heart throbbing so fast it hurt. I wanted to look behind, to see how much distance there was between myself and my pursuers, but I didn't dare for fear that I'd lose my balance again. All I could do was keep running, powered by pure adrenaline.

A flash of red in the trees caught my eye, and I turned, searching for an opening.

There was none, and it was clear that I wasn't going to outrun my attackers. Throat thick with fear, I slowed, stopped, turned. The branch in my hand was held out like a child's toy sword.

Angry voices and, incredibly, laughter, grew louder, and then the group of men burst through the trees. Nine, ten… now there was one more, and it was that unfamiliar one who hooked his thumbs in the waistband of his pants and sauntered forward.

His stare raked over me slowly, lecherously, somehow making me feel naked despite the baggy sweater that tented my body. The rest of the men spread out and formed a semi-circle of spectators that had my pulse hammering so hard I was sick.

"I won't make this easy." I held up the branch as though it was as wicked a blade as those held in the hands of the men that surrounded me. Adrenaline made the scene play out in high definition, and I scanned the circle, waiting for one of them to make a move. "I will fight you."

The man, who seemed to be the ringleader, called something back to the others that had them bursting out with raucous laughter. He moved closer, slowly, as though he had all the time in the world. His movements were sinuous, and I was reminded of that black mamba snake from so many years ago in the Kalahari.

Something told me he was every bit as deadly. I swung out with the branch, to keep him at least an arm's length away, fighting down the whimper rising in my throat.

"What a—how do you say—pretty little thing." Over the man's shoulder, I once again caught a flash of red through the trees, sending my stomach rolling.

Was it an animal? Another hostile person?

I trembled as I wondered what kind of fresh hell was in store. I couldn't focus on it, not with the men surrounding me, muttering to each other in a language I didn't understand. What I did understand was the tone, which was dark.

I had no illusions about what they wanted from me. But like with the snake, I wasn't going to go down without a fight.

My brain, clicking along rapidly thanks to the adrenaline surge, made the random connection between the predatory movements of the men and some of the wildlife encounter instructions that Sean had made me read before we arrived.

If approached by a black bear, your only option is to fight. Make yourself appear as large and aggressive as you possibly can.

I was being stalked by something a hell of a lot more terrifying than a black bear, but what the hell.

I gathered the scream up from deep in my core—all those hours of yoga had to have some benefit, after all—and, branch tucked under my arm, charged at the leader. He shouted, startled, a moment before the sharp head of the branch rammed into his throat.

The other men rumbled, swarming, but I swung the branch wildly. I thought the men would swarm me, but instead they laughed.

"*Jacques*, you have been hit by a girl!" The man with the apple laughed so hard that bits of masticated fruit sprayed from his mouth. "She did say she would fight!"

The leader—Jacques?—massaged his throat with a mud-splattered hand. His lips curled in a smile, but it held no mirth.

"That is all right." He arched a single dark eyebrow. I was reminded of the new superhero movies that were so popular, the Norse god of mischief—beautiful, but otherworldly, with evil seeping from every pore.

"I'll like it better if she fights."

CHAPTER EIGHT

Mountain Man

MY STOMACH DID a slow roll, and the bitterness of bile coated the back of my tongue.

This couldn't be happening. This kind of thing happened to other people, not to me.

My heart was racing so hard I was sure it was going to break my ribs. I swallowed, my throat painfully dry.

My ears began to ring as Jacques crossed to stand in front of me. I needed to run, I knew that I needed to run again, but I was suddenly frozen, held in place by the icy glint from those snakelike eyes.

He stopped walking, standing directly in front of me, and in a movement so quick it caught me off guard, he pulled a long sword from its sheath, tucking his shorter knife into the back of his pants.

A sword. An actual freaking sword. It made a slithering sound as he pulled it from the leather, a sound that changed to a whistle as he flicked the blade through the air in front of me.

I gasped. The lethally sharp edge bit into the thick wool of my sweater, slicing through it like a spoon through Jell-O. Frozen with fear, I couldn't move, couldn't even shiver with shock as the metal sliced my sweater and the tank beneath from top to bottom.

"Oh, now she is quiet." Lighting glinted off the blade as he pressed it to my cheek. The smell of hot pennies made my stomach turn—where was it coming from? The trickle of warmth on my stomach contrasted sharply with the icy rain, and I understood.

The bastard had cut me. He'd *cut me*.

"Let me go, *now*." The rain streaming down onto my bare skin was so cold it burned, but my insides were even colder, my bones turning to ice. "Who the hell do you think you are?"

My body was tense. If I saw an opening, I'd take it, but I was under no illusion that I'd get far. I knew what was coming. I knew, part of me knew, that it wasn't going to make a difference in the end.

The snake man ran his tongue over his lips, grinning at me. If not for the sinuous evil in his eyes and the icy blade against my cheek, he might have been attractive, which somehow made it all worse. "I'm someone you're about to get to know very well," Jacques said.

Whistling filled the air around my head, and I hunched in on myself, shrieking when metal clanged, and the sword that had been against my cheek went flying. The men surrounding me scattered with guttural shouts and I dropped to a crouch, shielding my face, my head, my torso from the flying blades that whooshed through the air dangerously close to me.

Scraping long tangles of my hair back from my face, I opened my eyes in time to make out a blur—a red one. I flashed on the spot of crimson that I'd seen in the trees, and quickly jerked myself back, crawling on hands and knees over a slick carpet of wet leaves.

"You are trespassing, *Jackal.*" This voice was different from the others, deep and rough, as though each word was scraped over a solid rock before being spoken. "Leave now, and we will let you go unscathed."

What now? Shaking rainwater from my eyes, I looked up and met a pair of raven dark eyes. I sucked in a deep breath, wincing as the movement tugged the skin on either side of the fresh cut on my stomach.

"Who are you?" My gaze was held in the glittering depths of the newcomer's stare, but I was still able to form an impression of him.

A big man—massive, really, certainly bigger than any of the men who had surrounded me. He was sturdy too, thick with muscle. Arms, shoulders, and chest were sculpted and pressed against the fabric of his red and black checked shirt. Narrow waist, a truly impressive set of thighs. And that face. Those dark eyes sparked from a countenance that screamed ferocity. He was sharp angles and planes, lightly tanned skin covering high jutting cheekbones and a nose that spoke of a break or two in the past. A wide jaw boasted a long, thick black beard that matched the wild mane of hair that fell loose around his shoulders.

In his hands was an axe, a rustic length of wood with a heavy, well-worn head that glinted dully in the low light.

My imminent rape had been interrupted by some kind of Viking lumberjack, but my senses still screamed at me to run. The wild warrior facing off with Jacques—Jackal?—had saved me, but the ferocity in his countenance didn't assure me that I was safe.

"That is not my name." Most of the men had frozen, but Jacques shifted his weight from foot to foot in front of the newcomer. Fury painted his features, and something else as well—affection? Surely not. But yes, there it was again. And frustration, too. "You will show me respect."

"I show respect to those who deserve it, *Jackal.*" The newcomer twirled his axe in a smooth motion that I might have admired if I hadn't been so terrified. "The life you have led can never be absolved enough to earn it from me."

I thought that Jackal—that name suited the man better—would laugh in the other man's face, but instead he screamed, the pent-up rage in the shrill sound bringing chill bumps to my skin. Raising his sword over his head, he sliced it through the air and down, where it thudded dully against the wet earth.

"Child of the forest, I should have killed you where you lay!" Raising his sword again, Jackal's eyes widened manically. "Changeling! You are cursed!"

He swung the sword down again, but this time the target was the giant of a man who stood opposing him. The warrior met the sword with a swing of his axe, and the metallic clash was deafening in the small clearing.

I expected Jackal's men to raise their knives and jump into the fray, and couldn't understand why they instead stepped back, observers of the battle, but not participants.

I didn't have time to wonder why. Pushing myself painfully up from the cold, hard ground, I wrapped my arms against the slash in my stomach and again turned to run.

I saw nothing, heard nothing new, and yet I pulled up before I could sprint off into the trees. The fine hairs on the back of my neck stood up as if electrified, and my senses kicked into overdrive, searching for the new threat that some primal instinct I didn't know I had was detecting.

One moment all that I saw at the edge of the clearing were trees—dense, dark, solidly green forest. One blink, and there they were, as though they'd never been anywhere else.

Fear turned my blood to slush in my veins.

A line of men stood shoulder to shoulder amongst the verdant canopy. Large, small, every size and shape seemed to be represented, but the chill came not from their sizes, but from their countenance, which was still yet menacing. They all wore... were those kilts? Yes— kilts. Red plaid that matched the shirt the giant was wearing.

Kilts weren't a big thing where I was from, and I'd always found the idea of them silly.

These men could have looked foolish—many men I knew would have. But looking at that impenetrable line...

I was looking at warriors, men even more dangerous than the ones fighting behind me.

My muscles trembled as the fight or flight response surged through me, my instinct again to run, but a tiny remaining sliver of caution froze me where I was.

Sean had fed me enough information about the history of the tribe we were coming to study to make my eyes roll back in my head. Bored I might have been, but I'd still absorbed a good chunk of it.

He hadn't said a damn thing about battles in the forest—he wouldn't, would he, because he was more concerned with the village and the tomb. I'd struggled to stay awake, however, as he chattered on ad nauseum about the minutiae of daily life of the Bras d'Or clan. He'd been particularly fascinated with their traditional dress.

"The clan wore a very specific red tartan, the design of which had been altered only slightly from that worn by their ancestors when they crossed the water. The cloth was rustic, woven by hand, then stitched and pleated the same way. A tartan was very large and had to be belted at the waist. It had enough fabric to be draped over the torso as a cloak, worn as a hood, or used as a blanket at night. Apart from the belt, members of the clan wore little other ornamentation, but going into battle or for special occasions, they used a closely guarded mixture of white and blue clays to paint runes onto the skin. These runes were meant to imbue the wearer with the properties the rune represented—protection, good health, speed, and more."

The kilted men forming an impenetrable wall in front of me had blue markings painted onto their arms, their bared chests and their faces. I blinked at them as my mind flipped through my memories of my conversations with Sean.

"The Bras d'Or clan were peaceful unless provoked. When threatened, they were the fiercest of warriors, stories of their brutality reaching across the sea."

Each kilted man held a sword that surely weighed as much as a small child, designed to cleave through armor or to crack open a skull.

My body seized. I couldn't turn and run back to Jackal and the giant. But neither could I rush the line of deadly warriors in front of me.

What the hell could I do?

"Chlanna nan con thigibh a' so 's gheibh sibh feòil!"

My head whipped around in the direction of the words. One of the kilted warriors stepped forward, an older man with sinewy muscles flexing as he lifted his sword to the sky. He repeated the chant, and the words, yelled with unyielding ferocity, sent shivers up and down my spine.

Those shivers were nothing compared to the adrenaline that surged through me when the rest of the men called back, answering their leader with screams. Piercing, ghostly wails erupted from each, and then they charged straight at me.

I turned and ran the way I'd come, right back toward Jackal and the giant. My arms pumped, my breath shuddered in and out of my lungs as the screeching warriors gained on me from behind.

The two men in front of me paused to take in the approaching battle, then rushed at each other again with snarls, metal clanging against metal.

Then the warriors were on me, swarming around me like I was a tree trunk in their path. Screaming, I dropped to the ground, curling into a ball as the battle sprang forth around me.

The kilted men had been charging those with Jackal, not me. I had to claw my way free of this bloody mess, but terror coated my throat, slick and bitter and hot.

The two men at the epicenter of the fight roared. The giant was bigger, faster, stronger, a better fighter in every way. Jackal, though, he fought dirty, biting and kicking and using whatever he could to take his opponent down. He battered at the larger man mercilessly, ducking under the deadly blade of the axe to get right into the giant's personal space.

Fury radiated from both faces. The men broke apart, sucking in air, then crashed together again. Steel locked against steel, and muscles bulged, faces contorted as something rippled through the air.

"The forest is mine." The giant bared teeth that flashed white above a dark raven beard. "Find somewhere else for your fun, or pay the price."

Jackal's lips curled up in a facsimile of a smile, the expression leaving me chilled. "We used to have fun together, Wood."

The man—Wood—growled, and increased the downward pressure. The blade of the axe seemed to scream as it slid down the length of the sword. Jakal's eyes darkened, glinting like obsidian as he licked rain off his lips.

"You say you want us out of your forest." The smaller man cocked his head. A murmur went through the others, and the tension swirling through the rain thickened, layered with undertones that I didn't understand. It almost seemed that the two men were embracing, so tightly locked together than one couldn't move without the other. "I know you, Wood. You used to stand by my side as we shared life's greatest pleasures. Those urges are still in you. I know what you want."

Shared life's greatest pleasures? Given that Jackal and his gang had already tried to get their hands onto *my* "pleasures," it didn't take a genius to decipher what he was speaking of.

His words meant that the giant—Wood—was no friend of mine.

Run, London. Run!

CHAPTER NINE

Altered Reality

THE VOICE REVERBERATED around my skull as my subconscious finally decided to unfreeze. Adrenaline sizzled through my limbs as I shoved up from the ground and ran.

Armageddon erupted behind me. A thunderous battle cry made me stumble. Thorny branches tore at the bare skin of my breasts, re-opening the shallow cut that Jackal had sliced through my torso. Twigs and rocks cut the soles of my feet, as I ran blindly. The copper tang of blood was in my nose, my mouth, turning my stomach as my feet pounded and slipped over the leaves and moss and pools of rain.

The sounds of battle faded behind me as I put distance between myself and the men, but the further I ran into the forest, the slower I moved until I finally stumbled to a halt. Bracing my back against a tree so huge, I wouldn't have been able to wrap my arms around it; I let the rough bark dig into my back as I sucked in great gasping mouthfuls of air.

My sweater and tank top had disappeared some-where along my path. I was wearing a demi bra, jeans that were soaking wet, and strangely enough, my Polaroid was still strapped around my neck, though I doubted it was going to be much good after my dunk in the lake.

The lake. The cave. Emmett. Sean. The crew. My thoughts tumbled, one over another until I wanted to sink to my feet and whimper.

Something was very, very wrong.

Head spinning, I sank to the wet ground. I was so turned around, I didn't know which way was out of the forest. Strange men were everywhere, and I didn't know who the good guys were, if any. I was freezing, bloody, and terrified as the nightmare I'd stumbled into trapped me and held me tight.

Things were clicking into place in my brain, but they made absolutely no sense. A clan of warriors with painted skin skulking around the forest. Another group of men with thick accents and an agenda.

And a giant with an axe caught between them. I knew the details of this story, but my brain refused to make the leap.

The rain slowed just the slightest bit, but the wind picked up in its place, knifing through my bare skin. I wrapped my arms around myself and shook as shock started to set in.

I wanted to believe that this was a reenactment of battles past by peoples current.

I wasn't sure that I did.

A blow to my chest shoved me into the trunk of the tree, the heavy pressure of a massive hand holding me in place like a butterfly cruelly pinned to silk.

I scrabbled at the thick wrist, the ropy forearm. I dug my broken nails into the skin hard enough to draw blood, but the pressure remained.

"Who are you?" I screamed as the voice cut through the wind and rain, slamming my head back against the tree so hard that I saw stars. I looked up to find the giant—Wood—looking down at me, his craggy face set in severe lines.

Jesus, he was huge. Up close, he was even larger than I imagined, probably around six and a half feet to my own five feet five. And it wasn't just the height—he was massive everywhere. Cords of muscle in massive forearms, in thick thighs beneath wet trousers, in shoulders so wide he looked like he could stop a speeding train with his bare hands. Hell, even his neck looked strong, like he could snap through a rope without even using his hands.

Above all that brute strength was a face that terrified me nearly as much as the colossal frame. Inky hair hung in wet ribbons around a face made up of sharp angles and broad planes. His beard was long, unkempt, and yet I couldn't picture him without it.

The eyes, though, they were what caught and held my attention. Glittering and nearly black, like stars without light, they were fixed on me with the attention of a mountain lion stalking a deer.

I stayed silent as he stepped back, the crushing pressure on my chest releasing. Gasping for breath, my fingers found a loose chunk of bark on the tree, and I yanked it off, fingers curling around the sharp edges. I needed a weapon, even if it was only a piece of wood.

His gaze slid slowly from the bark to my face. He huffed out a breath, the sound filled with exasperation and, unless I was way off the mark, amusement. "Who are you?" he asked again.

I swallowed thickly, body tense, bark digging into the tender skin of my palm. Shaking my head, words were stuck in my throat.

"Are you capable of speaking?" He arched an eyebrow, and my stomach did a slow roll. Part of me had hoped that maybe this guy was one of the good guys, but the impassive set of his face, the foreboding glint of his eyes, and what I'd heard Jackal say about him told me that maybe he was the most dangerous one of all.

"I just want to get back to my hotel." I sucked in another breath—my lungs were raw from my sprint through the woods. "Just let me go. No one has to know."

He leaned back against a neighboring tree, arching an eyebrow with condescension. "The desire to wander through these woods alone suggests that you either enjoy pain or that you're stupid. Which is it?"

The comment grated over my icy skin. I've been called stupid before, and I've always responded with a flippant comment or a single finger salute. My spine stiffened, and I felt inclined to do just that.

Don't flip off the scary giant, London. Don't. Do. It.

"Taking on a group of armed men alone isn't the smartest thing I've ever seen, either." Shit. My brain had no control over my mouth. Panic flared as something that might have been amusement flickered over the giant's face.

Of course, it might have been homicidal rage or something else dark, too. As he reached for the buttons of his red plaid shirt, bile rose in my throat, burning the already raw flesh.

"No." I pressed back against the tree, hard. I just needed a split-second opening; then I'd run. "Please. Just let me go. You don't even have to help me. Just please let me go."

Something—pity?—glittered in those dark eyes and a tiny fragment of my fear unfurled, only to be washed away in the rain. Growling under his breath, he peeled the sodden fabric from his torso and tugged his arms out through the sleeves.

I almost swallowed my tongue. I thought I'd understood the extent of his muscles before, but bare to the chest he was both impressive and terrifying. Broad and hard, ropes of muscle stacked on top of one another in the hardest male physique I'd ever seen. My eyes widened as I took in the solid wall that was his torso, the dark curling hair on his chest, the matching trail that striped a path into his low-slung pants.

There were so many muscles it was absolutely ridiculous. He looked like Captain America. If Captain America had been photoshopped.

Holding the shirt out to me, Wood looked me over from head to toe. Blood suffused my skin as his eyes trailed over me, lingering—to my surprise—not on what I wasn't wearing but what I was—my jeans, my bra, and my camera.

"What kind of garments are these?" His gaze flickered back up to my bra. Plain blue cotton, it wasn't anything special, but he was looking at it as though I'd wrapped myself in a paper sack. "Even the whores at the trading post wear more than this on top. Cover up, girl, before the Cabots come back."

I opened my mouth to hotly inform him that I'd been wearing far more clothing before Jackal had sliced the garments off me, but my mind stuttered on something he'd said.

The Cabots.

Click.

Just another puzzle piece falling into place.

I grabbed the shirt, wrapping it around myself quickly. It was as wet as I was, but still, the layer over my skin felt like heaven against the never-ending onslaught of rain.

"And trousers. A woman in trousers. Where did you come from?" Altering the question slightly, he tore his puzzled stare from my bra to my face. A strange sensation jolted through me. When he wasn't scowling, he was... well, he was still fucking intimidating. But those sizzling nerves inside of me settled just a bit, maybe some primal instinct that told me I wasn't in danger. At least, not from him.

Since I didn't plan on being any more of a damsel than I already was, I shoved that instinct right back where it came from.

Smart women didn't tell strange men where they lived, where they were staying. And I'd already been plenty stupid for the night, as Wood had so helpfully pointed out. I pressed my lips together, staring silently up at him.

He arched an eyebrow with more than a hint of confusion, as though he couldn't believe I wasn't leaping into his arms for rescue. With a heavy sigh, he patted his axe, which was now hanging from a loop in his leather belt. Darkening smears that smelled of copper colored one of the blades, and I couldn't help but shudder.

He moved so quickly, I never saw it coming. He lifted my Polaroid from around my neck, sliding it over one massive shoulder. I growled and grabbed for it, but he moved so fast for someone so big.

"Hey!" I lunged again, my fingers brushing against the strap but not finding purchase. "Give that *back*!"

The Polaroid was very old, thanks to Sean's Luddite approach to all things technological. After its dunk in the lake, it probably didn't even work. But it was one of my few remaining links to home. A thread of sanity that I could hold on to in the absolute insanity I'd found myself in.

I wanted it back.

Need to get my camera back overrode all common sense. Snarling, I threw myself against the giant.

"Oof!" He huffed out a breath as my elbow found his solar plexus. As he hunched over slightly, I was able to reach his neck as I stood on my toes, straining to reach.

"Ow!" My fingers closed around the rough woven strap, and I tugged, but I couldn't get the momentum to swing it up and over his head. He grunted as I tugged, thinking to maybe break the strap and get the camera that way. His hands swatted at me like I was a persistent mosquito.

"That's enough!" He didn't yell, but he spoke loudly enough to make me jolt. He took advantage of my surprise by picking me right up off my feet, jostling me enough that I let go of the strap.

I squawked as he lifted me with no apparent effort at all, swinging me up and over until my belly was resting on the wide expanse of his shoulder, and I hung upside down, facing his back.

"Let me go!" Panic surged, hot and bright. I screeched, trying desperately to get my fingers on the wickedly sharp blade of his axe. I had no idea what I was going to do with it if I got it, but I wasn't going to just let him haul me off into the woods. I was thrashing as hard as I could, enjoying his grumbles of frustration when my forehead smacked in his back, and his hand flew to...

Oh, hell no. His hand splayed right over the curves of my ass. Screeching again, I flailed as hard as I could. He shifted me and pressed a hand firmly over my mouth.

His palm smelled like tree sap, and I gnashed my teeth, trying to bite.

"Screaming like that will tell the Cabots where we are. Since Jackal and his men think that an unwilling woman is a cause for a party, I don't think you want that." The words made me still. No, I didn't want that at all.

"If I wished you ill, I would have left you with them in the first place." With that, he settled me over his broad shoulder like a sack of potatoes and started to stride forward. "And trust me, girl. If that happened, a hand on your ass to stop you from breaking your neck would be the least of your worries."

I stilled completely, chills raining down on my skin as he shifted me on his shoulder.

I didn't know who he was or where I was, but at this moment, he was the lesser of two evils. It took everything I had, but I forced myself to settle down. In response, his fingers dug into the flesh of my ass, gripping me tighter, though now I understood that he wasn't groping me. I expected him to grunt under the weight of my curves, but he wasn't even breathing hard.

"That's it. Settle yourself, girl. We've got a bit of a hike ahead of us." My face smacked into the rock-solid planes of his lower back as he started to move, and I found myself digging my fingers into his arm, his back to help myself hold on. I heard a rumble deep in his chest, and stretched, shaking my sodden hair from my face to try to get a look at him.

"You try to use my axe against me, girl, and you'll find yourself on the receiving end. Understood?" The slightest of smirks curved his lips. My glare faded as I gulped, nodding, my wet hair whipping against my icy cheek.

I understood. The giant might not wish me harm, but he wouldn't hesitate if it came down to him or me. I wasn't holding onto any delusions about who would win that one.

I latched onto the only sane thought amidst all the craziness—I needed to get back to that cave. Surely Emmett was looking for me by now. What would he do when he didn't find me there? What would Sean do? My parents?

I had to get back.

Opening my eyes, I took in the gnarled bark of tree trunks as we passed, the swirls of ash, amber, and cinnamon that covered the wood. I couldn't see much of it, but I knew that above was a dense canopy of leafy greens and silver-soft pine needles. It was the same no matter which direction I looked.

I had no idea where I was. I had no idea where the cave was. And with limited options, being carried through the dark, frightening woods by a big hulking warrior of a lumberjack was preferable to wandering, half-naked, cold and terrified of running into Jackal and his men.

I would go with the giant—with Wood—for now. I didn't have a choice. But as soon as I could, I needed to get out of these woods.

Just because this giant didn't seem to want to see me hurt… well, that didn't mean I was safe. I wouldn't be until I managed to find my way home.

CHAPTER TEN

Hidden Cabin

EXHAUSTION OVERTOOK ME as Wood carried me deeper into the dark forest. In the small gaps where the trees opened up to the night sky, I could see the moon grinning eerily down at me. My kidnapper carried me like I weighed nothing more than the axe secured to his hip as he moved at a steady pace through the trees. He clearly knew exactly where he was going, just as surely as I was completely disoriented. As much as I tried to memorize each turn, count his every step so I could figure out how to get back to the cave, my efforts proved futile.

What was that theory everyone learned about in high school? Occam's razor. With more than one possible explanation, the simplest was usually the truth.

So...

Explanation one. This could be a historical reenactment. Some of Mairi's relatives had dressed up in kilts and face paint and were running through the woods, and when I'd run into them, they'd stayed really, *really* committed to their characters.

While I'd love to believe that—God, how I'd love to believe that—the sharp blade to my clothes, the slice to my abdomen told a different story. These men weren't actors—they were dangerous. Then again, perhaps I'd taken a hard hit to the head when I'd tumbled into the lake, so hard it drastically changed my perception of reality. There was always that explanation. Sure. Likely. But I needed to cling to something solid before hysterics set in.

Explanation two. Some wicked reaction between the storm and the cave had catapulted me into another dimension, one where my motel, my friends and family did not exist.

And that was insane. The child of academics, my brain screamed and demanded proof. But the Cabots, and the clan with blue faces and kilts? I'd listened to Sean pontificate on every detail of their lives. Those people had been real—key word: *had.*

I thought of the tartans on the men that had come out of the trees to fight the Cabots. The clay markings painted onto their skin. These were things that Sean had told me about, *documented historical facts.*

So what was the simpler explanation? A historical reenactment where I'd been injured and no one cared? Or that what was happening around me was… real?

Wood chose that moment to shift me in his arms, interrupting my panicked thought process, and I absorbed his heat as I slid down the front of his body. Blood rushed back into my extremities after being dangled awkwardly over his back for so long, and I stumbled, suddenly dizzy upon seeing the world right side up again. I fisted and unfisted my fingers, wincing at the pins and needles as sensation returned.

When I looked up—*way* up, because my kidnapper was just so freaking *big*—those coal-colored eyes were studying me intently. I shivered with nerves as his stare raked slowly over my face, a careful, calculated assessment. Questions danced in the shining depths, but his lips remained pressed tightly together as if he didn't want to hear the answers to his questions.

I had questions of my own—hundreds and thousands of them—but the expression on his face did not invite me to ask them.

The big man grunted as he shifted me against him, rearranging me as though I was a rag doll. I didn't have much more life in me than a doll at that moment. Maybe I should have been fighting, but the tumble into the lake, the fading rush of adrenaline from when my skin had been sliced open—I was tired. So incredibly tired.

Plus, for the moment, I believed that he didn't mean to hurt me. If he changed his mind, then conserving some energy to fight back was the best plan I had. The thought of trying to escape this man, though—it didn't leave me with warm fuzzies.

I've mentioned he was huge, yes? Plastered against his chest like I was, I felt those muscles, rope after rope of them. His shoulders were twice as wide as my own, his chest just... massive. His waist was narrow but defined, leading to slim hips and to a truly impressive set of thighs.

Who was I kidding? If he wanted to hurt me, I didn't have a prayer. Didn't mean I wouldn't try, though.

I had no idea what I'd do if it came to that, but I'd figure it out. My memory flashed back to Emmett and the black mamba snake. I'd gotten us away from a snake with murder on its mind when I'd been just a kid.

I'd figure out a way to get away from a lumberjack too, if it came to that.

The big man continued to shift me, changing my position—maybe even his massive arm muscles were screaming from holding my not inconsiderable weight. One rough hand shifted under my backside, as the other guided my legs around his thick torso. I probably looked like a monkey clinging to its mother, but since the raw soles of my feet felt like a cheese grater had been taken to them, I was happy to remain in his arms.

This position, though… it was a little on the intimate side. Swallowing thickly, I slid my arms around his shoulders, and his back muscles flexed and clenched when I splayed my fingers, digging them in to hang on.

His touch was in no way sexual, not like that serpentine charge in the air when Jackal had slowly slid that knife down my torso.

I shuddered. I felt, more than saw Wood tilt his head to look down at me, but he remained silent.

And then we were in motion again. He tromped through the woods quickly, not quite at a jog but close. Every now and then his long beard would brush my face, scratch lightly at my skin. I'd never liked beards, had always thought they looked unkempt, but his was well-groomed, carrying the scent of soap and bonfire.

Probably a lot nicer than how I smelled right now. I shifted slightly, felt the dampness of sweat and lake water sealing my clothes to my skin and winced.

I was not in good shape. In fact, between the adrenaline, the terror, the shock of the icy water from my tumble into the lake and the cold I'd felt slicing through my bones ever since, I was feeling pretty sick.

My stomach turned, and I gripped Wood's shoulders, wondering what he'd do if I threw up on him.

I focused on the rhythm of Wood's steps, started to breathe in time until I dozed off. I came to when I registered that Wood was slowing down, the way you can wake from even a deep sleep in the car when you turn into your driveway. A faint hint of smoke reached my nostrils, indicating there was, or had recently been, a fire in the vicinity.

Fire. Heat. The cold in my bones sharpened, blades slicing through me. I trembled, then started to shake at the thoughts of getting warm, and without words Wood, as though reading my body language, dragged me impossibly closer, rubbing his hand over my back to create heat with friction. My breasts pressed against his chest, and I counted the pounding beats of his strong heart.

If he were going to hurt me, he probably wouldn't care if I was cold or not. I held on to that fact.

Daring to look up from his shoulder, I saw that the clearing we'd reached was small. In fact, if he hadn't been approaching it like he'd reached his destination, I wasn't sure I would have registered that it was a clearing at all. There was a semi-circle in front of a massive tree where the dense greenery of the forest was thinner. If I squinted, I could almost see where boot prints—massive ones—had crushed the tender foliage that covered the moist earth.

The giant grunted, heading steadily toward the immense tree. I stiffened, wondering for a moment if he planned to tie me to it, gasping instead when he carried me around the curved trunk, and I saw the secret the tree held.

One side of the tree was partially uprooted, roots as thick as my waist twisting and tangling until they formed a half-circle—a cave, almost. And tucked into that cave, looking almost as though it had grown there, was a little cabin hewn from rustic logs, rough planes of wood, and mossy stones.

"Oh." I felt as though I'd fallen into the Princess Bride or Lord of the Rings. This little dwelling was otherworldly, like nothing I'd ever seen.

Wood grunted again as he tugged open the door, ducking to clear the frame. The crispness of the air in the forest stayed outside, and I sighed with pleasure. I continued to absorb his warmth—he radiated it, as though he had a furnace at his core—as he carried me into the cabin. The tree. The cabin in a tree.

Inside it was dark, but not a chilling kind of darkness—more like what I'd experienced in the cave. Soft, welcoming darkness. The kind that invited you to curl up and relax. The scent inside was woodsy, earthy. Cedarwood. I had a bar of cedarwood soap back at home, and it smelled like the air inside this place.

Where in the hell was I?

What's the simplest explanation here, London?

My brain refused to accept it.

I heard a hiss and stiffened—ever since that dig in Africa, I'd associated hissing with snakes. A tongue of orange and violet flared, melting into a clear, cream-colored light, and I forced myself to relax as I realized it was only a lantern.

Still held tight by my captor, I glanced around the small space, easily able to take it all in with a long, sweeping gaze. The inside of the tiny cabin did not indicate that it was tucked into the side of a tree. Wood—at least, I assumed it had been him—had stacked logs to create walls, and only the sloping, slanting lines of the roof reflected the vee of the giant roots outside. It was a simple dwelling, cozy even, all one room.

Blinking in the dim light, I squinted and was able to make out a tiny wood-burning stove that vented outside, a solid wooden bed that would have sold for thousands of dollars in some upscale furniture store back home, a table and two stools that matched. There was a tin basin for washing, a few neatly stored bins, and not much else.

A grumble came from Wood's throat as he stepped back from the lantern. My pulse picked up, battering against the skin of my throat as he lowered me down to the bed, his touch surprisingly gentle for such a big man.

The rain picked up outside and battered at the roof as the silence stretched between us. I liked rain—one of my favorite things to do on a rainy day was to nap, letting the pitter patter of the drops on the ground lull me to sleep. Here, each splatter on the cabin roof was like a needle, piercing my skin with heat, filling me with adrenaline and alertness.

I sat up straight, pulling the sodden folds of his flannel shirt around me as he looked me over. The rough-hewn planes of his face were set in impassive lines, but the flicker in those inky eyes warned me that I wasn't out of danger.

"Don't move," he finally said, his deep voice little more than a growl as he slid my camera from his shoulder. He eyed it like I would eye a rat before setting it on the table, then he pulled his axe free and disappeared outside.

What the hell was he doing?

CHAPTER ELEVEN

Dressing Wounds

I FELT A measure of panic and worked to swallow it down, but my tight throat protested. *If he wanted to hurt me, he would have done it already.* I had to believe that at least. It was the only way to keep the terror at bay.

Needing a distraction, I cataloged my surroundings again, looking for anything that could be used as a weapon, but my tired mind stopped searching long enough to admire the smooth log wall, engineered from thick cedar trees. There were markings in the wood I didn't understand, yet every part of me understood there was something very special in the handcrafting. I shimmied back and touched the warm timber, impressed at the work that had gone into constructing the place.

Did Wood live here alone?

What the hell kind of name was Wood, anyway? It sounded like a nickname some frat guy had bestowed upon himself.

I curled into myself when the whistling wind and a

howling wolf cut the quiet. Gulping, and needing something to concentrate on, I searched the room again and let the warmth of the place chase the chill from my brittle bones. I tugged the massive, rain-soaked shirt away from my shriveled, waterlogged flesh, and took deep breaths as I aired it out. The shirt held the lumberjack's scent, pine, and an earthy soap infused with an herb I couldn't quite place, but would now always identify with Wood.

The reality of my situation crashed down on me with the weight of a boulder. I was in a lumberjack's cabin, deep in strange woods. With a giant named Wood. And a gash on my torso. From a sword.

The wind howled around the cabin, tree branches scraping against the sides, but it sounded more like an animal trying to claw its way to warmth and comfort. I shivered at the thought. What other kinds of animals were hidden amongst the trees and foliage, ready to pounce should I try to run? I wasn't sure, but I had the sneaking suspicion that Wood was more dangerous than any of them. Even though I had no idea who this mountain man was, or what he was capable of, for some inexplicable reason, I was more fearful when he wasn't here at my side, as opposed to when he was.

Alone in the dimly lit room, unease burrowed inside my belly, dissipating slightly when Wood came back into the cottage carrying logs and a big bucket, water sloshing from the sides. He glanced at me, expression surly, as though to make sure I hadn't fled. His thick muscles shifted as he fed the fire, stuffing huge logs inside. The golden embers sparked to life and heat washed over me in a burst. He settled the metal bucket on top of the stove and used a long metal ladle to scoop out the water.

He carried it across the small expanse, and settled on his knees before me. "Drink," he ordered gruffly.

I hesitated. How clean was this water? Was I going to get E. coli? Salmonella? Beaver fever? He frowned at me as I mentally debated with myself, but then thirst took over, and I did as he commanded. I sipped the cool water gratefully—so damn refreshing. Then I gulped faster, unaware of just how dry and scratchy my throat had become until the first thirst-quenching taste. Droplets dripped down my chin, landing on the wet shirt that suddenly felt heavier, weighted down on my body. I remained quiet as he refilled the ladle, and brought it to me again. I finished drinking and wiped my chin. I blinked up at him and waited for the questions. The wait was short-lived.

"What is a motel?"

I stared for a moment, adrenaline surging. I might have just rationalized that I was in a different time and space. Mentally, I knew that that was the most likely explanation. But that question, by all appearances sincere, and the confusion on his face solidified the fact that I was indeed a long way from home.

It was terrifying.

My heart raced as I stared at the man before me. I dodged his question, not sure that answering it was the wisest move. "I was in the cave, the one opening into the lake. Do you know it?"

He scrubbed a hand through his beard, then smoothed it out. Unlike Jackal and his men, Wood was clean. Looking around the cabin, I wondered where he bathed. "Yes."

Relief washed through me. If he knew it, he could take me back there. "There was a terrible thunderstorm, and I fell into the water. I hit my head. The next thing I knew I…you were rescuing me from that man. Jackal." I blurted out. "I don't know what happened," I said quickly, desperate for him to believe me.

My teeth started to chatter, even though my body temperature was quickly rising, thanks to the fire Wood had started. I shivered, chills skating up and down my spine as I recognized the signs of shock.

I expected him to continue his interrogation, but instead, he rose, straightening to his full height and turning his back to me. My gaze slid over him, and I blinked at the sight of his back.

Like everything about him, the expanse of his back was large, wide, with defined muscle that shifted as he did. But over his shoulder blades, his rib cage, his lower back… what was that? Everywhere the skin should have been smooth it was instead raised. Ridges and seams corrugated what should have been unmarked skin, and it took me a moment to realize what I was looking at.

Lash wounds. At some point in his past, Wood had been whipped horribly. The raised stripes were the result of skin trying to heal traumatic lacerations that had likely only had the most primitive of care.

My mouth opened of its own accord. How had he gotten these? Who had done this to him?

Looking over his shoulder at me, his eyes glittered over those cheekbones that seemed sharp as blades. His expression dared me to ask and warned of the consequences if I did.

I might have asked anyway if I hadn't detected the slightest hint of something else in those dark depths. Not pain, exactly, nothing as vulnerable as that. But those sparks told me that how he got those wounds was not something he liked to talk about. Ever.

I sank my teeth into my lower lip and inhaled deeply. I couldn't ask.

As if he knew what I was thinking, he twitched irritably, stalking across the small room to rummage through some metal container, though I noticed that he didn't make any effort to cover those scars, making me feel again as if he was trying to bait me into commenting on them.

It made sense. If I pushed, he had a reason to get mad at me. To kick me out and relieve himself of the role of my savior.

I wasn't known for my tact. I did have a compassionate streak, though, and I didn't have it in me to slice a blade over a wound that was obviously still raw, if metaphorical.

He muttered something under his breath, a single syllable that I guessed was something both directed at me and not overly complimentary.

I watched warily as he moved about in the dim light, the flickering glow of the lantern casting shadows both short and long over the small space. Reaching for one of the neatly stacked metal bins, he produced a thin white cloth, then ripped into it with a suddenness that made me jump.

The cloth ripped again, and my blood raced. It was a violent sound at the end of a violent day, and I was appalled to find my eyes welling with hot tears.

I hated to cry. My parents had dragged me through enough uncomfortable living conditions throughout my childhood that I liked to think I was tough. Those living conditions, though? They ran more along the lines of peeing in the bushes and eating rehydrated food for months on end and, yes, having terrifying encounters with deadly creatures like the black mamba snake that slithered around the Kalahari desert. But none of these things had been deliberately violent, none of them had had the decided cruelty that I'd seen on Jackal's face when he dug that blade into my skin.

None of them had kept me in a continual state of the unknown, the worry that came with wondering if I was safe or not. It was the sound of the fabric tearing that splintered something inside of me.

I had to get out of here. I had to run.

Batting his hands away, I struggled to stand. I made it two shaky steps before Wood picked up with a massive hand placed under each armpit and placed me back on the bed like I was a doll.

"Settle yourself, girl."

A tortured, whining sound keened from my throat. He looked down at me with those dark eyes, shaking his head just the slightest bit. Turning away so that I had a full view of those scars again, he poured water from a pot over the fire into a tin basin, slipping his fingers below its surface to test for the temperature.

Setting the basin on the floor beside the bed, he

slipped a piece of the fabric into the water, and I watched as curls of steam rose from its surface. He sank to his knees once again and inched mine open slightly to better position himself. His movements weren't sexual, but the position was hideously intimate, and I stiffened.

He tapped a long finger under my chin, and I looked back at him. Even on his knees, his eyes were nearly level with mine where I sat.

"I'm not going to hurt you." For the first time, I noticed that he had a hint of an accent, so light that it almost wasn't there at all. My parents had once introduced me to the daughter of another pair of archaeologists, one who was about my age. She'd had the same kind of sound in her voice—not exactly the same, but a similar way of letting something foreign brush over her words now and again.

Her parents had been from Bosnia. She'd grown up in the States, learning English at school, but also hearing it from her parents, for whom English was a second language. That was what Wood's words were like, as though he'd spent a good amount of time around people for whom English wasn't their first language.

What language was it? Who were the people who'd raised him? Looking at this fierce, gigantic man, it seemed impossible that he'd ever been a baby. I imagined he'd sprung into existence fully formed, like some immortal soldier.

Hands that possessed brute strength gently pushed the snarl of hair from my face, and the pad of his thumb traced my jaw, turning it left, then right, his gaze raking over me, through me. My stomach knotted tightly, but I wasn't sure it was fear.

"These cuts need to be taken care of before an infection takes hold."

With a light touch that contradicted the brutal strength of this man, he pressed the soft fabric to my face. I didn't want to show a physical reaction to the pain, so I clenched down hard enough to break my teeth as my open wounds rebelled.

Because of some of the remote places I'd been dragged to as a child, I knew how to dress my own damn wounds, and part of me knew that it would probably be smart to do so now, so I wouldn't be beholden to him.

The warmth from the fire and the comparative safety of my surroundings coaxed my body's adrenaline into receding. I was tired. So tired.

I found myself fighting to stay awake. I was tough. The crew of the Bras d'Or dig had seen me as weak and foolish, and I knew now that part of my reaction to that had come from surprise because it wasn't at all how I saw myself. I felt a desperate need to make sure that this man saw me as I truly was.

"Easy, girl," he said softly, seeing right through me, but there was a spark of anger in his eyes. Given that he was taking care of my wounds, I didn't think it was directed at me.

I know you, Wood. Jackal's words, spoken in that guttural French accent. The hint of otherness in Wood's way of speaking.

The two clearly had a history. An intimate one. And now they were enemies. At least, the whole trying to kill each other with sharp things told me they were. And

Wood seemed pretty sure that if the Cabots found me, it wouldn't end well for me.

Who was Wood? Who were the Cabots? How did they intersect?

I was pretty sure that Wood was the most dangerous of them all. But for some reason, he wasn't dangerous to me. At least, not yet.

"I can't decide if you were brave or reckless to be running around the woods," he grunted.

"I could say the same about you," I shot back without thinking. Lifting his head from his task, he glared.

Way to poke the bear, London.

His hand stilled halfway to my neck, and a cruel little half-smile quirked his beautifully brutal face.

Then those rough hands fisted in the front of my shirt—my borrowed shirt—and ripped.

CHAPTER TWELVE

Clan's Leader

THE BUTTONS I'D so painstakingly fastened went flying, and I heard the distinct ping of one hitting one of the tin basins.

A choked cry escaped my throat as he briskly peeled the fabric back from my shoulders, stare fastened on mine. I winced, but all he did was set the shirt aside on the bed.

"What the hell do you think you're doing?" I sounded a lot braver than I felt.

"I don't know where you're from, or why you seem to be having so much trouble accepting the danger that you're in." Each word was hard, brusque, like the thump of an axe into a tree trunk. "Here, you need to do what I say if you don't want to die."

I bristled; he sighed, as though I made him weary. *"Une fille stupide."*

I only spoke English, but I was pretty sure that he'd just told me I was stupid. I opened my mouth to argue, but he arched an eyebrow, and I snapped it shut, though not happily.

Dipping the cloth back into the water, he wrung out the extra, then started to stroke it over my collarbone. Again, his touch was at odds with his fierce demeanor.

"What are you doing?" I reared back as the cloth stroked over my chest. That was where the wound was, but it still far too intimate. Made me feel vulnerable.

"Cleaning your wounds." I detected sarcasm in his tone, and I didn't like it. Still, he seemed to expect me to keep doing the opposite of what he said, so I bore down and let him stroke the cloth between my breasts without another grimace.

I shouldn't have felt so naked. He'd already seen me shirtless and running for my life, right? When I'd put this bra on this morning, though, it had been with thoughts of Sean.

It seemed like a million years ago.

The gash now clean, Wood retrieved a small tin. When he removed the lid, licorice scent of turpentine, a hit of undiluted pine, reached my nostrils.

"What is this?" With the utmost care, he put it on my cuts, the coolness against my warm skin brought on a shiver.

"It's for disinfecting. If you are asking what it is made of, you'll have to ask the medicine woman at the trading post."

Medicine woman? Trading post? My heart jumped at that thought, and the pulling need to get there became a priority. There were answers there. I was sure of it.

"Where is the trading post?"

He grunted. "By the river."

Verbose, he was not.

"Where is the river?" When he painted the last bit of my gash with the salve, his rough fingertips scraped over my skin, igniting nerve endings, and I felt myself tense.

The sensation wasn't unpleasant. And that did, in fact, make me *stupide*.

"Through the trees." I couldn't tell if he was deliberately obtuse. "What were you doing in the cave?"

The cave. It was the cave that had hurtled me through… what? Time? Space? Into a different dimension? I had no idea. But it called me to with a fervor that was deafening. My answers were there; I knew they were.

I jerked my chin to where Wood had placed the Polaroid. "I was taking pictures."

I almost told him what I'd been taking pictures of— the long skeleton of the king, so lonely on the giant stone slab. But if indeed I'd been yanked back in time… how far back was I? Was the cave already a sealed-off tomb, the king lying alone on the cold slab of rock?

"What do you mean, taking pictures?" He scowled. "Pictures are painted. Or remembered in the mind."

His fingers again grazed the skin of my stomach, and this time I jerked back. The skin surrounding the cuts was hot, nearly feverish, and the sensation of a simple touch was intensified tenfold.

His eyes shot back to mine, and at that moment I felt stripped and vulnerable, the sensations coursing through me as thrilling as they were frightening. Something pulsed in the air, something that made my pulse accelerate, pounding through my veins.

He turned away, grabbed a rough woolen blanket from where it was draped over the end of the bed. I averted my eyes from the ribbons of his scars. The air surrounding us cooled ever so slightly.

"This should warm you."

"Thanks," I said. I wasn't cold. Not anymore.

He gave me a curt nod, and turned from me, hefting a split log and adding it to the fire. Straightening, he surfed his fingers over a high shelf and produced another shirt for me, the same red flannel as the first. I wondered if he wore anything else.

"You need dry clothing before you get sick." His brow furrowed as he looked back at me. His stare caught on my bra before he abruptly looked away again. It was hard to tell with the flickering light from the fire, but I thought that the slightest flush suffused his cheeks.

"Thank you." The words felt strange in my mouth. I pulled on the warm flannel, grateful for the barrier that I could hide behind. His stare made me feel naked, though in a very different way than Jackal's did.

A whistle cut through the air. I jolted, my fingers digging into the fabric so tightly it hurt.

"Easy." Wood whistled in return. The fact that he didn't seem alarmed eased my anxiety as much as possible, given the circumstances.

He didn't even look as he reached for items on one of the rustic shelves. Selecting a tin cup and three different jars, he placed them on the table. Opening each of the jars in turn, he gave each a sniff before spooning varying amounts of each into the cup. Topping it off with a ladle full of steaming water from the kettle above the fire, he rotated the cup in his hand to swish it all around, then handed it to me.

Sinuous curls of steam rose from the shimmering surface of the cup. I breathed it in. It smelled earthy, a strong herbal scent, but it wasn't unpleasant. "What is it?"

"Tea. Drink it." He furrowed his brow, looking me over as I sat on his bed, wrapped in his shirt and his blanket, drinking his tea. He was puzzled, and I think not at all pleased to find himself with a stray woman in his space.

Muttering to himself again—I got the impression he spent a lot of time alone and had no idea that he talked to himself—he snatched a bottle from his table. Lifting it to his lips, he took a long drink.

"What is that?" I was betting that it wasn't tea. He held the bottle out to me, and my eyes watered as I sniffed the contents. "Holy shit. Where the hell do you get moonshine from?"

His face registered astonishment. "Where the hell did a woman learn such language?"

"What?" I let go of the blanket as a wave of heat suffused my body. "You're kidding, right?"

He snorted, turning to tug on a clean shirt—apparently red flannel *was* all he owned. As he covered those scars from my eyes, I couldn't help but watch. He saw me watching, but said nothing.

"Drink the tea." With one last glance my way, he stepped outside to meet the whistler, leaving me alone in his space.

He wanted me to stay here, snuggled up in his bed,

drinking tea. Comfortable as that sounded, I wasn't going to sit here like a little woman while Wood discussed my fate.

Setting the tea aside, I stood on my tiptoes, not wanting to rub the soothing salve off the soles of my feet. My soaking wet jeans rubbed the skin between my thighs roughly as I soft-footed it to the door. Holding my breath, I opened it just a crack.

"You would go against your clan?" Two shadowy figures stood outside. One was very obviously Wood— the lines of his gigantic frame were already familiar to me, even in the dark.

The other figure was very nearly as large; the lean muscles draped in red tartan, his legs bare. I couldn't see the clay markings, but I knew they were there.

I hadn't thought of it earlier since I'd been a little bit consumed with thoughts of running for my life, but now the kilted man made me think of the strange figure I'd seen outside the cave. The one who had recited the morose poem to me.

The one who had disappeared.

I sucked in a breath at the memory, cold fingers dancing over the back of my neck. At my gasp, both men craned their heads in my direction.

"Show yourself!" The stranger's voice was harsh, and I found myself looking to Wood. He shook his head slightly, his eyes glaring at me to go back inside.

To hell with that. This was about me. I might have stepped into a world where women didn't wear pants or swear, but that wasn't where I belonged. I'd have a say in my future.

I pushed through the well-hidden doorway, standing just outside. The carpet of leaves was soft on the bottom of my feet, and I wiggled my toes against it, seeking the comfort to my raw flesh.

The man grabbed Wood's arm, turning him bodily to face me. I gasped softly at the gesture, sure that Wood would pull out his axe and smite the stranger for laying a hand on him.

Wood's eyes met mine, and I saw the flicker of anger. Instead of lashing out, however, he visibly struggled to bank it, letting the other man push him in my direction, though he did breathe out irritation. "Guthrie. Enough."

The man—Guthrie?—made a show of looking me over. He snorted when he saw my wet jeans. I recognized him now—he was the leader of the men who had materialized out of the woods to fight Jackal. The one who had looked at me with murder on his face and sent me flying back toward the enemy.

"For this, you would go against your clan?" The derision in his voice made it clear that I was the *this* he was referring to. "I won't have this. I'll give you the night to do as you will with her, and then you will do as you must."

A roaring filled my ears. I flattened myself against the door, sure that a bear or some other large animal was charging. My pulse thudded, making my heart pound against my ribcage.

Nothing charged, and in the ringing silence following the thunderous sound, I realized that the sound had come from Wood. He stood chest to chest with the other man, hair bristling, teeth bared as though he was exactly the animal I'd feared.

"I cannot believe that you would suggest such a thing." He leaned impossibly closer to the other man, their noses almost touching. "You, of all people. I demand respect for her memory."

The older man was still, as immovable as if he'd been carved from stone. There was no telling what he was thinking. The silence stretched forth, and I wondered if they would stand there all night, neither man giving in.

There was nothing I could say. Contrary to what I'd thought, this disagreement didn't seem to be about me at all.

Who was the *her* they were referencing?

I didn't think I was going to find out tonight.

Slowly, silently, I backed into the cabin, closing the door behind me. In the warm light of the fire, I peeled my wet jeans down my legs and, with a shrug, my underwear as well. I laid them out at the end of the bed, and the simple fabric against the rough wool looked strange. Alien.

I supposed it was.

Swinging my legs up into the bed, I hesitated, then reached for the tin mug of tea. Now cool, I gulped down the contents, which tasted like grass but were surprisingly soothing.

Easing back on the pillow, I craned my neck, listening for more conversation outside. There was silence, but not the same silence of the two men as they'd stood toe to toe. A gunshot sounded, and I hunched into a ball on the bed. Another followed it, then another, then a grunt, and a thud. The scent of freshly cut wood drifted in through the small window as the noises resumed. Crack, crack, crack, grunt, thud.

Wood was chopping… well, Wood.

The other man was gone.

Frightened and alone, I curled into the bed and pulled the blankets tighter as the rhythm continued. My eyelids grew heavier, weighed down with fatigue until I could keep them open no more, and I fell asleep.

CHAPTER THIRTEEN

New Day

I ROLLED OVER, a square of lemony sunlight hitting me in the face. I jolted up with a start, my heart pounding in my ears.

I was a light sleeper, a restless one. My mother had always said I slept like an eggbeater, tossing and turning and kicking until I'd beaten the blankets into a tangled submission. Right now, though, the woolen blanket was lying smoothly over of me, as though I hadn't moved all night.

What the hell had been in that tea?

I hugged the blanket to me, memories of last night firing my blood and filling me with unease. I blinked, rubbed my eyes and stole a quick glance around. My stare swept the entire room once before being pulled back to where Wood sat in one of his chairs in front of the fire. He was examining the contents of my backpack—the one I'd lost in the cave. He must have gone there while I'd been sleeping.

Anxiety, stress, and grief crashed over me as though I'd stepped under a waterfall. I'd slept through a chance to get back to the cave—to get back home.

In the bright morning light, I could see Wood's face more clearly. I hadn't had a moment to think about his age yesterday, but this morning, the pale sunshine revealed some fine lines around his eyes. They were enhanced by the slight shadows underneath his eyes.

The blankets beside me were smooth, untouched. He hadn't slept in the bed, and I swallowed, hard, when I realized that I would have had no idea if he had.

Had he slept at all?

I propped myself up on my elbows, studying him. The movement made him glance my way, and when he did, distrust danced in the depths of his eyes, which seemed even darker now that it was day.

Fear gripped my throat.

"What do they call you?" Yesterday, he hadn't exactly been warm and fuzzy, but he'd showed a whisper of gentleness when treating my wounds. The one across my chest and stomach pulled uncomfortably as I shifted in the bed, but I knew it was far less painful than it would have been without his care.

Right now he was eyeing me with the same distrust and hostility that Guthrie had. I'd appreciated his fierceness when he'd charged from the forest and swung hiss wicked axe at Jackal, but having it directed at me made frost settle into my blood.

"What do you mean?" I asked as I shimmied backward, pressing my back against the rough wooden logs.

"I am Wood." That hint of an accent was thicker

today, his words slow and forceful, as though he was speaking to someone he thought was an idiot. "Who are you?"

"My name is London." I had to bite my tongue to keep from using the same tone back. The night before, I might have. In the cold light of Wood's distrustful gaze this morning? It didn't seem like the brightest idea.

"Lon-don." I could almost picture the syllables rolling across his tongue as he tasted them. "What kind of name is Lon-don?"

"What kind of name is Wood?" I shot back, then cringed.

Maybe you are stupid, London.

His eyes darkened even more as he glare at me. "I didn't choose it. It was given to me because of my birthplace."

Wood was born in the…woods. Of course he was.

"Yeah, me too." I snorted, but his expression didn't change. "I guess we have something in common."

"I've never heard of such a place."

"It's a long way from here." Was there a London at all in this… time? Dimension? Planet?

I couldn't hold back the snort of laughter. Yeah, maybe when I'd fallen into the water, it had shuttled me straight to the moon.

He furrowed his brow as I laughed. He didn't see the joke.

"How did you come to have these?" He waved a stack of square papers before me. I wanted to jump up and grab them when I realized that they were the Polaroids I'd taken the day before. He held them above his head, a place I'd never be able to reach without a ladder even if I jumped up and tried.

"Those are pictures. Photographs." I eyed the stack with longing. Seeing those would prove to me that I wasn't insane—my real life existed. "Remember, I told you that's what I was doing in the cave. I was taking pictures."

"Pictures are painted or remembered," he reminded me, thumbing through the stack. He stopped on a photo Sean and me, examined it, then turned it over to look at the blank back. "I have never seen paintings such as these. Did you paint them? Is that what you are trying to say?"

"No." I couldn't hold back the frustration. "I can't even draw a stick person. I took them. With that."

I pointed at the Polaroid, which still sat on the table.

"What is a stick person?" He seemed as startled as he'd been when I'd said *shit* the night before.

I sighed, shaking my head. "It's not important."

Pushing back the blankets, I started to slide from the bed. Wood exhaled softly. His stare seemed frozen to my legs. My bare legs. I'd forgotten that I wasn't wearing pants. Or underwear, for that matter.

But I couldn't hide in the bed all day. Deciding to brazen it out, I tugged at the plaid shirt I still wore. It was massive on me, hanging nearly to my knees. As long as I watched how I moved, I'd be fine until I got dressed, which I couldn't do with Wood here.

Pulling that shirt down so far I thought the worn flannel might rip, I stood on shaky legs.

"Ow." I winced as I realized how sore I was. Everything ached—my muscles, even my bones. Pausing for a moment to let my limbs wake up, I looked up through my eyelashes at Wood. He was… well, he was looking at me. I can't describe it any other way. He was looking at me as though he'd never seen a woman before. It should have made me uncomfortable, maybe, but it didn't. Instead, a tiny spark ignited in my belly, growing steadily, warming me from the inside out.

Ignoring it, I moved to the table, the wounds on my feet far less swollen and angry than the night before, thanks to the salve. For this I was grateful. I grabbed at the camera like a lifeline, opening the plastic casing in the place where the film was loaded.

To my surprise, it was still fairly dry. The camera itself was bulky, old-fashioned, fitted together more tightly than the mass-produced devices used today. I wondered if that had made a difference, if the device would still work.

"Look." I held up the camera and pointed at the film pack still lodged inside. "These are called plastic negatives. They're covered in chemicals. When I press this button, one of the negatives moves in front of the camera lens. It captures an image of whatever you're taking a picture of."

I clicked the film compartment closed, lifting the camera. I thought I'd try to take a picture of Wood and kill two birds with one stone—see if the camera was still working and, if it was, demonstrate to him what the device did.

I aimed the camera at him and froze when I saw the confusion on his face, confusion mixed with not a little bit of apprehension.

"Where is this London you come from?" I could see that he wasn't afraid of me—I wasn't sure there was anything that this man *was* afraid of—but it was obvious that he had no idea what to do with me. I didn't even know what to do with myself at this point. "How did they come to have things such as this? I have never heard of negative chemicals. Or plas-tic. What is it made from?"

Questions about my hobby awakened my inner nerd. Nothing would have made my day like sitting down in front of that fire and explaining the history of photographic images.

Wood's disbelief made me pause. What would he do if I took a photo of him, if he saw his own eyes and mouth and beard coming to life on a little square of plastic-paper? What would it mean to him? To his beliefs?

What would it mean for my safety?

"It's not important." I swallowed against a dry throat as I placed the camera back on the table. "Yes, these are common in London … well, where I came from."

He picked up the camera gingerly, as though he thought it might be cursed. It looked like a baby toy in his massive hands.

"So if I understand, it helps you to paint the picture?" He poked a giant finger into the lens, making me wince.

I opened my mouth to explain again, but after a moment I closed it. He wasn't a primitive caveman—no, if anything, I thought he was likely quite smart. But he had absolutely no frame of reference for this kind of technology. No way of understanding.

Making him understand might make him fear. And making him fear might put me in danger.

Sinking my teeth into my lower lip, I stroked a final finger over the hard plastic shell of the camera.

"Yes, it helps me to… paint the picture." It wasn't exactly a lie, I supposed. The camera harnessed the image I wanted to capture, a vision I had in my mind's eye.

I wasn't going to explain any further.

"You went back to the cave." I indicated the contents of my backpack, which was on the floor. "Did I… was it…"

How was I supposed to ask this?

"Spit it out, girl." His voice was a low rumble. It reminded me of thunder on those summer nights when rain beat down on the top of our tent, wherever in the world it was staked.

"The cave. Were there lanterns set up…a tomb?"

"A tomb?" His eyebrows shot up.

"Never mind," I said quickly and started putting all my things back into my damp backpack. His hand closed over mine, stopping me, his grip so tight, and firm, my gaze snapped to his.

"I do not understand you."

Well, I didn't understand him, either. Looked like neither of us were going to figure things out any time soon, either.

"I told you, my name is London. I'm a…" What did I tell him? An archaeologist? A student? I somehow knew none of those things would make sense to him. "I'm not…from around here."

"That is obvious." His nostrils flared. He stared at me another moment, his expression perplexed. Without another word, he stood, and the scraping of his boots on the lumber sparked every frayed nerve in my body.

My gaze followed him, watching carefully, cautiously as he tossed another log into the fire. That's when I noticed my jeans and panties strung up to dry in front of the stove. I hissed out a breath when Wood tugged my cotton panties from the rope and held them up. I had a… how shall we say it? I had a big butt. Still, my underwear looked positively miniscule in those thick fingers. For a long awkward moment, we stared at each other, silence hovering like the sharp blade of his axe.

"What is this?"

CHAPTER FOURTEEN

In The Present

*O*H, *GOD*. I felt… I didn't know what I felt. I had the wildest urge to laugh.

"They go under my…trousers," I said finally, face flaming. "Girls, um, wear them."

He angled his head, his eyes moving slowly over my body, traveling the length of my legs and coming to rest on the hem of the shirt. I tugged at it, suddenly very, very aware of my nakedness beneath the worn flannel.

A line pinched between his brows. "These are your…drawers?"

"Yes." I reached out and grabbed them from him. I quickly balled them in my fist, and stuffed them into my backpack, away from his curious eyes. "My drawers."

He studied me like I was an alien in a foreign land, and I suppose I was. "They are very… small."

"Not really." I wondered what he'd have thought if, instead of the panties, I'd worn the skimpy thong that I'd packed for the trip. You know, just in case.

He went still, deadly quiet, and I tugged on the hem of the big shirt again, feeling like a bug under a microscope.

"Guthrie thinks you're a whore who stole from the Cabots."

What?

"I'm not a whore." I squeaked with indignation, slipping back onto the cot to cover myself with the linen. "Why would he say that? What did I do to him?"

"You are in my bed without any drawers on," he reminded me, and I felt my blush grow darker still.

"They were wet!"

He raised an eyebrow, and I closed my eyes, hearing what I'd just said. Since what I was saying wasn't helping, I shut up.

"If you are not a whore who stole from them, then he believes you are a spy. That the Cabots paid for a whore, which would be you, then staged the scene in the woods to insert you into their clan."

"A whore *and* a spy. How flattering," I snapped. "To what end? Who the hell are the Cabots, and why on earth would they care about having a spy in a village?"

Wood crossed his arms over his massive chest and regarded me coolly. "You are the one who should be answering questions, but I am curious, so I will play your game. The Cabots are loggers. They cut timber, then drive the logs down the river to sell to various trading posts. It is dangerous work. They are dangerous men."

"Still not making any sense. What the hell would loggers want with a spy?" I got a brief flash of memory; a video watched during one of the times I'd attended a brick and mortar elementary school. It had had a brief two-minute segment about log driving, men who rolled the logs beneath them with their feet while they impossibly balanced on top of them, driving them down a body of water.

"The Cabots want to find the village because they want to find me." Wood spoke slowly, his voice rougher than I'd heard it yet. "They will punish the clansmen because of me. I will not allow that to happen. Do you understand?"

Oh yes. I understood the blade-sharp edge in his tone. He would not let me lead the Cabots to the village, though I still wasn't sure of the connection between the clansmen and himself.

I needed to get back home. Then I'd be right the hell out of everyone's business.

"Are you?" Wood pinned me with a stare.

"Am I what?" I couldn't have moved while he looked at me like that. His eyes—those deep, dark depths. When I'd first arrived in Nova Scotia, I'd looked into the depths at Bras d'Or lake at night and wondered if it had a bottom at all, or if someone could just keep diving down, down, down and never stop.

Wood's eyes were like that. They were dark—too dark, almost, against his sun-lightened hair and tanned skin. I couldn't look away—I was hypnotized.

"Are you a spy?" He took a step toward me. One step for him crossed half the floor. He was now close enough that I could feel the heat radiating from his body.

"No," I whispered. I trembled.

"Are you a whore?" He took another step, bringing

him directly in front of me. The top of my head barely grazed his shoulder, and my neck hurt when I craned it to hold his gaze.

I didn't want to be held captive like this, a tasty treat stuck in a web, waiting to be consumed. I had to break the spell.

"There isn't enough money in the world to pay me for this." Flicking open the top button of the shirt, I bared my collarbone, where the gash from the sword started. "Don't you think?"

The silence stretched, and my stomach coiled so tight I thought I was going to throw up. I wasn't a whore, or a spy, just someone very far from home, but I was pretty sure they weren't going to believe that.

"I think you have a lot of questions to answer."

My throat tightened, and tears pricked my eyes. *Don't cry, London. Don't cry.* I *hated* to cry, and here I was, tearing up for the second time around this man.

No more. I squared my shoulders and pulled myself together. I needed to get back to the cave. That was my goal, and I needed to focus on it.

"This is the truth. I was at the cave, and there was a storm. I fell into the water. When I crawled out of the lake, Jackal and his men were there. They chased me into the woods, and you know the rest." He continued to stare at me, and I shifted uncomfortably under his gaze. "Who is Guthrie?"

Barrel arms folded across his chest as he dipped his head and stared at me. He hesitated before offering a short answer. "The leader of the Bras d'Or clan. He wants me to bring you to him."

Like hell.

But now Wood needed something. And I needed something. I'd never been very good at haggling—in markets in countries across the world, I often wound up paying *more* for my purchase instead of less. But survival now demanded I give it my best try.

"I'll go." I crossed my arms over my chest, mimicking his stance. "But only if you take me back to the cave first."

He arched an eyebrow, and I knew what he was thinking. If he wanted to take me to the clan, there wasn't a damn thing I could do about it, not if he decided to haul me up over his shoulder again like he had the night before.

But I could scream. I could kick and yell and draw the attention of anyone who might be close by—anyone who wanted to find the village and who the clan wanted to stay hidden from.

"The cave is just a cave," he finally said, cocking his head. "Whatever you are searching for, it is not there."

"Please." My voice broke. What was happening back… back where I'd come from? Had time frozen? Or was it tick-tick-ticking by, leaving everyone who knew me in a panic?

Emmett. I'd texted him to come to the cave. What had he thought when he'd found nothing but my backpack?

I eyed the bag on the floor. Had he even found that? Did the bag exist in two separate dimensions, or was it solely here with me?

My head hurt.

After what felt like an eternity, Wood heaved a rough sigh. "You cannot go back into the woods dressed like that. You claim not to be a whore, but I cannot imagine who else would wear such a thing."

Giving the finger to the big, bad lumberjack was probably not the smartest idea.

He reached into my bag and held up my underwear again, and I felt blood suffuse my cheeks. Jumping a little, I grabbed at them.

"Well, no one will see them under my jeans, will they?" I tried to reach around him for my pants, but he shifted to block me.

"You cannot wear those." From the end of the bed, he lifted a… dress? Yes, a dress, holding it up for me to see. He seemed vaguely proud. "You will wear this."

"I—" I was speechless. The dress was ankle-length. Nut-brown. It had long sleeves that ended in a tight cuff, and it buttoned down the front.

I looked from it to the small pile of other garments still sitting on the bed—a pair of baggy cotton shorts, a loose undershirt type thing, and a pair of shoes that reminded of those ugly Doc Marten-type shoes worn by everyone in nineties sitcoms.

Losing my breath, I sat down heavily on the bed.

"I went to the trading post this morning." Wood was eyeing me warily, though why he would be worried about my reaction, I had no idea. I was too busy wiping cold sweat off my forehead to do anything else.

That dress—it was something that might have been worn in Little House on the Prairie. Maybe even before that. And it wasn't one of those costumes made from polyester so cheap that it snagged on the skin.

This was the real deal. This was what had been available in the trading post when Wood had gone, which must have been in the middle of the night, which explained why he looked so tired. But if this was what had been available, then this was what was in fashion.

When I'd first set foot on Cape Breton Island, when I'd looked at the lake and felt that I'd stepped into another world—that was what I was feeling now. Because I had. I'd fallen into the water in the cave, and it had somehow, impossibly, sent me somewhere else entirely.

It should have been the Cabots that drove that home.

Or the appearance of Wood and his axe.

Or the clansmen when they'd silently appeared from the woods.

No. No, those things had made me panic, but what drove home the reality of my situation was a simple, somewhat ugly brown dress.

"Girl?" Wood shifted uneasily from one boat-like booted foot to the other. If I hadn't had nausea roiling greasily in my gut, I might have been amused that I'd managed to disconcert the giant. "London?"

It didn't matter, though—none of it mattered. It didn't matter that part of me maybe, kind of felt a spark of gratitude for Wood. Or that the rest of me was terrified of the situation I'd landed myself in.

Right now, I had no one to rely on but myself.

"I'm fine." Sucking in a deep breath, I forced myself to brush the last of the sweat from my brow and to stand. I turned away from the dress, trying to gather my composure.

"I appreciate the gesture, but I'll wear my own things."

I wouldn't—I couldn't—wear that dress. The dress that smacked me in the face with its otherness. It would be a constant reminder that I was trapped here, with no way to get back to the dig, to Emmett, to Sean and my parents, even to Mairi.

"It is not a gesture, girl, nor is it an option." The faint glower on his face told me he was not used to being refused. "Cabot's men are looking for the girl in the blue trousers."

"You'll be with me, right? In the woods?" I was not going to wear that dress. Even if it hadn't made me sick to my stomach, it wasn't practical. I'd never worn skirts or dresses. They weren't practical on a dig, and I couldn't see them being any more practical here.

If I saw the cave, or another chance to get back to my place in the world, then I needed to be able to run.

"What does that have to do with anything?"

I turned back to Wood and leaned against the solid wood table. "Are you going to hand me over?"

He went silent and stared down at me, face inscrutable. "No."

"Then I have nothing to fear." The quiver at the end of my words told a different story.

"You have a lot to fear, girl." Wood allowed himself one of those little half smiles he'd offered before, the ones that seemed more full of wicked intent than mirth.

"I don't think I do. Not when I'm with you." I held

my breath. I wanted to nurture this protectiveness that he seemed to feel toward me, even though I planned to make my way to the cave first chance that I got.

For the briefest of moments, his warrior's features softened, the fine lines around his eyes smoothing out, making him look younger. Less fierce.

My heart did a strange little shimmy.

Scowling, he turned back to the fire. Taking up his axe, which was resting against the wall, he began to polish the head with a cloth. He held the blade up to examined the sharp edge. The metal glinted in the rays of sunlight streaming in, and in that instant, my mind rewound to the discovery at the cave, the ceremonial axe lying beside the lonely skeleton.

Stay in the present, London. Or, you know, the past. Just focus on getting home.

CHAPTER FIFTEEN

Finding Home

"Um...I NEED TO go to the bathroom." Wood's eyes narrowed. "You know. I need to relieve myself."

He wasn't getting it. I did a little shimmy, the tea having suddenly caught up with me. Understanding crossed his face.

"Outside." He gestured toward the door with a jerk of his head. Uh, of course it was outside. I prayed that he had something more elaborate than a hole in the ground.

Unbearably conscious of the fact that I still wasn't wearing any pants, I tugged on the socks that he tossed me. Thick and woolen, they were huge—obviously his. When I slipped my feet into them, they came to nearly my knees, the heel sticking out strangely around my midcalf. Still, they were soft and warm, cushioning the lacerations on the bottoms of my feet when I forced my feet into the shoes he'd gotten me as well.

The shoes were too tight, but I couldn't imagine

wandering around barefoot when my feet looked like ground meat.

I followed him outside, about ten paces away from the artfully disguised cabin. Tucked against a tree was a bucket filled with sand, a carved-out seat—wooden, of course—on top.

Primitive, but I'd seen worse. *Used* worse. I resisted the urge to cheer. I ducked behind the wood to do my business, painfully aware that he could hear me, which, thanks to my upbringing, wasn't anything I'd been self-conscious about before.

Still, my cheeks burned when I'd finished and waded out from behind the tree to find Wood maybe ten feet away, standing with his back to me, searching through what appeared to be an icebox.

"Do you, um, have soap?" I asked, and rubbed my hands together, indicating I'd like to wash up. I suddenly felt grimy all over.

"I know what soap is." His voice was wry as he closed the lid. "I've even been known to use it on occasion."

I cocked my head. Had he just made a joke? I didn't know what to think about that and was certainly too startled to laugh as I followed him back to the cabin, trying to memorize the shapes of the trees we passed so I could find my way back.

I was pretty sure that was a hopeless endeavor.

"Here." Inside, he took up the same basin he'd used to wash my wounds with last night. It was empty and dry. From the kettle he kept over the fire, he poured two inches of water into the basin, then set a rough cloth and a sliver of soap beside it before striding back outside.

I frowned at the water. Where did it come from? Obviously, there was no running water. The lake was too far, so he must have gotten it from the river he'd mentioned. He would have had to hike there, then haul it back. Having me with him meant he needed more water. Water, tea. Shoes and soap.

Why was he doing this? I didn't understand.

While I waited for the water to cool off, I lifted the sliver of soap and sniffed. Dry, it didn't have much of a scent, a far cry from the heavily scented bars available at drugstores. When I swirled it through the water experimentally, I wrinkled my nose. The water made the bar slimy and unpleasant to touch, and it smelled a little bit like oil. Still, it lathered up on the cloth, and the cloth removed the layer of filth from my skin, so I was happy enough.

I scrubbed every inch of my skin with soap and water, sliding the cloth under the oversized shirt to wash beneath since I wasn't about to get completely naked when Wood could walk in at any moment. Once my skin was red from scrubbing, I dunked my head into the soapy water and lathered again, working a repulsive amount of grit and even some bits of leaves from the strands.

Finally, I removed the socks and shoes and washed my feet. The trading post might have had a medicine woman, but I didn't want to chance an infection without a doctor.

Damp and clean, I worked my legs back into my now dry underwear and jeans. I worked on my bra beneath the massive plaid shirt, which was still clean enough, since all I'd done was sleep in it. To make its size less cumbersome, I tied a knot at my waist, reducing the bulk.

There. That was better. Except that my hair was dripping and tangled and in my face, and I had no comb. Looking around, hoping to miraculously find a barrette or a pack of Goody hair elastics, I finally landed on the strip of cloth that Wood had torn a piece off of to tend to my cut the night before. The cut had knit closed overnight, and I didn't feel the need to redress it, so instead I ripped off a ribbon of the thin fabric and used it to pull my hair back into a bumpy ponytail.

I was working my feet back into the too-big socks and the too-small boots when Wood came back in. I noticed that his eyes were averted when he walked through the door, as though he expected me to still be naked and scrubbing away.

"I'll empty the water." Now that I'd realized that having me here made extra work for him, I was anxious to do something. I carefully carried the basin outside and threw the water into the bushes, then stood for a moment, listening to it drip down to the ground.

If I closed my eyes and pretended hard enough, I could imagine that this was just another dig in just another part of the world.

I thought of Emmett and the snake, and my heart contracted.

I carried the basin back inside, setting it carefully on the table. While I'd been outside, Wood had set food on the table. He grunted and gestured to me to sit down.

For once I listened, my stomach growling embarrassingly loud.

When was the last time I'd eaten? I'd had a few bites of my cold bagel while taking Polaroids of the cave, and that was it.

"What is this?" I was starting to feel bad for being a drain on Wood's resources when I planned to bolt for the cave the second I could. I shouldn't eat his food as well.

My stomach cramped. I needed to eat.

"Cold bannock." I took a piece in my hand. It was a dense bread-type thing, and when I nibbled on the end, it was dry as dust. "Here."

He shoved a small bowl with a serving of something that looked like stewed fruit across the table before dishing one out for himself. Gingerly I dipped the end of the bannock into it. It was some kind of preserve—blueberry, maybe. Not quite as sweet as jam, but it wet the bannock enough to swallow.

"Take a piece of bannock with you." Wood shoved back from the table as I was swallowing the last of my blueberries. "We have a long walk ahead."

"Where are we going?" My fingertips turned to ice.

"I will take you to the cave." He scowled down at me as I brushed crumbs from my shirt. "I do not believe you will find anything other than what I saw this morning. It is just a cave. But on the very small chance that you have not dreamt all of this, it would suit my purposes to be rid of you."

I felt inexplicably hurt.

What the hell is your problem, London? You don't want to be here any more than he wants you here. He's taking you to the cave! That's what you want!

I was silent as I followed him out of the cabin. I looked back at the tiny house hidden amongst the roots of a tree, and wondered if I would ever be there again.

We set off through the brush. Despite his size, Wood was light on his feet, clearly at home here amongst the trees. I, on the other hand, found myself tiring after twenty minutes, though I supposed I was still exhausted from the day before. I also kept reaching for the straps of my backpack and the Polaroid around my neck, neither of which were there. Their absence made me feel hugely naked. I couldn't remember the last time I went anywhere at all without at least a purse to hold my essentials.

Twenty minutes more and the wounds on my feet started to sting. The too-small shoes made the woolen socks abrade my skin, and I knew I was bleeding.

I refused to complain, limping when Wood wasn't looking at me, and forcing myself to walk normally when he was. If I mentioned my pain, I was pretty sure I'd find myself back over his shoulder, and that was the last place I wanted to be. No, where I wanted to be was home, back in my comfy bed. Hell, I'd even settle for the uncomfortable bed at the Cheticamp motel.

The others had to be worried about me. An undignified sound caught in my throat. Okay, well at least Emmett had to be worried about me. Sean obviously wasn't.

That wasn't entirely fair. Sean had known me for a long time. At the very least, he would have been worried enough to call my parents, though I doubted he would have mentioned what, exactly, had sent me running to the cave in a thunderstorm.

Would I ever see either of them again? Just like that, terror at my situation swept through me, and my knees buckled. I heaved in a deep breath, then forced myself onward.

"How much farther?" I asked, voice tight. I'd thought I was in decent shape, but emotional upheaval, my second strenuous hike in twenty-four hours, minimal food and my wounds were showing me that an Olympic athlete, I was not.

Wood turned, narrowed those dark eyes of his and looked me over. "Are you not well?"

"I'm well enough." I couldn't help snapping. I was pretty sure I was entitled to be cranky. "I'm just not used to this much hiking. Walking," I amended, in case he didn't know what hiking meant.

His brow furrowed. "How do you normally travel?"

Car. Bus. Plane. Train. Subway. Bicycle. Rickshaw. Buggy.

I doubted he knew what any of these were.

"Never mind, I just…are we close?" I shifted my stance, putting pressure on one foot then the other, all the time trying not to wince.

I shrieked when, before I could catch even a breath, he scooped me into his arms. "You should have told me your feet hurt."

His face was set in a glower. I waited for him to call me *une fille stupide* again.

The man was way too astute for his own good, but I

guess that was what it took to survive in a time like this.

But what time *was* this? All I'd seen were the woods, the cabin, the clothing and the toilet. It spoke of primitive times, yes, but he did have an icebox, and a trading post.

"The boots…they're just a bit tight," I explained, guilt washing over me. He'd been kind enough to provide me with footwear when my presence was clearly a pain in his ass, and here I was complaining about it.

"I will get you a new pair." His words were stilted. I winced as I thought of the trouble that would take him. "Until then, I will carry you."

Great.

CHAPTER SIXTEEN

The Cave

HE CONTINUED FORWARD. At least this time he carried me fireman-style, rather than slung over his shoulder like he'd just clubbed me over the head and was dragging me back to his cave, though as I thought of his cabin, I supposed that that description was surprisingly apt.

Another ten minutes, and I thought that I could hear water when I strained my ears. We were close, and the longing for home suffused me. I wanted to leap from his arms and sprint for the cave, but I forced myself to be patient.

My body bobbed in his arms as he walked, and his warm scent reached my nostrils. Cedarwood and pine and smoke. It shouldn't have been so appealing. It was also quiet. Quiet let my mind wander, and if I let my mind wander, I'd start to think about what would happen if the cave had really become just a cave.

"Do you live in these woods alone?"

Wood grunted his response and not only did I take that as a yes, I also got the sneaking suspicion that he'd done more talking these last twenty-four hours than he'd done in a month.

"How come you live alone? Don't you get lonely out here?" I frowned as a thought occurred to me. "If you owe loyalty to the clan, why don't you live with them? Or is this a thing? Are there lots of lumberjacks that live all alone in the woods?"

"Lumber-what?" He squinted down at me as though I'd spoken in another language. He was avoiding my questions.

"Do you have a wife?" I suspected not because a wife likely would have protested a strange woman in her husband's bed without her drawers on. Plus, his cabin was so… stark. Sterile. If a woman lived there, I was sure I would have seen some trace of it.

His entire body stiffened, and a deep guttural sound caught in his throat, though he didn't speak. Okay, I'd obliviously hit a soft spot.

Moving on.

"Well then, how about a girlfriend?"

He grunted.

"A boyfriend?"

"Silence does not always have to be filled." His teeth clicked, and even though I couldn't see his jaw through that long beard, I could visualize the muscles rippling. "We're here."

He stepped through the edge of the trees, and free of the canopy of leaves, I could hear the waves of the water as they lapped on the shore. We'd emerged right by the mouth of the cave, right where that strange man had scared ten years off my life. Where I'd seen the white buck.

I cranked my neck, looking around. Neither was there.

The opening of the cave yawned in front of us. No rubble to show that it had only recently been unblocked. It was obviously the same cave, but it was as though I was looking at a slightly blurry photograph—it wasn't exactly the same. Made sense, since natural formations changed over time.

I thought of the skeleton that I knew wasn't inside here and now. Everything changed over time.

I squirmed, and Wood set me down on the uneven ground. Breathing deeply, I tried to open up my senses, searching for that crackle of energy from the night before.

I heard the soothing motions of the waves, smelled the sweetness of decaying algae. I could taste the dampness on my tongue, and feel the humidity in the moist breeze that kissed my cheek. But when I looked around, all I saw was the cave, the bright clear sky, the trees whistling in the wind.

Not a single goddamn spark of otherworldly power rent the morning air. My heart sank at the stillness around me, but surely, surely if I searched I'd find my way home.

Pushing away from Wood, I scrabbled over the rocks in front of the cave. They'd been worn into steps by the repeated passing of feet in my time, but now were simply large outcroppings of rock.

The cave opening was still small, and though I could pass through, Wood had to duck.

Inside the cave it was empty. No giant slabs of stone carved with runes. Not nearly as many stalactite and stalagmite teeth threatening to swallow us whole.

The chamber where the dead king's body should have lain wasn't accessible, the yawning corridor only a slender crack. Beside it, though, was an opening that I didn't remember, and something frantic overtook me as I shoved my way through.

"*Merde!*" Behind me, I heard Wood curse. His massive frame was too large to squeeze into the opening. I couldn't wait for him, using my hands to feel my way forward through the dark.

At the end of the cavity, I paused, struggling to hear over my heaving breath. I could hear the lake beneath me, could feel the dampness in the air. But there was no warm water pooling around my feet. I was fairly certain that this wasn't even the same corridor I'd been in before.

There was certainly no magic here. I collapsed with a small cry.

"London!" Wood slammed a fist against the wall of the cave, his voice echoing off the vaulted ceiling. "What happened?"

I barely heard him. My blood roared.

No. No. No.

Slowly, aching as though I'd aged half a century, I crawled back through the corridor on my hands and knees. When I poked my head through, coughing against the dust that my movements had disturbed, Wood caught me under the arms and hauled me out from the rock.

Those large hands patted me down, ascertaining that I was still in one piece, that some cave-dwelling monster hadn't gotten me in its jaws and taken a large chomp. That done, he simply set me back on my feet. It was hard to see his face in the dimness of the cave, but I thought I could detect the lightest dusting of sympathy on that fierce face.

One big hand pushed my hair from my face.

I cried. It didn't matter that I hated crying, the sobs ripped themselves out of my chest, and I felt every fiber separate. Terror was black, slick and oily as I gulped at it and it slithered throughout my body, filling my veins, making me sick.

Up until this moment, I'd been certain that the cave was the answer. That all I had to do was get here, and I'd be able to slip back through the crack between this time and my own.

Reality sliced through me like the blade of Wood's axe. I couldn't get back. I was trapped here, in this primitive time, with a lumberjack who didn't want me. A gang of immoral loggers with rape and torture on their minds and a clan of kilted warriors, however, very much did.

I was never going to see my parents again.

I was going to die.

Wood stood, a silent sentry to my grief as I had a complete breakdown at his feet. When my sobs had quieted, and I looked up at him with wary eyes, he sighed and, catching me by the elbows, hauled me back up to my feet.

"Gird your loins, girl." He set me down, and the severity of his expression sent another stone sinking in my stomach. Hysteria clawed at me from within, desperate to get out and take hold of the world.

"I'm sorry you didn't find what you were looking for. That would have been easier for us both. Now I'm going to have to take you to Guthrie."

CHAPTER SEVENTEEN

Protector

"No!" The scream ripped from my throat, echoing off the rocks. Panic flooded my veins as one of my hands found the slash on my torso, pressing into it until it protested as if the pain would wake me from this nightmare.

I didn't think—I just ran.

I hadn't gotten three feet before Wood had overtaken me, wrapping those tree trunk arms around my waist, lifting me right off my feet.

"No!" I shrieked again, kicking back against his shins, my voice bordering on hysteria. I felt the now-familiar sensation of him throwing me over his shoulder, and rather than hold on to the stiffness that anger brought to my muscles, I let myself flop, turning to deadweight. It surprised him enough to loosen his grip, and I flew out of his arms, hurtling myself forward.

"Get back here." The growl in his voice was no joke, but pure adrenaline had taken over. I darted forward, away from the cave and back into the woods, the ill-fitting shoes slowing my progress, not that I was that fast to begin with.

"London." I felt his breath against my ear seconds before his arms again banded around my midsection. He hauled me off my feet again and simply stood, holding me tightly while I flailed. A grunt escaped him when one of my feet connected with his shins, but he didn't loosen his grip.

My movements slowed. I was still tired, so tired from running around the woods, and I hadn't had much to eat. Add in shock, and I wasn't going anywhere. As I started to lag, Wood hauled me up higher, high enough that he could speak directly into my ear.

"Where do you think you're going to go, girl?" His words were rough with exasperation. "What do you think you're going to do in the woods? You'd be dead within a day. Bears, lynx—you'd be a tasty meal. That's if you don't stumble across Jackal, and if you do, a bear attack would be a better fate."

My breath was coming hard. I quivered, all of the pent-up rage and terror that had flooded my system in the last twenty-four hours ready to make a repeat occurrence.

"London." Loosening one arm, he ran a massive, calloused hand over the length of my hair, then repeated the gesture. Was he petting me? "Your best chance is with me."

"I—" I wanted to go home. Being here, by the cave, listening to the crash of the lake's waves on the rock, made me long for it so desperately that the taste was bitter on my tongue.

I had no way home. I was stuck. Stuck here, wherever here was. And I was scared.

"Why are you helping me?" I finally asked wearily. Maybe if I understood that, I'd be less terrified. I'd been nothing but a hassle ever since he'd charged into that clearing last night, and I couldn't understand why he'd protected me in the first place.

He eyed me, something I couldn't decipher flickering through the depths of those inky eyes. The silence was ropy with tension.

"It's the right thing to do." He finally spat the words out, but I was surprised at the bitterness behind them. Still, I wasn't going to look a gift horse in the mouth. If he was feeling obligated, I was going to push it as far as I could.

"I want to go to the trading post." The idea occurred to me as I spoke. The cave was closed, and Wood was right, I couldn't wander the woods. I knew a few things about survival, actually, given the time I'd spent on digs, but those had always been prepared for with research into the location.

I didn't know how to hide, though.

I wasn't entirely sure what a trading post was, but there had to be people there. And if I were amongst people, maybe Jackal wouldn't be so eager to haul me off into the woods.

Maybe I could get a job. Something to pay for food and someplace to live while I figured out how to get home. *If* I could get home.

Terror crept into my throat, threatening to choke me

at the thought, and I pushed it away. No more hysterics for me.

I had to survive.

Rather than applauding my determination, Wood snorted with disgust, setting me down on my feet. With one hand on my shoulder, he turned me to face him.

"And how do you think people at the trading post are going to react to you?" He gestured to my jeans. "I can't figure out who you are myself. They won't be able to either, and fear will have them treating you in a way you won't care for."

"You're treating me pretty well." I spat out the words, enraged at having my plan—my only possible plan—thwarted.

One corner of his lips lifted, just the slightest bit. "I am not afraid of you."

"Why?" I planted my hands on my hips, so angry that I though sparks might shoot from my skin. "You don't know where I'm from. You don't know who I am. You don't know anything about me. Maybe you should be afraid."

I half expected him to laugh at the suggestion that he, the very large, very muscular woodsman, should be afraid of me. Instead, the hint of mirth disappeared from his lips.

"Once you've lost all that you cared about, there isn't anything left to fear." Setting his face back into impassive lines, he pointed back through the woods. "Face it, girl, I'm your best chance."

"I want to go to the trading post." I clung to the idea desperately, probably because I didn't have any others.

"Take me. Now."

He shook his head, stonily. "Even if it was a good idea, which it isn't, I can't do that."

"What?" I froze. "Why not?"

"Your appearance has brought attention to the clan I once considered my people. Jackal searching for you threatens their peace. Guthrie has demanded to see you, and if you can't satisfy him with some answers about who you are and where you're from, then he will take you to Jackal himself."

He pointed again to the trees. "We're going to meet him. Now."

"What?" Even though Wood owed me less than nothing, I felt the shock—and the fear—down to my bones. "You can't take me there. What am I supposed to do?"

"I don't know yet." He shook his head slightly as I tensed again, my body preparing to run. "Don't do that, girl. You know you won't get far. To the clan we will go, whether you walk, or whether I carry you over my shoulder."

"Why?" I whispered as I followed him into the woods. Betrayal washed over me, irrational though it was. "Why are you doing this?"

He didn't reply. I followed him silently into the forest.

"IT IS NOT our way." Guthrie was the older man I'd met at Wood's cabin, the one who had hated me on sight. He sat on a massive stone seat built into the wall of the low building, pounding the blade of his sword into the floor, which was nothing but dirt. The dust kicked up by the movement tickled my nose, and I almost sneezed, saved only because I was half holding my nose.

Approximately thirty men were crowded into the building along with Guthrie, Wood and me, and in such close quarters, I was painfully aware of the lack of indoor plumbing. The air in the small stone building was dense and musky, and it combined with the fear in my gut to make me nauseous.

The men, each shirtless but wrapped in the same swath of plaid fabric, an intricate pattern with several shades of red and blue, were eerily silent. Today there were no runes painted on their skin with clay, and I found myself faintly disappointed. I'd wanted to see them closer.

"I found the girl. She is mine to be concerned with." Wood captured my arm and with a sharp tug, pulled me beside him as he regarded Guthrie.

"The Cabots are currently swarming the forest, searching for her." Guthrie cast me a furious glare. "What happens if they come across the village? We will fight, but we should not have to. I will not stand for the unnecessary slaughter of my men, the rape of my women. You already carry our weight on your shoulders. Do you wish to increase it twofold?"

You already carry our weight on your shoulders. I cast a sidelong glance at Wood, wondering what the hell that meant.

His face revealed nothing but ferocity, an intensity I

hadn't seen yet.

"I found her," Wood repeated, and I heard the danger in his voice. "I will take responsibility."

"You don't have to take responsibility for me!" I stood straight, spine stiff with indignation. "I don't understand the problem. I'll go to the trading post. I'll find work. Cabot's men surely won't bother me around so many people."

Guthrie cast me a single withering stare, ignoring my words.

"You understand what this means?" Guthrie stood. He was slightly smaller than Wood, but he was still a large man, lean and wiry. He was also surrounded by dozens of clansmen spoiling for a fight—their eagerness sparked along the air.

"I do." Wood held the older man's stare. Something passed between them in the tense silence.

"What?" I caught at Wood's arm; he shrugged me off irritably. "What the hell is happening?"

"Very well." The rest of the men acted as though I wasn't there. With a terse nod, Guthrie sat again, though his eyes had narrowed to slits. "She is your responsibility. Let's hope she's not your downfall, too." He lifted his sword, and his men cleared a path, their movements sharp, military precision.

I slowly crept out from behind Wood's back, still tugging at his shirt. He looked at me with exasperation as I stood beside him, a combined force.

Unease weighed on my shoulders. We'd won this battle, but I sensed that there might still be a war.

Wood gripped my arm, and none-too-gently led me

though the path the men had provided. I drew a deep, relieved breath when we reached outside. But the fresh air caught in my throat when I saw the cautious glances cast my way. No one here trusted me. Looking down at my filthy jeans and the strange shoes, I knew that I wouldn't have trusted me either.

"Stay here." Wood deposited me beside a semi-circle of tree stumps clustered with young girls. I glared at him, and he caught my chin in his hand. "Girl, for the love of the forest, just do what I say for once."

"Fine." I huffed out a breath, but as he strode away, his long legs eating up the distance, anxiety settled in, hot and sick.

"She is wearing pants, like a man." The group of young girls whispered together, then broke into laughter, and I remembered the bonfire. "Perhaps she is one."

Doesn't matter what century it is, then. Young people are always cruel.

I felt a flush climbing the back of my neck as I thought of the slick humiliation of hearing my colleagues say nasty things about me. Things that weren't even true.

I also remembered Emmett speaking the truth, standing up for me, not caring what anyone thought.

Well, I might have cared what Guthrie thought, but I didn't need to put up with crap from a bunch of teenagers on top of everything else.

My skin was hot with self-consciousness, but I sucked in a breath and turned my direction directly to the girls. I looked them each directly in the eyes, and one by one they turned away, flushing themselves.

All of them turned away, except for one, the second

to last one I made eye contact with.

The girl was tall, slim but with more going on in the chest area than I did, though I was probably a good five years older than her. A couple of curling russet strands escaped a braid that reached her waist, framing a face with young, creamy skin that makeup had clearly never touched.

Eyes a startlingly dark shade of blue were set off by the long, full tartan skirt in the clan's pattern. A separate piece of the same tartan was draped like a sash over a simple white blouse-type garment.

The other girls all leaned in slightly toward this one girl, the queen bee. And the queen wasn't intimidated by my eye contact. She looked right back, making no secret of the fact that she was looking me over, and was clearly not impressed with what she saw.

Okay, then. She looked for so long that it got weird. The other girls began to whisper, but I found myself staring right back. I couldn't look away, and yet I could feel the toxicity of her aggression pouring into my already vulnerable self.

The sharp cry of a baby caught my attention. Relieved for an excuse to break the staring contest, I jerked my head in the direction of the sound. Just past the circle of stumps, a painfully young mother was doing that pacing, jiggling walk that so many of them did. In her arms was a baby wrapped in a swath of plaid, howling at the top of its lungs.

The mother, rail thin, with long auburn hair tied back in a tight braid, caught my eye just long enough for me to see the deep smudges beneath her pale blue eyes.

She was exhausted. And the way the baby was hunched up over her shoulder, stiff as a board as it strained, tugged at my memory.

As an infant, I'd apparently had something called colic. Basically, I had an upset tummy, almost all the time. My mother had listed off the symptoms to me countless times over the years as she recounted the stories, the different remedies she'd tried depending on where in the world we'd been at the time.

Different remedies—hadn't she recited those to me, over and over again? It hit me, how I could prove myself to these people. I wasn't stupid—I couldn't stay in Wood's cabin forever. The day he decided to stop helping me, what would I do?

The Cabots… I didn't know how to handle that situation yet. But I could make myself useful to the clan.

I looked away from the young mother only when I saw Wood walking back toward me in my peripheral vision. At his approach, the group of girls burst into giggles. I saw Queen Bee fasten that creepily intense stare onto him.

Aah, I thought. Someone had a little crush.

To my astonishment, he acknowledged her, dipping his head in her direction. "Keltie."

There wasn't time to ponder it further.

"Wood." He didn't slow. I planted my feet. "Wood!"

His eyes narrowed. "Move."

"I need to go to the medicine woman. At the trading post."

"You are going back to my cabin until I can figure out what to do with you."

Part of me was overjoyed that he wasn't planning to simply wash his hands of me now. The other part dreaded whatever it meant for him to "take responsibility for me."

Later. I would worry about that later. *Focus, London.*

I pointed to the baby. The mother eyed me suspiciously. "I can help that child."

"There is no help for that child." As it so often was, Wood's voice was thick with exasperation. "It cries all the time. It is a sickly baby."

"That's the thing. I can help him. I know what's wrong with him." I dug my feet into the dirt. "Please. This will... this will make them trust me. I think. I need herbs."

Wood folded his arms over his chest, eyeing me narrowly. "You do not need them to trust you. They have agreed that you are my responsibility now."

I shook my head, and strands of my hair stuck to my sweaty cheek. "Then let me ease that burden. Please."

"Are you going to try to run?" He eyed me suspiciously. "I'm weary of manhandling you."

From the side, I saw the Queen Bee, Keltie stiffen.

"I won't run." My words were indignant, even though my cheeks warmed at his words. I didn't want these young girls thinking that Wood manhandled me in any way at all.

Though the way they all looked at him... I hadn't thought of him in that light. I'd been too preoccupied trying to survive. But the obvious attraction that all of these young women had for him...

Well. Yes, he was handsome, if you liked gigantic

men who didn't know how to smile.

I didn't like it, but now that Pandora's box had been opened, I could see what they liked.

"The trek is long." He arched a brow. "I will not carry you."

The whisper of attraction vanished. *Smartass.*

I hold one foot up. "My feet have gone numb. I'm good to go."

He grumbled something, bent, and put his mouth close to my ear. "If this is some trick, I will personally put you over my lap and tan your hide."

The visual of Wood doing that to me, his big hand coming down over my backside, stopped me cold. That would hurt. But threaded with what I considered very healthy fear was something else. Something I didn't want to examine too closely.

Finally, he heaved an exasperated sigh, jerking a thumb toward the woods that we seemed to be tromping through willy-nilly every time I turned around.

"Go."

CHAPTER EIGHTEEN

Nature's Creatures

"How long of a walk is it to the trading post?" We'd left the village an hour ago. The last thing I wanted to do was complain, but after the events of the last two days, my body was in complete shock. Everything that could ache did, and I hadn't been lying when I'd said my feet had gone numb. Too bad that didn't take away from the pain of my blistered heels. After everything I'd been through, a little bit of raw skin on my feet maybe shouldn't have been such a big deal, but after an hour of walking, every step nearly brought me to tears.

"Not much further." I saw Wood cast me a sidelong glance. After the stern lecture he'd given me in the village, I expected him to mock me for insisting on this trip when he didn't see it as necessary.

But when he slowed and pulled a flask from his pocket, making a show of stretching out those insanely large arms, I knew that the tears stinging the back of my eyes and his timing weren't coincidence.

"We will rest for five minutes." Unscrewing the metal flask, he took a large sip, wiping his mouth with the back of his hand before passing the small vessel to me. The scent reached me before I even closed my hands around it, making my eyes water.

"Is this your moonshine?" I grimaced, then felt like that was in poor taste. He was sharing; I should partake.

I tried not to wince as I lifted the lip of the flask to my lips. The liquid burned on contact, but I poured a little out onto my tongue.

I almost dropped the flask when fire burned a path down my throat and straight into my belly.

I gagged, coughing as Wood nipped the flask back out of my hand, then helpfully thumped me on the back. I looked up at him, tears pooling in my eyes from the strength of the liquid.

He thumped me again, and my coughing lessened as the liquid settled fully into my gut. When I was able to blink the tears out of my eyes, I found him looking at me curiously.

"What is moon-shine? That is the second time you have said this word." He pronounced it as two separate words. "This is liquor that I make myself."

"Same thing." I swallowed again, trying to get the fiery taste from my mouth. "Is there any water?"

He furrowed his brow. "You do not bring water on a hike. You drink when you get to the river."

Of course. How silly of me.

We started forward again, moving from a fairly sunny patch of the woods to a denser, thicker area of forest. The sweet scent of decaying vegetation was everywhere, and rotting leaves were a soft carpet under our feet.

I was enjoying the brief respite from the sun, because the strenuous hike had sweat trickling down my back under the flannel shirt. Clutching the fabric in front in my fingers, I pulled it in and out, trying to create a breeze.

I was so intent on cooling off that I didn't notice Wood had stopped in front of me. I stepped on his heels, smacking into that long, tall wall that was his body. I expected him to growl at me for stepping on his heels, but he stayed silent and absolutely still.

Mystified, I followed his gaze, sucking in a quiet gasp when I saw what he was focused on. Ten feet in front of us, nibbling on a patch of grass still damp from last night's storm, was a deer.

We had deer in Pennsylvania, but since I lived in a city, I'd never seen one up close. The animal was tall, slender, with impossibly long legs that looked so fragile. Tawny brown, it had a patch of white on its tail.

Unlike the ghostly white stag I'd seen outside the cave, I could see this creature breathe as it enjoyed its meal.

Beside me, Wood slid his axe from his belt. He lifted it as I stared at him, confusion quickly clearing as I realized that he meant to kill it.

"No!" I shrieked, grabbing Wood's arm. The axe went flying, whipping end over end through the air. I dug my fingers into his bicep, dragging his arm down as he cursed and shook my hand away.

"What are you doing?" we both shouted at the same time. A wooden *thunk* punctuated our words, and I turned my head to see Wood's axe buried in a tree trunk directly behind where the deer had been.

The animal had vanished. Smart creature.

"You were trying to kill it?" My voice squeaked with indignation. "Why? Why would you do that?"

"Because I like to eat." He reached into his pocket and pulled out something wrapped in cloth—bannock like he'd told me to pack. I'd left mine on his table.

My stomach growled, and he lifted an eyebrow as he broke the bread in half. "It would seem that you do, too."

He offered me a piece of the bannock on an outstretched palm; I shook my head stubbornly.

"How could you eat it if you'd… I mean…" I ate meat. I liked meat. But I preferred not to think of where it had come from. I couldn't imagine deliberately sinking a blade into the flesh of a living creature, then using it as food. "How could you do that?"

"That is not hard. I've done it since I was a child." His voice lightened. "After the first hit, you slice the throat. To make sure the creature does not suffer."

His eyes met mine, and his stare was earnest. He wanted me to know that he could kill the deer and eat it, but that he made sure it didn't suffer.

Fantastic.

"Then I—" I held up a hand to cut him off.

"I wasn't asking for you to tell me how you killed the deer and cut it up for meat. I was asking how you could take its life." Again, I knew this was hypocritical. Buying my chicken breasts from the grocery store didn't make them any less a dead animal, but I just… I couldn't. I couldn't eat an animal when I'd been the one to cause the life to drain from its eyes.

"Finding a deer on this part of our journey was fortuitous." He was still staring at me as though I'd grown a second head. "I could have strung it up, and it would have drained by the time we returned."

Drained? I gagged.

"I do not understand." He closed the space between us, head tilted with confusion. "Food is survival. That deer was our dinner. What do you propose we eat instead?"

"I—" Shame washed over me. Not because I felt how I did, because I couldn't help that. But here I was a burden to him yet again. I still didn't understand why he was helping me.

I wanted to go home.

Something thick was gathering in my throat. Shaking my head brusquely, I turned away. Berry bushes had appeared here and there along our trek, and while I hadn't recognized some of them, right now I saw what were undeniably raspberries. Desperate to be some help instead of trouble, I unknotted the hem of the large plaid shirt and held it out in front of me like an apron. Suddenly frantic, I started to pull the ripened red berries from their buds, laying them in my makeshift basket. "Here. Eat these. Please."

"The deer is back." Wood said this idly, as though testing my reaction. I turned slowly, watching as the animal crept back our way. Wood's axe was still embedded in the tree. I looked at him sidelong to see if he was going to pull out some other kind of blade, but he simply looked from the deer to me and sighed.

I was shocked when the deer sidled closer, then closer still. It stopped when it was about five yards away, eyeing us placidly before dipping its head to munch on the grass again.

"Stupid animal." Wood shook his head.

"Ssh." The deer looked up at the great rumble of his words. "You're not stupid. You're beautiful, yes you are."

Entranced by the creature, I tossed the handful of berries that I'd already collected toward the deer. It blinked at me, swiping them up delicately with a large, rough tongue. No sooner than it had its mouth full than it froze, hearing something we didn't, and bounding off into the trees.

I watched it go as Wood stalked over to the tree, freeing his axe from the wood with a grunt. He stomped his way back, stopping in front of me. Looking down at me, he sighed again.

"You are a very strange woman." Sliding his axe back into his belt, he jerked his head forward, gesturing that we needed to move on.

"I've been called worse." As we started to walk away, I couldn't help but smirk up at him.

He just shook his head again and sighed.

CHAPTER NINETEEN

Trading Post

T HE TRADING POST was large and wooden, a fortress
on the edge of the lake. It didn't look welcoming,
and a sense of foreboding tickled uneasy fingers down
my spine.

"Stay here." We were standing in a small copse of
dense pine on the edge of the forest. He gestured to a
smaller version of the tree that he'd worked into the
design of his home, indicating that I should take cover in
the dark tangle of roots.

A silvery cobweb glistened in the light, a curtain in
front of the little den. The tiny space was probably
crawling with spiders, with ants and grubs and who knew
what else. Unlike so many people, I wasn't afraid of
bugs. That didn't mean I relished the idea of little crawly
things creeping all over my skin.

That wasn't my real motive, though. I was determined to find a way back home, but I couldn't rely solely
on Wood until that happened. I needed to explore my

surroundings, the world in which I was trapped.

I wanted to see the trading post. I needed to.

"I'm coming with you." I stood straight, chin raised. Annoyance flashed on his face as he hesitated.

"I could make you stay."

"How?" I almost rolled my eyes, but my breath caught in my throat when he leaned in so close that I could smell the cedarwood scent on his skin.

"I would wrap twine around each of your wrists and tie you to that tree right there." He pointed; I couldn't look away from his eyes, which darkened with his words. "You wouldn't have a choice but to do as I wished."

"I—" My mouth went dry. I should have felt terror, but instead, I felt something hot and sticky and tangled in my belly.

"I suppose I can't trust that you won't shout the fort down, though." He pulled back rapidly, leaving coolness where there had been warmth. He looked me over, shaking his head.

"Unknot your shirt." After leaving the deer, I had tied it back up. I did as he said, stilling when he took the snarled length of my ponytail and tucked it up so that my hair looked shorter. "You have far too much hair."

"My hair isn't nearly as long as the women in the village!"

"The women in the village do not need to hide." He looked me up and down. I thought his gaze might have lingered for just a second on my breasts, but I probably imagined it. The curves of my chest couldn't be seen at all underneath the baggy flannel. "You look nothing like a man."

Still, I felt as though I'd taken another hit of moonshine—a searing burn, straight to the gut.

The moment passed, and all I saw on Wood's face was irritation.

"You will stay right by my side. Do not look at anybody, do not talk to anybody. We will go to Freya's shop, and that is it." He started striding toward the wooden fortress. I struggled to catch up.

"Freya is the medicine woman?"

"Yes." Wood took one stride for every three of mine. Practically running, I was out of breath by the time we reached the gate.

The perimeter of the trading post seemed to be at least twice Wood's height, made of long logs that had been sharpened to points at the top. The gate wasn't visible until we were in front of it, and only then could I make out the rustic hinges that marked it as a door.

Wood heaved and, with effort, opened one outward. The other stayed bolted in place.

"You can just walk in?" I asked when Wood beckoned me in. The place looked so… well, it looked hostile. Like it had been built to withstand a raid, which I supposed it had. "No one guards it?"

Wood pointed up above our heads. A small shack sat squarely on top of a sturdily built tower that was twice again as tall as the fortress walls. If I squinted, I could just make out a figure. And the barrel of a rifle.

Wood saluted whoever was in the watchtower, then ushered me through the gate, heaving it closed again behind us.

"Remember. Head down, speak to no one." I

frowned; I wanted to look. But the first time I even started to lift my chin, Wood yanked on my elbow, bending to growl in my ear.

"The Cabots rarely come here, but they are not the only logging camp. River pigs are rough men. Jackal wants you especially because I took you away, but other men would be more than happy to bring you to their camp as a treat to share."

I swallowed, pressing a hand to my stomach, where the flesh was tender from the tip of Jackal's sword.

"I understand," I whispered. My tongue was bitter with fear.

What kind of world had I fallen into?

I stayed directly behind Wood as he strode through the trading post. Rather than a series of shops, as I had expected, the semi-sheltered layout made a ring that followed the inner perimeter of the post's walls. Though I didn't look at anything higher than about knee level, I noted that goods were interspersed with craftsmen, heavy woolen blankets and barrels of beans, raisins, sugar, and rice alternating with a blacksmith, a boat builder, a woodworker, and more.

Twice men greeted Wood. Once he grunted in return, and the second time he exchanged a few words. Once he stopped to purchase something, though I didn't see what it was until he gruffly shoved them into my hands and told me to put them on. Head down, I hurried into the new boots, and a little warmth zinged through me, touched by the gesture. For the most part, people seemed to skirt around us, avoid us. Since Wood stood head and shoulders above the other men, I thought I understood why.

The heavy scent of herbs hit me two displays before Wood stopped. It nearly killed me, but I kept my stare on the planked wooden walkway until he spoke.

"Freya." His voice sounded so low, so wild compared to the melodic blend of French and English around me.

"Wood." I looked up to find a woman seated on a stool behind a counter and staring straight at me.

I did my best to hide my surprise at her appearance. I'd been… well, I'd been expecting an old crone. Like one of the witches in Hocus Pocus. Someone stooped and wizened and bent, with long, wild hair and gnarled fingers.

This woman was perhaps in her early thirties—probably around the same age as Wood. Something tightened in my chest as I acknowledged that, as well as the fact that she was quite lovely. Lovely and Wood's age. Average height and more than a bit plump, she had rosy cheeks in a fair face. And she was smiling at him with appreciation.

She did have long hair, though hers was up in a massive golden knot on the back of her head. Her eyes were a peculiar shade of violet and regarded me so intensely that I knew my half-hearted disguise was useless here.

"What do you need?" All business, she slid off her stool. Wood gently shoved me forward—apparently, my silence wasn't meant to be kept here.

"Um." I cleared my throat and shifted from foot to foot. The woman's stare was so intense; I had no idea where to look.

"Speak up." Freya rapped the counter with a tin spoon, barely missing my knuckles, and I felt a flash of irritation.

"I need chamomile. Fennel. Um… ginger or cinnamon, if you have it." I closed my eyes, trying to remember the ingredients in gripe water. I wouldn't have had a clue, if not for those digs where so many children were forced to tag along. Many of the locations were nowhere near a Walgreen's, so parents made do with what they could get. "Peppermint."

"Stomach trouble, is it?" Freya nodded briskly, as though my standing had improved a notch in her books. "This will give you a rough night, but you'll be the better for it in the morning."

Wood snorted; I flushed when I understood what she was referring to. "No! It's not for me. It's for a baby!"

"A baby, you say?" She looked up at Wood, amusement playing around the corners of her lips. "Hiding some secrets in the trees, are you, Wood?"

I thought he would vehemently deny it—most of the men I knew would be dancing about red-faced if anyone had so much as said *baby* in connection with a woman they barely knew. Wood, though, just snorted again, waiting for Freya to tie the herbs up in a square of clean cloth.

"Steep a spoonful of these in hot water. When it's cool, the baby can drink." She looked curiously from me to Wood and back again, but I wasn't about to comment on the baby situation. Hell, no.

"What will you trade for?" Wood took the herbs and

tucked them into a pouch on his belt. Freya pursed her lips, thinking.

"Mackerel." She nodded briskly. "Yes, mackerel. They're running now, yes?"

Wood nodded again. "Tomorrow."

"Good enough."

Wood didn't have to tell me again to resume my silence and keep my head down. He started to lead me back the way we came.

A bubble of excitement welled up inside me. I wasn't sure if this would help me earn the clan's trust, but it felt good to act on something. I felt as though I'd been doing nothing but reacting to things thrown my way since I'd tumbled into the lake.

"Wood!" Another man stopped us. I stared down at a barrel full of something called saltpeter. I listened with half an ear as Wood was questioned about the price of timber.

Was it timber? I strained to hear, though I wasn't that interested. It was so loud here. Had it been this loud the whole time?

A very large, very loud group pushed through the gate.

"*Je suis chaud!*"

"*Beau cul!*"

"*Où sont les femmes?*"

I didn't have a clue what any of this meant, but the voices shouting sent ice through my veins an instant before I saw the man at the head of the group. Nearly as tall as Wood, handsome in an arrogant way, I knew that if he turned to look at us, I would see cruelty shining in his eyes.

Jackal.

"Fucking Cabots." The man Wood was talking to spat on the floor. "Every single time they get paid. They come, they complain, they harass the women, they make a mess."

I tried to hold my breath but only succeeded in becoming ever more aware of it.

I had to bite my tongue to hold back a scream as Wood whipped a woolen blanket from the display. He wrapped it around both of our shoulders, I guessed to hide the plaid, and pushed me toward the shadows at the back of the store.

"They occupy the whores. They drink and fight," the man was still intoning, though no one was listening. He half turned to follow us. "Hey! My blanket! That's going on your account!"

"Merde." There was something dark in Wood's tone, something that frightened me. I didn't have even a second to ask, though, because he tugged me along the backs of the displays, racing for the front gate. "Someone will mention we are here."

"But you have your axe." I was breathless from adrenaline. I didn't want to come face to face with the man who was hunting me, but I trusted Wood. I would never forget the image of him roaring into the middle of the ring of Cabots, like Thor. Thor with an axe.

"Girl, it is an axe, not a rifle." We had reached the end of the ring of displays, close to where we had entered. We hunched over, Wood peering around the entrance. He took a moment to look back at me, face incredulous. "One Cabot, two. Perhaps three. That I can handle. But the entire group of them? Not without the clan behind me."

I would have felt stupid if there had been time. There was not. I could hear the boisterous group, scattered throughout the center area of the trading post where I now noticed several women were. Women dressed in clothing that covered a lot less than the outfit Wood had brought me that morning.

"They left two men at the gate." Wood cursed again. The urge to flee welled up inside me, threatening to boil over.

Was this what life here was like? Threat after threat, again and again? How did people live like this?

I couldn't handle the suspense. Ducking under Wood's arm, I peered around the corner myself. Two men stood by the gate that they hadn't bothered to close. Both were sipping from flasks.

"We will turn back. We will make our way to the exit by Freya." I winced. That was a long way, especially when we were hiding under a blanket. "Then we will climb the watchtower."

"*What?*" I tried to stand, a reflex, and the top of my head smacked into his chin. He growled.

"Get ready."

A long, lightly furred limb flashed from behind the gate.

"What..." I exhaled, grabbing hold of Wood's shirt. He tugged, and I pulled back.

Another long, fragile limb. A delicate nose, face, and ears.

It was a deer.

"What is it doing here?" I could feel the warmth of Wood's breath in my hair. "*C'est stupide.*"

"Boys! Dinner is here!" One of the Cabots by the gate slapped the deer on the flank as it sauntered through the gate into the trading post.

The deer tiptoed into the center of the post. One of the tradesmen wandered over, then two of the Cabots. Soon the poor animal was surrounded by people, and clearly regretting its decision to check out the party.

"This is our deer! Ours!" I recognized the shouting man as the one who had been eating an apple in the clearing. "How many women will this get?"

"What would I do with a deer?" One of the whores grimaced at the animal. "No trade."

"I will trade pemmican for it." A rotund man wearing an apron spattered with blood approached the animal. He stroked under its neck before looking into its eyes. "It will make good meat."

"No!" I cried out before I could stop it. Wood swore again, shoving me forward. I resisted, not able to tear my gaze away from the animal.

This time it looked back. I swear it looked right into my eyes. I could almost hear its thoughts.

"Go, you stupid girl! Run!"

"It's the same deer," I breathed, jolting as Wood finally gave up trying to get me to move, wrapping his arms around me from behind and lifting me off my feet. "Wood, it's the same deer!"

"It cannot be helped, girl." I stiffened in his arms as he dragged me to the gate that was still open. My breath hitched as I shoved at his chest, kicking at his shins. "London! Enough!"

He hauled me through the gates and back to the small copse of trees that he'd wanted me to stay behind in. Once we were hidden in the trees, he pinned me between one solid trunk and his massive chest, wrapping his hands around each of my flailing wrists.

I didn't cry when I tumbled into the lake. I didn't cry when I got sliced open with a sword. But I couldn't stop the tears that overflowed for the poor, dumb deer.

"London. London!" Wood lowered his face until it was pressed against mine, and I was forced to look into his eyes. "I am sorry. I am sorry about the deer, but we have to keep moving. Do you understand? We have to keep moving, or it will be the deer *and* us. Do you understand?"

I nodded, even though I could taste the salt from the tears that were still coming. My nose started to run, and my face crumpled, but when he grabbed my hand, I followed him from the small copse of trees and back into the depths of the forest.

He let me cry. And not once did he remind me that I was crying over a deer.

CHAPTER TWENTY

Building Trust

I WAS STILL upset about the deer when we got back to the village. The sun was hanging low in the sky, a heavy ball of fire, and I forced myself to look into the light.

"Thank you," I whispered, half to myself and half to the animal. Wood cast me a strange look, and I forced myself to push the animal that had likely saved my life from my mind.

It was clear that Wood was puzzled by my sadness over an animal. I didn't know how to explain it to him. He saw animals as food. I, on the other hand, had never looked into the eyes of a creature, knowing that it was going to die.

My spirits were heavy, but as we passed from the forest into the village, I felt myself standing straighter, becoming more alert.

I didn't see Guthrie anywhere, and for that I was thankful. I did notice Keltie standing by a primitive cabin, this time with only one other girl instead of an entire gaggle. I wasn't pleased when Wood guided us her way, though at least with him there, her attention was on him and not me.

"Keltie. We need a cup and some hot water." He didn't say please, and I thought about telling him that the least he could do was say please. The obvious pleasure that the young girl had at doing his bidding stopped me from speaking.

I watched as she left the fish she'd been drying on a rack to dart into a cabin, returning with the steaming cup of water. When she presented it to Wood, she tilted her head coquettishly and smiled up at him from beneath long, naturally dark eyelashes.

I felt that tightness in my chest again, the one I'd noticed when I'd gotten an eyeful of Freya and her voluptuousness, and had noted the ease with which she and Wood spoke. Surely I wasn't… jealous?

Wood grunted at me, holding out the cup for me to take as he reached into his pouch for the packet of herbs. Untying the fabric, he sprinkled some into the water, and the herbal scent of the fennel, the chamomile, the peppermint, and ginger hit my nose.

Closing my eyes, I inhaled the steam. It reminded me of the only time I'd gotten a pedicure. A girl in one of my history classes couldn't believe I'd never had one, so she dragged me along. I still didn't see the point of painting my toenails pink, but I'd enjoyed the relaxing scent.

Wood looked at Keltie. She pointed to the cabin she'd just exited. Their wordless communication had that tightness spreading in my chest again.

"Stay here." Wood took the cup back, and his expression just dared me to argue. I was so discomfited by the threads of jealousy that I wouldn't have even thought of it. Instead, I stood awkwardly, aware that Keltie and her friend were staring at me, and that they weren't too friendly about it.

I listened to the exchange inside, which was a little hard to hear over the baby's crying. The crying changed to shrieks, and I winced, praying that I was doing the right thing.

I waited for what seemed like forever. Keltie made a production of watching over me, sighing dramatically every time I shifted. As the sun dipped, the night grew cooler, and I hugged myself, Wood's shirt doing little to keep me warm once the chill crept in. I remembered the way Wood had cradled me against his torso on the way to his cabin, lending his body heat to my shivering frame. That would be a nice way to get rid of my chill.

Wait, what? No. I could walk by myself.

I distracted myself by trying to memorize the layout of the village; what I could see of it, anyway. Many of the clan cast distrustful glances my way as they passed, but soon the village grew quiet, blackberry twilight creeping in on a whisper.

When Wood finally emerged, the night was velvety and dark. The moon was big and high, but little filtered through the high trees, forcing me to strain to see him.

I realized belatedly that the baby had stopped crying, and stood so abruptly that the stump I'd perched on fell over. I heard Keltie's snicker, but focused all of my attention on Wood.

"How did you know?" He stood close, hovered over me. His voice was hard but hushed.

"Where I come from—"

"London."

Why did he keep doing that?

"Yes. London. The place." I sighed inwardly. "There's something called gripe water. It helps babies who cry. All I did was make some."

He scrubbed his chin like he was mulling that over, then he glanced past my shoulders, took in the darkened village. "We are finished here."

Keltie made a sound of disappointment. I turned to go, but the door to the small cabin slammed open. The young mother I'd seen earlier came running out of her hut. Her eyes were wide, and her hair was down, tangled as though tiny hands had been tugging at it.

She tugged on the sleeve of my shirt to stop me.

"Thank you."

THE EARTHY SCENTS of pine and moss were refreshment for my senses after the slightly smoky air in the village. I took deep, cleansing breaths as the forest closed in on us, hugging us from all angles. Wood slipped through the trees and brush with his usual grace. I followed along, the journey that much harder in the dark. Now and then I scraped up against a tree that seemed to come out of nowhere. My jeans were covered with dust and mud and my sweat. They needed to be washed.

I lifted my arm to smell myself and my eyes watered. I needed a wash, too.

"I need a bath."

"I will not disagree."

"Hey," I said and grabbed a twig. My cheeks flushed. Did I smell bad to Wood? I'd gone for days without bathing before, when running water wasn't available, but I'd never done so around someone that... well, that I had some complicated new feelings for.

He turned slowly, and all the nightlife in the forest seemed to go quiet. "Put the stick down, London."

His voice was gruff and deep as his fingers curled into fists at his sides. I took in his warrior stance, but there wasn't a single bone in my body that worried he would hurt me.

Why was that?

"I was only playing," I said, to make light of it.

"Playing?" His voice was deadly serious, but... there. Yes, there it was. The moonlight caught the twinkle of amusement in his eye.

The terrifying giant was playing with me. Against every shred of better judgment that I possessed, it made me a little bit weak in the knees.

I shifted from one foot to the next. Even though the new boots fit, I still had blisters from the first pair.

It wasn't important. What I had to say was.

"I have to thank you." Even though the village was far behind us, I gestured behind me with a crook of my head. "I'm sure it wasn't easy standing up to Guthrie, going against his orders for a stranger."

Why, I wanted to ask. Why did you do that for me?

I was afraid of the answer. Afraid that he would tell me that he would have done it for anyone.

"Do you mean harm to the people of the village?" He cocked his head, looking me over. Sweat dripped down my spine. I wasn't much to look at in that moment, and I was fully aware of it.

"Of course I don't." Though I wouldn't mind if Keltie developed some condition that meant she had to stay away from Wood.

"Then we will prove that." He exhaled a long, slow breath, and scooped me up. "No more talking."

"I can walk," I say, but despite my protest, I curled into him, delighted with the sudden waves of heat.

"And I can carry you."

I closed my eyes for a moment. I knew that any feelings I was having were likely a reaction to the extreme stress of my situation, but no matter how I looked at it, being held weightless in arms that I wanted to stroke was far from unpleasant.

As he'd ordered, I kept my mouth shut as he glided through the forest like he knew every tree, every twist, and every turn. Soon the scent of smoke reached my nose, and I knew we were home.

Home?

I snorted at that, and Wood eyed me curiously as he opened his door. I squirmed, expecting him to set me down, but instead, he grabbed something from his shelf and stepped back outside, carrying me through some more trees, trees, trees and more trees—and down a slope. At the top of the hill, I thought I could hear the unmistakable sound of moving water. By the bottom, I knew that we were close to the river.

"Why are we at the river?" I'd been quiet long enough.

"We promised Freya mackerel for the herbs." *We.* That shouldn't have made something heat in my belly.

"You're going fishing, tonight?" I squinted in the darkness. Yes, all I could see were trees.

"We promised mackerel," he repeated like I was dense. "And you need a bath."

I was probably lucky that he couldn't see the scowl I leveled at him in the dark.

He deposited me gently on the embankment, and I glanced up to see the big moon shining down on us. Broken into slices by high-arching tree branches, the fractured silver provided just enough illumination for me to see the outline of Wood's body and the glint of his eyes.

"You want me to bathe here?" I ask. I glanced around the darkness, oddly comfortable with my surroundings. I'd bathed in worse than a clean, running river.

What gave me hesitation was that Wood was right here, and given that it was dark, I knew that he wouldn't go far.

Instead of answering, he started to unbutton the front of his flannel shirt. We were close enough that I knew his gaze was on me as he let it hang open, then slid those huge, capable hands to the waist of his trousers.

This was a dare. I knew that I didn't imagine that. What I couldn't fathom, though, were the stakes.

I gasped and turned as he shed his shirt entirely, then

let his pants fall to the ground.

"You are very modest for a woman who wore garments such as I first saw you in." Amusement was thick in his voice as I listened to him enter the water. Right. The bra he'd been so fascinated with. I wondered if he would be shocked if he knew how skimpy lingerie could get.

A splash reached my ears, and I gulped in a deep breath, stripping as quickly as I could. I slid into the water before Wood could resurface, knowing that in the moonlight, my pale ivory skin would be illuminated like a candle.

"Oh, my God," I barely swallowed the scream. The water was so cold it took my breath away. I hunched in on myself as my nipples puckered painfully.

"You are praying?" Wood surfaced, sleek as a seal. His voice came from several feet away but knowing that that massive body, those sleek muscles were completely naked meant that he wasn't far enough.

"The water is freezing." I ducked down until only my ears and face were out of the water. I'd reached the point where the water seemed warmer than the air around it. "How can you stand it?"

"The cold is good for you." I heard him slicing through the water, coming closer, and my breath caught in my throat. What was he doing?

"Here." I smelled that oily scent that I now knew was soap, and when I squinted, I saw him rubbing his hands together, working up a lather. He passed the bar to me, and I felt the scrape of his calloused fingers over my palm as he did.

I was on fire. Was this simply because Keltie had made me look at him differently? Was it because I'd experienced so many surges of adrenaline in the last forty-eight hours? Because surely I wasn't burning for a strange woodsman while I was also wild with grief for the life I was currently barred from, for Sean and Emmett, too?

Yes. Surely it couldn't be that this was actual chemistry, that primal reaction that happened at random and without warning? One of those inexplicable connections that hooked two people together for no reason at all?

London, get a grip.

I stared. I couldn't help it. I watched as he ran his soapy hands over his beard, his face and hair. I watched as he moved those capable hands over his torso and lower.

My mouth was dry by the time he slid beneath the water to rinse, and I blinked rapidly to pull myself together. I stayed crouching in the water, waiting for him to leave before I washed myself.

I wasn't at all sure that he'd mind if I soaped myself up in front of him. I also wasn't sure that I was ready for what would happen if I did.

"Your turn." He stood, water lapping around his hips. His really well-defined hips.

"Turn around." No. No, I was not ready for this at all. I was terrified.

"I have seen the female body before." I could hear the smirk in his words. I scowled. I didn't want to hear about how he'd seen the female body form. Or rather, whose female body he'd seen.

"You haven't seen mine," I shot back, louder than I intended. My voice seemed to echo off the empty sky.

"Do you have a tail?" Bathing naked in a freezing river just lightened him right up.

"No," I huffed out, exasperated. "I do not have a tail."

"Horns."

"Wood!" I couldn't withstand the one-two punch of that body so close to mine and the softening of his gruff demeanor. "Go!"

I pointed to the embankment.

"I am going to fish." I averted my eyes as he pushed through the water, the moonlight illuminating the planes of his muscles. "Do not drown."

I didn't bother to respond. I couldn't, because he chose that moment to exit the water. His dripping hair, his broad shoulders and strong back, narrow waist and tight ass. Those massive thighs. Even his calf muscles were chiseled and pleasing to the eye.

He must have known that I was watching, but he moved unselfconsciously, bending to retrieve the spear he'd dropped at the river's edge before wading back into the water.

"Wood." I meant to ask him again for some privacy, but my voice was weak. In response, he made a show of turning around, presenting me with his back.

"I will not look." He sliced a hand through the water. "You have my word."

His word would have to be enough.

I stood. The river that had lapped around Wood's hips hit just below my breasts, making it far more difficult to lather the soap in the appropriate places.

I tried not to think of all the parts on Wood that the slippery bar had just touched.

An unwanted quiver moved through me as I washed between my legs, then dipped back into the freezing water to rinse. Wood, who by now had two fish on the spear, didn't seem cold at all.

I climbed from the water, goosebumps prickling, mind racing. Was he watching me the way I'd watched him?

I didn't want him to. Except that I did.

The embankment was steep and slippery, and my feet weren't in the best of shape after all our walking. I dug my toes into the moss, but when I pushed forward, I lost my footing.

"Fuck," I cursed under my breath as I righted myself. I balanced precariously as I slipped back into the flannel shirt, tucking my bra and underwear into the pocket.

I felt the heat of his body before he spoke, straightening, with my jeans dangling in one hand.

"What does fuck mean?"

CHAPTER TWENTY-ONE

Les Poissons

WHAT DOES FUCK MEAN?

"It's a bad word," I answered, flustered by his presence. "A swear word. Something you'd say when you were upset."

"Like *Tabernac*."

"I don't know what that means." I was distracted by the way his voice flowed over the unfamiliar word. "But if it's something you say when you're upset, then yes."

"Fuck." Wood sounded the single syllable out like a toddler, and I resisted the urge to laugh. "It has a pleasing sound. *Fuck*."

And when he said it like that, it put other images entirely into my head.

"It also means—" I slammed my mouth shut. Telling him the other meaning of the word, after the charge in the air between us when we'd been in the water? Not wise unless I intended to do something about it.

When we reached the top of the slope that led to the

river, I found that I was sweating anew. The effect was like going for a run after having a nice long shower. I looked at my filthy jeans, which were clutched to my chest. I glanced at my clothes, picked them up and held them to my chest. They, as well as the shirt I'd put back on, were filthy.

"I…"

"You will wear another of my shirts," he said, clearly picking up on my distress. "I will wash these. Tomorrow, I will get you more clothes."

"You don't have to…" I needed more clothing, but how was I to procure that without Wood's help? I'd taken note of what kinds of goods were exchanged at the trading post. I didn't have herbs, or furs, or blankets. I couldn't fish, and obviously, I wasn't going to be able to hunt. I wasn't a blacksmith or a woodworker.

Even if there wasn't the threat on my life, for reasons I still didn't entirely understand, I was completely dependent on Wood.

It didn't sit well.

Loneliness was bitter on my tongue. I missed home, missed my family, even though I rarely saw them. I wanted to be back in my apartment, surrounded by my things, my camera, and photos.

I no longer much cared what Sean thought of my disappearance, but what about Emmett? Did he care?

Did it even matter? I might never see either of them again. Never see my parents. How long did someone have to be missing before their apartment was emptied, their belongings sorted through? How long before everyone thought I was dead?

Turning, I regarded Wood out of the corner of my eye. He was hiding something from me—he was hiding the reason that he was so fiercely intent on keeping me safe from Jackal, from Guthrie.

But he'd saved my life, was continuing to save it.

Every dig that I'd ever been on, there had been a sense of camaraderie. Each camp, whether we were in tents or a motel like the Rumbledethump, had been like a tiny village. Everyone had offered help where help was needed, but there had been a strong sense of reciprocity. If someone sourced the ingredients for gripe water for your colicky child, then you offered them something in return.

I wanted to offer something to Wood, but my resources were rather limited. What could I do?

I shook my head to pull myself together. There was nothing I *could* do right this moment, but I'd think on it. I knew that I couldn't live in his cabin, eating his food and wearing his clothing, forever.

"Wood, I—" I wanted to express my thanks yet again, though I suspected by this point he would just ignore me. But after I turned toward him, my eyes widened, and I dropped my jeans to the ground.

"Why are you still naked?" Oh, surely that squeaky voice wasn't coming from me. I looked up, side to side, but couldn't seem to keep my gaze away from the frame that was illuminated in a sliver of pale moonlight.

Something that felt like adrenaline but was something else entirely trailed lazily through my body, the sensation similar to the pleasure of slowly slipping into a steaming hot bath.

Arousal. That was what the sensation was. A low, drugging hum of arousal.

He was closer now than he'd been in the water, and I could feel the heat of his skin, steaming after the frigid bath.

"You are very concerned with nudity." He frowned, but didn't do anything to cover up... well, anything.

Look away, London. Look away.

Oh, who was I kidding? I looked.

His cock was thick and long, in proportion to every other part of his massive body.

I was a virgin. I wasn't ashamed of this. I'd had some teenage fumbling under clothing, some college ones without. But I'd never had my fingers itch with the need to touch like this.

Touching wasn't a good idea. Not when I was dependent on him for so many things right now.

Needing a distraction, anything, before I gave in to the need to touch, I forced myself to look around. That was when I saw the fish, seven of them, twitching on the spear they'd been impaled on.

I gagged.

"You do not like fish?" he asked. Either he hadn't noticed my struggle to keep my hands off him, or he was ignoring it. Either way, I was grateful. "Please do not tell me you think of fish as you think of deer."

"I like fish." And no, I didn't place them in the same category as deer. "I just prefer them on a Styrofoam tray, wrapped in cellophane."

"Sometimes I think you speak another language." He shook his head. "I will teach you to fish with the spear."

"You're too kind." I grimaced. This would be a useful skill, but...

Yeah. They were still twitching. I shuddered.

Wood cast me a perplexed look. I suddenly had the strangest urge to laugh. I couldn't because I knew that if I started, I might not stop.

This was my life now. Conversations about the absurdity of the word cellophane with naked giants holding wiggling fish.

It was both the funniest and saddest thing I could think of. I couldn't hold back a shiver.

"You are cold." Wood held out his arms. "Here, I shall carry you."

"No!" I jumped out of his reach.

"What are you doing?" He moved closer again. "You let me carry you just earlier today. I shared my warmth with you. You liked it."

"You weren't naked then!" I couldn't hold back a giggle as he rubbed his temples with his hands, clearly confused and not a little vexed.

Still, he stopped chasing after me. "You are very strange, London from London."

"You don't know the half of it."

SINCE WE'D BEEN gone all day, the interior of the cabin was chilly, the fire nothing but a pile of smoldering ashes. Still, the tightly planked wooden walls blocked the brisk wind.

Wood followed me in, thankfully leaving the spear

full of wiggling fish outside. He pulled another of his seemingly endless supply of flannel shirts from a shelf, tossing it my way before taking down another for myself.

He snorted when I pointedly turned away as he dressed himself in that and a pair of trousers. Granted, it was probably silly since I'd seen, well, everything by this point. Still, it was ingrained in me.

"You are cold. Why are you not putting on the clean clothing?" He looked at me pointedly. I twirled my finger in the air, gesturing for him to turn around. He arched an eyebrow, incredulous. I waited.

Finally, he turned, sighing with exasperation as he did. I hurriedly swapped shirts, tossing the dirty one onto the bed before staring regretfully at my jeans.

I wished I had a spare pair, but such a thing didn't seem to exist here. My other options were the dress or the bloomers, or, I supposed, a pair of Wood's trousers, which would be about a foot too long.

The bloomers were going to look ridiculous. I pulled them on anyway.

"I'm done." Wood had busied himself building a new fire while I changed clothing. I studied the flames, the brilliant sunrise colors dancing in the small stove, chasing away the chill.

When he turned, he took one look at me and burst out laughing.

My lips curled into a wry smile. I knew I looked ridiculous. Sitting on the edge of the bed, I tugged on the socks and shoes. Standing again, I started to gather up the excess material of the shirt, planning to knot it at my waist as I had earlier.

Wood cleared his throat loudly. I looked up at him to find his face tense, his expression intent.

"What?" I looked down at myself, then back at him. "I know I look silly. I won't wear this to the village or anything."

"It is not that." He swallowed, looking away again. "Tying up the shirt is fine in your... your *jeans*. But the bloomers have, ah. They are made to make it easy to relieve yourself. Since you are so strange about nudity, you might leave the shirt hanging down."

"What?" He turned his back to me again, presumably so I could discover what he meant. I wiggled around a bit in the bloomers, then finally slid a frustrated hand down run over the seam between my legs.

It didn't exist. The bloomers had a gigantic slit through the middle. This would be very handy if I needed to head out to the woods in the middle of the night.

But if I'd tied the shirt up, I might have given Wood a glimpse of something I hadn't intended to at all.

My face flushed red. "Um, thank you."

Broad back to me, he declined to comment on that, instead adjusting the logs in the fire. "Can you clean and cook fish?"

For a moment, my spine stiffened. My mother had always been one to make a fuss over traditional gender roles. I appreciated that she had taught me that I didn't have to do something just because a man might think I should, but here and now?

Wood had provided the fish. The clothing, the shelter. My mother would be horrified, but I wasn't going to complain if I was assigned kitchen duty.

"I've never cleaned it, but I can cook it."

"Good." He nodded with satisfaction, and I felt a ridiculous sort of pride that he was pleased with my one measly survival skill. "I'll teach you how to clean it, so you know how to do both. Then you can cook while I wash our clothes."

He was going to wash our clothes. I supposed when you lived alone in the middle of the woods, gender roles didn't exist.

He grabbed a long knife from one a small bin of utensils, and we stepped outside. The fish had stopped wriggling, and I winced as Wood slid one from the spear, leaving blood and guts behind.

I'd made such a fuss over the deer; I was determined to buck up and learn now. Plus, I liked to eat. I needed protein, and if I was too squeamish to eat meat that had been hunted, then fish was my only choice.

"You hold the fish like this, and cut from here to here." He placed the fish on a large slab of wood, then started to scrape off the scales. He poured water over it to rinse, then removed the fins, the gills and sliced it open with one long cut while I watched. I'd thought the process would bother me more, but maybe I was just too hungry to care.

Wood tossed the guts into the woods. I leaned in to watch and inhaled the clean scent of his skin.

"You do the next one."

Clumsily, I mimicked his actions. When I stole a quick glance at him, the barest hint of a smile played around the corners of his lips, and I was filled with probably more pride than I should have felt over cutting open a fish.

"There. Ready to cook." He gestured at the pile of cleaned fish. "Choose two for our dinner. I will package the rest for Freya."

"Uh…" I looked from Wood to the fish. "They still have heads."

He furrowed his brow. "Yes."

I sighed. Here we went again. "How do I cook them with heads?"

I thought he might laugh at me, but instead, he cocked his head to the side. "I have never cooked a fish without its head. When you have the fish with the cell-o-phane, do they not have heads?"

I closed my eyes. "No. They do not. Someone removes the heads before I purchase them."

He was silent for a moment. "If the heads bother you, I can remove them." Picking up two of the fish, he laid them side by side on the board, but I caught the knife before he could slice.

"No. I should… I should try." Swallowing thickly, I placed the blade of the knife against the fish. Then, with a grimace and a squeal, I cut off their heads.

The chef's song from The Little Mermaid played through my head.

"Les poissons, les poissons…" I sang under my breath as I finally dared to open my eyes. When I did, I smiled. Wood had already discarded of the heads, so slicing the remaining parts into fillets was easy enough.

"You speak French?" I looked up, questioning. He mimicked the tune I'd just been singing. "Les poissons, les poissons…"

Wood the giant warrior lumberjack was singing a Disney song. I couldn't compute.

"No, I don't speak French." I turned away to hide the twitching of my lips. "That's just a song that I know."

"It is catchy." He gathered the rest of the fish, then gestured to the remaining two. "The pan is inside. You cook. I will be back shortly."

He walked away humming the song under his breath, and this time I couldn't hold back a giggle.

CHAPTER TWENTY-TWO

Working Together

I USED THE board to carry the fish fillets back into the cabin. Apart from the pleasant crackle of the fire, there was utter silence, and I paused for a moment, soaking it in. I hadn't been aware of how much background noise there was in my daily life until I'd arrived here.

I was surprised that I didn't feel the need to fill the silence. Instead, I felt myself relax a bit as I searched for the pan, then rummaged through the shelf that he used as his pantry. I found salt, and a sniff at a glass bottle told me that it was oil of some kind. I sprinkled the fish with the former and added the latter to the pan, then set it on the fire.

The fish began to sizzle, and I shook them in the pan. Soon enough the scent filled the room, and I felt a sharp pain in my stomach. The bannock of that morning seemed a very long time ago.

Did he usually eat anything with his fish? Surely he

ate vegetables or no way would he be as healthy as he was. Not wanting to snoop through his things, but wanting to make a nice meal, I looked over the neat row of shelves.

On one shelf was a wooden crate with a lid. I opened it, thinking that perhaps it held bread. I gave a little hum of pleasure when I instead found potatoes.

I peeled them painstakingly with a knife, cut them into cubes, and added them to the pan with the frying fish.

Wood startled me when he entered, our wet clothing draped over his arm. For such a big man, he moved almost silently.

"Potatoes?" He sniffed the air with appreciation.

"I found them on the shelf." For some reason, I felt awkward. 'I hope you don't mind."

"You are cooking my dinner. Why would I mind?" He began to clip our clothing to a rope that I hadn't noticed before. It ran the length of the wall. My stomach did a slow roll when I saw his massive hands on the delicate cotton of my panties. He handled them awkwardly, as though he wasn't sure whether they went up or down.

"I don't know. Maybe you were saving them for a special occasion." I shrugged.

"You are a strange one, girl." He shook his head. "One day is the same as the next here."

That was… sad. Frowning, I watched as he walked over to the table where my camera still sat. A stack of the plasticky developed Polaroids sat beside it. Picking them up, he began to flip through them, lingering on one of

Sean and me.

The one in which we'd been kissing. I stirred the fish and potatoes in the pan, then came to look over Wood's shoulder. I expected the picture to make me sad, embarrassed, even a bit hysterical—all of the things I was supposed to feel over Sean's betrayal.

Instead, I found myself snorting with derision. I was glad that I hadn't wasted my virginity on someone who saw women as replaceable in his bed.

And for the first time, I noticed that he had a weak chin.

"Who is this?" Wood waved the Polaroid in the air. He was frowning.

"That's Sean." I turned back to my cooking. "We… worked together."

"This does not look like someone you simply worked with." His observation was blunt. I grimaced.

"We worked together," I repeated. "And… I thought he was something more."

"Like a boy-friend?" The word sounded strange on his tongue, and I looked at him quizzically. He shrugged. "I listen when you speak, even if what you say sounds strange."

"Yes, like a boyfriend." I flapped a hand with irritation. "But it turned out he wasn't."

I didn't want to think about Sean, which would make me think about Emmett, and about home. I poked at the pan. "Dinner is ready." I didn't want to think about Sean, which would make me think about Emmett, and about home.

"This is how you paint pictures at home." He wasn't

ready to drop the subject.

"Yes, I suppose that's one way to put it." I pulled the pan from the stove, taking down the two plates that sat on the shelf above it.

He turned the photo over, examined the back. "You miss it."

"I do." My stomach rolled, and suddenly the delicious cooking smells made me feel a bit sick.

"I don't understand where you came from." Placing the picture back on the stack, he looked up at me, those dark eyes piercing. "But I understand that it isn't... the way that you came here. It wasn't the same as traveling on foot, or by boat."

"No," I whispered, hugging my arms to my torso. The cave and its secrets had been all that I'd thought about the last two days, but now the reality of what had happened to me took on a dream-like quality. "It wasn't like that at all."

This was a nightmare. I would wake up.

But as I looked at Wood, and felt that little click when his eyes met mine, I thought that perhaps it wasn't a nightmare after all.

He scrubbed his chin, a habit I was now becoming familiar with when he was perplexed.

"Do you have forks?" I asked. He gestured at the cutlery bin. Using the large spoon I'd been cooking with, I placed a portion of fish on each plate, then added a portion of the potatoes, filling Wood's plate much more than mine. He made a sound of appreciation as I placed it in front of him.

Picking up the fish with his fingers, he passed it

under his nose while I searched over the shelf for a fork. I found a three-prong utensil that would do and seated myself across from Wood at the small wooden table.

We ate in silence until our plates had been cleaned. Wood stood, taking the dirty plates to the stove, and bringing back two tin cups. He filled them with something from a bottle before handing one to me.

"This isn't moonshine, is it?" I sniffed warily, delighted when, rather than the overwhelming fumes I'd been expecting, I scented the rich notes of wine.

"Do you make this?" I sipped, pleased at the rich flavor that flooded my tongue.

He shook his head. "It's made in the village. I trade for it."

"Fish?"

"Sometimes. Sometimes I use gold."

"Gold? Where do you get that?"

He sipped, regarding me over the edge of his cup, as if deciding whether or not to answer.

"The river," he finally said, setting his cup down on the table.

"The river?" I frowned, sorting through my memory banks. "Like… panning for gold?"

"Doing what?" His eyes narrowed. "No. Logging."

What I knew about logging was what I'd seen in a YouTube video that I'd stumbled upon when researching Bras d'Or before heading to the dig. In the short clip, which claimed to be a Canadian childhood classic, a skinny, animated character called a log driver danced from spinning log to spinning log, driving the wood down the river. It was set to the tune of something called the Log Driver's Waltz, which had been stuck in my head for a week.

I squinted at Wood, trying to picture him in place of the gangly cartoon lead. It was surprisingly easy, given the grace that he'd already displayed every time he moved.

Wait. Logging. Wasn't…

Understanding hit. "You used to log with Jackal."

Something flashed in his eyes, but he remained silent. With my cup inches from my lips, I went silent as well, studying his face.

This, I realized—this was why Jackal was hunting me. Wood had saved me from what he seemed certain would have been my fate if he hadn't intervened, but in doing so, whatever had passed between them meant that Jackal wanted me more than ever, just to hurt Wood.

It was an impossible situation. And as I sat there, I realized just how much my very existence was costing this man.

I couldn't be the reason that he—and the villagers, I realized, given their still confusing connection to him— had to look over their shoulders all the time.

No wonder Guthrie had wanted to hand me over and be done with it.

Damn it; there went the waterworks, the stinging at the back of my eyes and the top of my nose. I had to go.

Where would I go?

Wood was staring at me with that obsidian gaze that seemed to pierce right through my skin to my soul. I stood to get away from it, turning to the stove.

"How do I do the dishes?" A slightly hysterical laugh

bubbled up in my throat. I had made Jackal hunt for him, and I didn't even know where to fetch the water to wash the plate I'd just eaten off of.

This time I heard him come up behind me, the tread of his boots on the wooden floor. I suspected that this was deliberate so that he didn't startle me.

I felt the heat that seemed to forever radiate off of his body, warming the skin of my back. We stood like that, mere inches between us, for a long moment.

I jumped when I felt the weight of his hand on my shoulder. He settled it there, not squeezing, not rubbing, just letting me absorb the comfort of his touch.

"I do not understand where you came from, but I am not sorry that you are here."

My breath caught in my throat. I tried to turn, but he held me in place, dipping his head to speak into my ear.

I shivered as I felt his breath fan out over my lobe.

"You are very tired. Whatever you are thinking of, it will hold until morning." Now he let me turn, and I looked up at him cautiously.

He knew. He knew that I thought I had to go.

If I left tonight, he would follow. He would keep me safe.

Finally, I nodded. He was right. It could wait for morning.

Wood cocked his head and looked me over. "You are tired."

"I am." Brushing my still-damp hair away from my face, I looked at the stove. If I settled on the floor in front of it, I would be warm enough to sleep, though I'd be sore in the morning.

Wood watched me like I would imagine he'd stare at a gorilla in the zoo as I toed off the boots, setting them neatly against the wall. I lowered myself to the ground, stretching out uncomfortably on the hardwood, cushioning my head with my arm.

He let out a sound of pure exasperation. I squawked when he squatted and lifted me right off the floor with his hands under my knees and back.

"What are you doing?" I kicked. He carried me to the bed, and my pulse sped up. Rising to my knees, my mouth fell open as I watched him remove his boots, then start to unbutton his shirt.

He tossed the flannel to the end of the bed, his hands dipping to his waistband. A choked sound escaped my throat, and I looked away.

His trousers made a soft thud as they hit the floor.

Oh, God. He was acting on that tension that had been between us since the river.

Nerves made my legs tremble even as heat settled low in my belly.

So help me, I wanted him to.

Screwing my eyes shut, clenching my hands into fists, I waited for the dip of the bed beneath his weight.

Instead, I heard the creak of a floorboard. My eyes flew open in time to see Wood lowering himself to the floor.

Naked.

"What are you doing?" I planted my hands on my hips, telling myself that it was relief I felt, not disappointment.

"Getting ready for sleep." His tone was wry.

"You are so frustrating!" Growling, I slid from the bed. "I am the one sleeping on the floor. That is that."

He rose, approaching me. My neurons began to fire wildly when he stopped an inch in front of me, mirroring my stance.

He was naked. He was completely naked, and if I shifted my hips…

Don't even go there.

"There is one solution." His voice was gruff, making my pulse skitter.

"What?" I gave an exaggerated huff.

"Have you ever shared a bed with a man before, London?"

And here we went around again.

"Yes," I lied, jutting my chin out stubbornly. I was breathless. "Lots of times."

"And these men," he growled, bending so that his face was directly in front of mine. If I'd stuck out my tongue, it would have brushed his lips. "Did they expect sex when they shared your bed?"

Shaking my head, I gulped for air, finding that there was none. It crashed back into my lungs as he wrapped his hands around my waist, depositing me back on the bed.

"That is not how it's done in Bras d'Or."

I LAY ON my back, clutching the sheets tightly to my breasts as Wood looked down on me. My heartbeat had sped up, thudding so rapidly that I thought I might be sick.

If I didn't want this, now was the time to make my protests known.

Who the hell was I kidding? I wanted this. My entire body wanted this. No one at home had any claim on me that way, so what was stopping me?

He lowered himself to the bed, sliding beneath the sheet. My breath started to come faster.

I was in Wood's bed. He was naked, and I had a gigantic slit between the legs of my bloomers. Delicious tension coiled inside of me as he shifted onto his side, and I felt his stare, the lightest of touches on my skin.

"Most men in Bras d'Or would expect sex from a woman sharing their bed." His breath was warm on my neck. "I am not most men. I will never expect something you are not willing to give."

"I—" I wanted to say that I was, in fact, very willing. The heat in my belly had grown, leading to a very real ache between my thighs. I wanted, so badly, to offer him the comfort of my body, to share his heat in return.

I didn't want him to think that comfort was all this was.

"London." He lifted a hand, and I thought I sensed hesitation before he stroked it gently down my cheek. My heart contracted painfully.

"Go to sleep."

CHAPTER TWENTY-THREE

Primitive Living

I CLOSED MY eyes, and when I opened them again, sunlight was slanting through the crack in the door. I stretched out my limbs one by one, my muscles rebelling with the movement.

Why was I so stiff?

Memories of the day before flooded back in. The trek to the village, to the trading post and back.

To the river.

To the bed.

Sucking in a deep breath, I rolled over. I was the only occupant of the bed, the sheets beside me cool.

I'd slept beside Wood. I'd slept in his bed.

I'd liked it.

Closing my eyes, I remembered the way he'd looked when he'd stalked from the floor to the bed. I'd been sure, so sure, that something was about to happen. Something big.

The fact that it hadn't only made me want him more.

The air outside the bed was chilly, but when Wood came back from wherever he'd gone, I didn't want him to find me just lounging the day away while he worked. With the same sensation I felt before I dunked myself in the river, I shoved off the covers, getting the shock of the chill over with.

Padding across the floor in bare feet, I tossed one of the last logs onto the red embers, and flames jumped to life, the heat licking over my bare legs. As the smoky scent filled the air, I hugged myself, blinking sleepily.

What time was it, anyway?

I had no way of knowing.

It was past sunrise, but still early enough that the light seemed weak and thin, though that might have just been because of the weather. Outside, the wind whistled and leaves from the tree that the cabin was tucked into brushed at the roof.

The fire had been nearly out when I'd added the log, which told me that Wood had likely built it two or so hours ago. He'd likely been up before dawn. Where on earth had he gone?

I wasn't scared, not exactly. But I was discomfited by the quiet, the hush that came from being alone in the middle of the forest.

With Wood here to fill some of the silence, I didn't notice it so much. But with the big man's commanding presence absent, I felt very, very alone.

The door swung open suddenly, and I jumped, gasping as I clasped a hand to my chest. For the first time since I'd met him, Wood seemed startled as well, though he recovered in the blink of an eye.

"I did not expect you to be awake yet." Closing the door, he set a large flannel bundle down on the table. He quickly undid the knot he'd tied in the top of it, and when the fabric fell open, I saw that it was one of his plaid shirts.

"Where were you?" Where was there to go so early? And how did he know where he was going in the dark?

"We owed Freya the mackerel. I do not like to leave debts unpaid." He pulled a stack of clothing out of the bundle, and then a basket. The fresh scent of bread filled the cabin, and my stomach took that moment to growl.

Brushing my hair back out of my face, I moved closer to inspect the contents of the basket. Besides a handful of rolls that still had tiny curls of steam swirling through the air, there was a small jar of something that looked like jam, a hunk of white cheese wrapped in cloth, and a roll of some meat.

"Is this salami?" My mouth watered at the thought of the salty taste. Some salami and cheese in a roll? I could pretend that I was at the popular Jewish deli that took up the ground floor of my apartment building in Pittsburgh.

My stomach growled again as I thought of the last meal I'd had there. A friend from school and I had shared matzoh ball soup, an order of noodle kugels, and a massive sandwich made of salami and corned beef on rye, garnished with Russian dressing and coleslaw.

My mouth filled with saliva.

"It is headcheese." He retrieved a knife and two plates, bringing them back to the table. I'd been anticipating the meat, but now I slowly set it down on the table.

"What…" Oh, I didn't want to be rude, but the word *headcheese* didn't fill me with excitement. "What is headcheese?"

Please don't let it be made of a head.

"Headcheese is made from the head of a pig." Oblivious to the gag reflex working in my throat, Wood carved off a thick slice and set it on my plate. "The meat is cured, then stuffed into a pork stomach."

"Sounds… delicious." I nudged the slice to the edge of my plate, reaching instead for a roll. I added a sliver of cheese and some jam, ignoring the quivering slab of pig.

Wood placed a thick piece on his own roll, adding cheese and jam and sandwiching it all together. His moan of pure pleasure when he bit in was more than a little distracting.

"Fish and potatoes are well and good," he said after he devoured his first roll and started to build a second, "but good headcheese is a treat."

"You don't eat like this often?" I eyed the slice on my plate. If Wood had purchased this thinking I would be thrilled to eat it, then it would be rude of me to turn my nose up.

But it was made from a *head*.

"It is too much trouble." He shook his head; I flushed. It took only seconds for him to realize what he'd said. "What I mean to say is, when I can hunt and fish, there is no need to trade for anything else."

"Right." He'd gotten this especially for me. Maybe even to… impress me?

Trying to keep my expression impassive, I picked the slice up with my fingers. I lifted it to my lips, thinking frantically of all the other strange foods I'd come across in my life.

Chicken feet in Asia, tripe in Britain. Fermented shark in Iceland, fried spiders in Cambodia, and cow's blood with milk for the Maasai tribe in Eastern Africa.

Comparatively, headcheese wasn't all that strange.

I opened my mouth. I took a bite. The taste of ham filled my mouth, and I swallowed.

Opening my eyes, I found Wood watching me. I smiled as convincingly as I could.

"It's so good." I smiled encouragingly as I laid the slice back on my plate. I was surprised at the taste, which was fine. But I still couldn't bring myself to eat an entire piece. "I wish I'd eaten it before the bread. Now I'm too full."

Wood shrugged and ate the piece himself.

Finished eating, I cleared the plates, placing them in the bin I now knew was for doing dishes. When I turned back, I found Wood looking at me with apprehension.

"The cave," he said slowly. "I went back. There is nothing there."

I understood suddenly why he'd brought a basket of treats back to the cabin—he'd wanted to sweeten this crushing news.

Slowly, I lowered myself back into one of the chairs. I knew I should probably have flown into hysterics at this news, but I was strangely calm.

We'd already been to the cave together, and I'd already discovered that whatever had hurtled me here wasn't active.

Did that mean it wouldn't ever open up a passage

again? I wasn't sure, but at the moment, there wasn't much I could do.

I smiled up at Wood, trying to reassure him that I wasn't about to lose my mind. His sober expression remained. I couldn't help but notice the way his gaze kept dipping, moving over my face. A prickle of awareness flared through me, and I smoothed my hand over the tangles of sleep.

"What?"

"After we eat, I will cut your hair," he said soberly.

My stomach knotted, and I swallowed past the instinct to argue back. After the incident at the trading post, I knew that I needed to change my appearance. At this point, survival was more important than vanity, not that I'd ever spent a whole lot of time on my makeup or clothes.

But my hair. I loved my hair. I'd always worn it long. I'd never had it dyed.

I couldn't think about it.

Standing again, I began to pack the remains of the meal back into the shirt. Not knowing what else to do with it, I folded the flannel back over the top of it.

"What are we doing today?"

"Cutting your hair." One brow arched as he cast me a look. "You do not have the best memory."

The man was always so literal. "What are we doing *after* that?"

He frowned at me.

"What do you do with your time? What do you do when you're not hunting or fishing?" I huffed out a breath at his blank stare. "What do you do for fun?"

He looked a bit exasperated with all my talking. "In the village every fortnight, we play games for entertainment."

"When is the next fortnight?" I wasn't sure how I felt about returning to the village.

"Soon."

"What kind of games?" I was picturing Monopoly. "Is it something I can practice?"

So I don't embarrass myself, I added in my head.

Wood snorted. "Only the men play the games."

I stiffened, my mother perching on shoulder with a pitchfork in her hand. "And what do the women do?"

"The women watch."

I was appalled. "Maybe I want to play."

"You can't." I was not impressed at the amusement on his face. "London, you truly cannot."

"You don't know that." I lifted my chin in the air. "I'm going to try. You can't stop me. I think the women should have fun too. That's all I'm saying."

He muttered something in French, and I was fairly certain that it wasn't complimentary. Standing, he smirked down at me. "If you're so eager to prepare yourself for the games, then you can come chop wood. That will toughen you up."

I looked down at my arms. I wasn't a fan of the gym, but I was in decent enough shape. I didn't think I needed to toughen up.

I didn't want to argue, though. "I will, then."

"First, though." He took a clean knife from the stove, running his finger along the length of it.

I cringed inwardly when I realized what the knife was

for. "That's how you're going to cut my hair? Don't you have any scissors?"

"Scissors?"

I had no idea when scissors had been invented. I demonstrated a cutting motion with my fingers. "Scissors. The blades cross and cut."

"Here we use a knife."

My stomach clenched. I didn't relish the idea of a knife near my head. I looked up at Wood, at where he stood with the hilt clutched tightly in his hand.

There weren't many people that I would trust to do this. Strangely, this terse man was at the top of the list of people I *would*.

I arranged myself in the chair. I said nothing but knew that my stillness told him I was ready.

His boots echoed on the floorboards as he came close. The wooden legs on his chair scraped over the floor, then groaned from his weight as he sat. I shook my hair out, tossing it over my shoulders, and pinched my eyes shut.

Wood lifted the knife.

CHAPTER TWENTY-FOUR

Learning the Land

I FLINCHED AT the brush of Wood's hand on my neck, and he swore.

"If I am to do this, you must hold still."

"Sorry," I whispered, steeling myself for his next touch.

His fingers swept over my neck again as he smoothed my hair out and gathered the long strands in his fist.

"Breathe," he said as the knife connected with my long blonde strands.

I sucked in air, but I suddenly I had a huge lump in my throat, and I was sure I was going to vomit. I had no idea what was coming over me, or maybe I did, but as the knife sawed through my hair, my chest tightened. I struggled to fill my lungs as the severity of my predicament crashed over me. I was tired and alone…lost.

This was about more than cutting my hair. My hair represented the life I'd unwittingly left behind.

There was nothing I could do to swallow the big hiccupping sob rising in my throat.

Wood finished cutting in one fluid slice, and when I felt the obscene lightness where the curtain of my hair had once hung, a cry burst from my lungs, a shrill sound that serrated the quiet. Wood stilled behind me, his breath changing, becoming harsher. His arm dropped, and from the corner of my eye, I caught the fistful of my severed hair in his big hand.

"London?"

I shook my head; lips pressed tightly together.

Caught off guard, Wood stood, lifting me off the chair. He carried me to the bed, seating himself on the mattress before settling me in his lap. His hand went to my back, and he rubbed soothingly. I buried my face in his chest, breathed him in and tried very hard not to let myself completely lose my shit.

I hated to cry. I was stronger than this.

"It will grow back," he said finally, the calmness in his voice washing through me.

"It's not the hair," I whispered and exhaled slowly as a measure of tranquility filled the space. "I just..."

"I will help you." His voice was gruff. "You are not alone."

I sniffed and blinked back the last of the tears.

"Can I see it?" Panic trickling out of me, I pushed away from his chest, his comfort, and ran my hand over the short cap of my hair. Wood cupped my face and held me for a moment, tension in his mouth as a soft hiss escaped his lips. A laugh rumbled through me. "Is it that bad?"

Instead of answering, Wood shifted, and lifted me from his lap. I gingerly sat as he rummaged through a metal bin, then produced a jagged piece of glass. He blew on it and rubbed it against his shirt to clean it, then he held it out in front of my face.

I blinked to focus my blurry vision.

What caught my attention wasn't the shortness of my hair, but the dark half-moons beneath my eyes and the paleness of my skin. My cheeks seemed slimmer, and no wonder—I hadn't eaten a Dorito in a week.

"It's not so bad." I took a deep breath.

"Not so bad," Wood repeated and when I glanced up at him, caught the intensity in his stare, a frisson of heat trickled through my blood. Wood turned, made a grunting sound, and put the mirror away.

Wood walked over to the table and picked up the stack of clothing I'd noticed earlier.

"Here," he said, holding out a pair of trousers. "Jackal is looking for a woman with long golden hair."

A snort of laughter escaped me. "And I now look like a boy."

"Not a boy," Wood said as I held the pants up in front of me.

"A man then." I ran a hand over the rough fabric. It wasn't denim, but it would do.

"Not a man."

I glanced up, caught this expression, held his gaze. "What, then?"

He scrubbed a hand over his beard, then turned from me, bending to one knee to poke at the fire. The flames rose, and he stood again. "I need to cut more wood."

Wood grabbed his axe and tossed it over his shoulder. I followed him outside, still in the clothing I'd slept in, and took a great mouthful of the fresh, clean air. Mist lifted from the forest floor, as the morning sun rose higher in the sky. Birds took flight and leaves kicked up under my feet as I trekked behind Wood. The forest closed in on me, the cabin no longer visible when he came to an abrupt halt. He held his hand up to quiet me, and I tucked in behind him, straining to hear whatever it was that caught his attention.

He sank to one knee and tugged on my shirt to pull me down with him. He touched my cheek and angled my head. I glanced into the distance, and my heart leaped when a big bear crossed the path in front of us.

"Black bear," Wood whispered under his breath. Adrenaline surged through my veins, and I fought to keep still as I watched.

Fur that was more a dense chocolate brown than black rippled as the huge animal lumbered along on all fours. I instinctively reached for my camera, only to come up empty. I inched closer to Wood, exhaling deeply when the bear was finally out of sight.

"Do you come across bears often?" My heart was hammering so hard I felt dizzy. I sucked in a deep breath.

"Yes." He looked me over, and I'm sure he saw my fear.

"Be respectful of the animals, and they will respect you."

I stared at him. "You sound like a fortune cookie."

"A what?" He shook his head. "What I mean is that most animals simply want to be left alone. They will not bother you unless provoked. Don't provoke them, and you will be fine."

Turning his attention to the trees around us, he snorted softly. I heard him mutter *fortune cookie* before he reached out to run a hand over the bark of a trunk.

"This one," he said. Swinging his axe over a shoulder, he pointed to a stump. "Sit there."

I backed up, eager to be out of the way before he swung his axe.

When he did, I had to swallow to keep from humming with appreciation. This was how he'd built those arms, that chest.

He grunted as he tugged the axe out of the trunk, then swung again, slicing the blade into the small notch he'd created with the first swing.

The noise of his third swing reverberated through me. I yelped when something furry ran across the clearing.

"Rabbit." He smirked at me. "Good for a stew."

I rolled my eyes.

He continued to swing. After five or so minutes, when the sweat had started to pour down his face, he tossed the axe to the side. Shrugging out of his shirt, he swiped the flannel over his forehead, then tossed it to the ground as he went back to the tree.

I stared.

Wood stepped back moments before I heard a loud crack like a gunshot. I was transfixed as the tree began to fall, moving through the air in slow motion.

It fell with a thud, and Wood stood back to look at his work. I stood and walked over to him. "What can I do to help?"

"You are not chopping wood." He snorted at the idea.

I arched an eyebrow. "You can't stop me."

He rubbed his hand over his chest, and his muscles ripple. "You truly want to do this? It is not easy."

Nostrils flaring, I held my hand out for the axe and when he placed it in my palm, I nearly staggered.

I'd had no idea that it was so heavy, but no way was I going to show him that I found it challenging.

"You need to cut the branches off first." My heart sank. The tree was large, and there were easily thirty thick branches up toward the top.

Wood did this all the time, so I wasn't going to complain. I lifted the axe and it came down under its own weight. One of the branches snapped.

"Like this," Wood said. He came up behind me, his body pressed against mine as he repositioned my hands on the handle. "Now lift it, over your shoulder." He kept his hands on mine and guided me.

"Now put your body weight into it." I did as he said, and the axe came down harder, and a bigger branch broke off.

"You are strong."

I beamed at his comment, which wasn't even a little bit true. Still, I continued to chop at the tree, moisture breaking out on my forehead. After a few more swings, my shoulders burned, and my arms quivered.

Wood took the axe from me, and I frowned.

"I can do it," I said.

"You did do it." He nodded at me. "Now I need you to gather those branches for kindling. Pile them there."

Wood made quick work of the tree, much quicker than I would have, and proceeded to cut it into round segments, which he then chopped into logs.

We spent the rest of the morning carrying them back to the cabin. I strained under four or five, but Wood hefted a dozen on each trip.

When I finally dropped the last of the wood into a pile, I brushed the back of my hand over my forehead to wipe away the sweat. My face was hot, my body ached, and my hands and arms were covered in bark dust.

I needed yet another bath, but thoughts of getting into the icy river again made me shiver.

"Stay here." I sank gratefully into one of the chairs by the stove, watching as Wood filled pots with water and placed them on the stove. He didn't seem even the least bit tired, and he did ten times the work that I had.

Would I get that strong?

I looked down at the soft curve of my belly and grimaced. It wasn't likely.

Steam started to rise from the pots as Wood slipped back outside. I heard some thumping, reverberating through the trunk of the giant tree, and then he was back, a huge metal basin in his hands.

"What's that for?" I winced when Wood dropped it to the floor, a metallic clang reverberating through the small space.

"It is for your bath."

"What?" I looked from the pots on the stove to the

basin. So much work for a bath, but the idea of sliding into hot water made my aching muscles weep with delight.

"Last night, we bathed in the freezing water when you had this." I hurried to the tub, running my hands lovingly over the rim. "You've been holding out on me."

He dipped a finger into the pot of water to test it, then filled the basin. "Last night you hadn't worked so hard."

He continued to heat water and fill the basin, and the lengthy process showed me exactly why we'd bathed in the river before.

When the basin was half-filled, he pointed at me. "I suppose you wish me to leave while you wash?"

"I do." I cast him my sunniest smile. If he'd been the kind of person to roll his eyes, he would have then. I knew he found my modesty ridiculous.

He moved toward the kitchen table. "The door is that way," I said and pointed.

"Soap," he muttered and dropped a fresh sliver, as well as a rough cloth, into the basin on his way out.

"Thank you." Waiting until the door had shut behind him, I slipped from my sweaty clothes, draping them over the chair before slowly easing myself into the luxurious warm water.

Heaven. I sank back, letting it cover my bare body as I briefly closed my eyes. Who would have ever thought I'd find bathing in a metal basin by a fire in the middle of nowhere so wonderful? Certainly not me, but I did appreciate Wood doing this for me.

I grabbed the soap and brought it to my nose. Over

that oily smell, I thought I could smell Wood. A smile touched my mouth as I ran it over my body.

I stayed in the tub for a long time, until my fingers began to shrivel and the water began to cool. I let loose a moan, not wanting to get out, but knowing it was time.

Closing my eyes, I dunked under one last time, and when I surfaced, there was a shadow hovering over me.

What the hell?

CHAPTER TWENTY-FIVE

Attraction

"WHAT DO YOU think you're doing?"

I shrieked at the unexpected voice. Hunching in on myself, I looked across the small room to see Keltie, one hand on her hip, the other holding something wrapped in a gingham cloth and cradled close to her chest.

"What do *you* think you're doing?" I grabbed the flimsy washcloth and covered myself, my gaze darting to the open door. A cool breeze whistled through the cottage, chilling my damp skin. Goosebumps rose, and I sank deeper into the tepid water. "You almost gave me a heart attack."

"A what?" She shook her head as if swatting away an annoying fly. She tapped a foot on the floor, and I realized that she was waiting for me to answer her question.

"I'm bathing." My tone was heavy on the sarcasm. I waited for her to realize that I was naked and clearly in need of some privacy.

She rolled her eyes at me instead. "That is obvious, but why are you in *that* tub?"

What was *with* these people and their lack of modesty?

Wait. What if Wood had been the one bathing? Would Keltie still be standing there unconcerned if she'd walked in on him while he had a rub-a-dub-dub?

I hadn't recovered from the delicious torture of sleeping next to him the night before, and I didn't care for the idea of this young girl walking in on him naked. I flapped my hands with irritation. "Get out while I get dressed."

"I asked why you were in that tub." Her face reddened. I blinked when I realized that she was angry.

I was missing something. Craning my neck, I looked at the metal basin. It was old. The tin was scuffed and dented. I didn't see anything to get mad about.

I opened my mouth to tell her she could bathe in the damn tub if she'd just let me get out of it first when she gasped.

"Your hair."

Self-conscious, I touched the wet strands that fell to just below my chin. In my time, it would have been considered a bob. Might have even been stylish, but I'd never worn it so short. I watched as Keltie drew her waist-length, midnight black braid over her shoulder, and felt the loss of my long gold ponytail quite keenly. "I...Wood cut it."

She crinkled her nose. "It's dreadful. You look like a boy."

"I think that was the plan," I responded quietly, even though Wood had assured me I did not resemble a boy…or a man. As if my thoughts had conjured him up, his massive frame suddenly filled the doorway, blocking the natural sunlight.

"Keltie." Wood's voice softened as he greeted her. "What brings you this way?"

Did every villager know where Wood's cabin was? He seemed too private for that. But if only a few knew, then how did this young girl?

The venom that had been in her expression when she looked at me melted into sweetness and light as she smiled up at him, holding out her gingham-wrapped bundle. "I made cinnamon braids and thought you might like some. I know they're your favorite."

After handing the bundle to Wood, she settled her hand on his arm, just for a moment. I cleared my throat loudly, not at all sorry to interrupt the tender little moment.

"Wood, I need to get out of the tub." Still clutching the cloth to my breasts, I widened my eyes, trying to express my agitation.

His eyes dipped to the cloth, which was very thin. And I was very cold. I knew I wasn't mistaking the interest in his eyes.

I cleared my throat again. He shook his head as if coming out of a trance.

"Thank you for the bread. Will I see you at the games tomorrow night?"

"You will." She cast me a quick but triumphant look before sniffing. "Father said to bring her."

"Her name is London." Wood turned to place the wrapped bread on the table. I almost shouted with exasperation at the fact that they were still talking and I was still naked, but he flicked his stare toward me quickly, and I watched as unwrapped the bread and laid the cloth over my camera and the stack of Polaroids.

He doesn't want Keltie to see.

Wood was protecting me. Again.

"Shall I tell Father that you will be there?" She smiled again, and something tight lodged in my chest. She wasn't faking her interest in Wood just to upset me. It was easy to see that she had genuine feelings for him, or at least that she thought she did.

Wood scrubbed his hands over his face. "Tell him we will be there."

"I am so pleased." Her entire body leaned toward him, signaling her interest. "It is a beautiful morning. Perhaps we could enjoy these cinnamon braids together."

"London needs to get dressed." He turned away from me deliberately. I'd only known him for three days, but I already understood that he was trying to get her out the door for my sake.

"I'm not stopping her," Keltie said, not bothering to hide the coldness in her voice.

Her attitude seemed to trigger a reaction in Wood. Sighing, he took her by the elbow. "Come with me."

She smirked at me as he led her outside. I heaved a sigh of relief as the door closed behind them.

Either I needed to get over my hang-up about letting it all hang out, or Wood and company needed to develop some modesty. Three guesses who was going to win that one.

Grateful for the privacy for now, I listened to their footsteps crunching over the leaves outside, fading as they walked away from the cabin. When I could no longer hear their steps, I hauled myself from the tub, folding the washcloth neatly over the edge of the basin.

What about me in that tub had made Keltie so angry? I eyed the thing balefully. Maybe if I rubbed it, a genie would appear.

Genie, I wish for you to send me home.

Wood wasn't at home.

Pursing my lips, I stood by the warm fire for a second, amused by the steam that rose from my skin as the moisture dried. Conscious of the minutes ticking past, I turned to the clothing that Wood had retrieved from the trading post for me that morning.

Trousers that were too big for me, even with the belt Wood had thought to bring as well. A thin white shirt.

Jackal was searching for a woman. Next time I left the cabin, I would look like a man.

I'd just dressed when the door opened again, slowly this time. Wood ducked his head through, opening it the rest of the way once he saw me dressed by the fire.

"Where's Keltie?" My voice was flat. She was just a girl, but I didn't have much warmth for her.

"Gone."

"Who is her father?" My fingers worried the hem of the shirt.

"She is the daughter of Guthrie." He looked me over. What I was wearing wasn't so different from anything I would wear at home—pants and a shirt—but knowing that they were supposed to make me look like a boy made me feel unattractive.

The heat in Wood's eyes told me that he found me anything but.

"She is interested in you." I studied his face for his reaction. I wasn't sure what I'd been expecting, but it wasn't mild panic.

"She is not." He took a step back as if to distance himself from my crazy notions. "She is family. It is not that way."

"Family?" I grasped at the notion eagerly, curious for anything about his background. "Is she your sister?"

I was pretty sure that her intentions with those cinnamon braids hadn't been sisterly.

"In a way." He turned away, effectively dismissing me. I wasn't done.

"She was angry about me using this tub. Is it hers?"

Something flickered across Wood's face, and for the first time since I'd met him, I saw complete coldness.

His boots stomped as he disappeared out the door, closing it tightly behind him.

He didn't want to talk about the tub. What the hell was so special about the damn tub?

Pulling a chair over to it, I sat and stared at it, willing it to reveal its secrets to me.

It didn't. It was, after all, a metal tub.

"Let me see your feet."

I nearly jumped out of my skin. I hadn't heard the door open, but Wood was suddenly behind me, the tin of salve that he'd used before in his hands.

"They're fine." I tucked them beneath the chair, my bare toes sticking to the hardwood.

He simply knelt in front of me and, with strong hands on my calves, pulled one foot onto his lap.

"They are raw." He traced a finger over one of the blisters, and I winced. "Do you not understand the importance of treating a wound? If you do not, you could get very sick."

Infection. He was talking about infection. This was important, but as the fingers on my feet started to rub my sore soles, I found it hard to pay attention.

"I do not want you to be sick." Looking up, his eyes met mine as he opened the tin and dipped his fingers inside. He held my gaze as he stroked the salve over one foot, then the other.

By the time he reached for a clean pair of socks to slide over the top, I was breathless.

"I do not wish you to get sick. Do you understand?" Something pulsed between us, and I wondered why I'd ever allowed Keltie to get under my skin.

"I understand." My lips parted. It wouldn't take much movement at all to slide from the chair, to straddle those massive thighs and place my lips on his.

He stood, leaving a chill where there had been warmth.

"I am going to teach you how to fish."

The non-sequitur left me struggling to catch up.

"You do not like being dependent on me. If you learn to fish, you will not be so dependent. Do you see?" He huffed out a breath.

"I'll learn." I jumped to my feet as prickles of awareness assaulted my nerves. We stood there a moment longer, eye-to-eye, before he abruptly turned away.

He walked over to a hook and grabbed a big fur coat, holding it out to me. I blanched as I wondered what fuzzy little creature it had come from. He sighed.

I knew what he was thinking. Never mind where the coat had come from, it was cold outside, and the fur would keep me warm. I was going to have to just get over it.

"What will you wear?" I slid my arms into the gigantic fur. If only PETA could see me now. "It's not fair for you to have no coat."

"I do not chill as easily as you." He grunted before heading outside. I followed him and the air, brisk at this time of the morning, bit at my face. I followed him over a carpet of fallen leaves, cursing when I slipped on the dewy moss.

Frustrated with the brisk pace he set, the bulky coat slowing me down, I called out after him. "Where are we going?"

"Fishing. Did you forget already?"

"I didn't *forget*." I surreptitiously raised my middle finger at his back, not that he would have any idea what it meant if he saw me. "I just mean how far?"

"Then you should have asked how far."

I raised the middle finger of my second hand.

"Okay, then." I made my voice overly pleasant. "How far?"

"Not far."

The man was infuriating. Still, I followed him down to the river, to the same embankment we'd been at the night before. In the valley below, the water rippled in the wind, a sight that made my hands itch for my camera.

Wood clearly had no time for such things. With long strides and a sharp, pointy spear in his hand, he led the way, forcing me to duck and dodge tree branches as they sprang back toward me. Now and then he'd turned to check on me. "Keep up, girl."

"I am," I shot back, my frustration from the morning simmering. "I'm just not used to traveling this way, and I don't know my way around as you do."

Something buzzed by my head. I twitched to shake it away, opening my mouth to shout.

Something hit the back of my throat, and I choked.

"Oh, my God," I squeaked out. Wood stopped, his muscles rippling as he turned to face me. His eyes narrowed, assessed me, as I coughed like an asthma patient and jumped around frantically, my ankle nearly twisting on a twig. "I think I just swallowed a fly. Yuck. Yuck. Yuck."

He sighed the way one might with a misbehaving toddler. His nostrils flared as he stepped up to me, cupped my arm, and led me down the embankment. "Drink," he said.

I went down on my knees, leaning over the water with cupped hands.

"Try not to fall in this time."

My gaze flew to his. Was he teasing me about how I'd landed in this time and place to begin with—my tumble into the lake? Did the man have a sense of humor?

If I weren't so disgusted by the fly sliding down my

throat, I would have come back with a smart-ass comment. Instead, I scooped water with my hands and gulped it back greedily.

"That was disgusting," I said and coughed some more.

"Maybe if you didn't talk so much the flies wouldn't get in." The corner of his mouth quirked, and I cast him a glare. When he looked away, though, I couldn't stop a tiny smile.

He started walking again, and I hurried to my feet to follow.

"I wasn't talking too much. It's just that you don't tell me anything," I mumbled to myself. I fell into place behind him, lost in my thoughts as I watched the way his flannel shirt moved over his shifting muscles. My mind went back to Keltie's invitation, and the lightness I'd felt over Wood's humor vanished.

A worried knot tugged at my stomach. "What are the games?"

I pictured an ancient Roman arena, me in the middle fighting for my life without so much as an axe.

"Do not worry so much." His words said one thing, his tone another. Anxiety flared inside of me.

"Why does Guthrie want me there?"

"We will find that out tomorrow night."

CHAPTER TWENTY-SIX

Repent

"TIME TO FISH." Not giving me a chance to think too much about the games, Wood's steps finally slowed, and he pointed up ahead. "The fish swim thickly here. Even a child could find success here."

I glanced at the fast running, shallow stream. Numerous rocks, worn smooth from years of rushing water, jutting out of the surface. It would make a beautiful picture, too. Me flailing around, trying to stab a fish with a spear? Not so much.

Wood jumped onto one of the rocks. "Follow me."

He hopped from one rock to the next with an ease of a logger, and one I'd never be able to duplicate.

"How about I just fish from here." I'd faceplant in a second if I tried that.

He came back toward me and held his hand out. "Come on."

"Ah, I don't think these boots were made for rock jumping."

"You can't learn to fish from over there. Now come on."

I wanted to tell him I didn't need to learn, that I'd be back to my own time soon enough, but that wasn't true, was it? I needed to learn how to survive.

Gingerly, I accepted his hand and scrabbled onto the first rock. He held me until I balanced, and surprisingly enough, the boots did have a good grip.

"Keep your arms out for steadiness," he suggested. "Like this."

I did as he said. Once I was stable, he jumped to the next rock, then reached back for me to guide me out deeper and deeper. We did this for a few more minutes until we landed on a big, solid rock that would support us both.

My breath caught in my throat when his compact chest pressed against my back, and he bent, his mouth close to my ear. "Look," he said and pointed.

I leaned forward to peer into the water, and Wood's arm slid around my body, his big hand splayed over my stomach to hold me to him. His touch sent little jolts of pleasure zinging crazily around my body.

Secure in his arms, I bent forward a bit more, and he tugged at me so I wouldn't topple. That's when I realized I pretty much had my backside pressed against his…front side…the position far too personal. I shifted, and a deep tortured noise sounded his throat. Wait, was that…

Holy shit.

His hold on me loosened, and I snapped up straight. Heat moved through my body despite the cool breeze, and I gulped air. I darted a glance around, looking everywhere and anywhere except at Wood, and his…wood…as my mind raced.

"London," he finally said in a deep rough voice.

"Yes." I turned slowly and worked to keep my eyes from dipping to take in his body, as the air around us charged. Birds took flight, and the water seemed to rush faster, pounding in my ears, behind my eyelids.

He scrubbed at his beard, his brow furrowed, but there was something hungry and wild in his eyes. He inched closer, the heat from his body wrapping around me, and I could no longer seem to breathe. "Wood?" I asked, and lifted my chin, my lips parting slightly.

He stared at my open mouth for a second; then a change came over him. "I am not a good man."

"What?" My gaze moved over his face, the tension lining his face. "Why do you think that?"

"I used to do very bad things." Suddenly fierce, he pinned me with the intensity of his stare. "Things that would make you scream in terror."

"You used to be part of Jackal's crew," I said slowly, mind racing. The full implications of that hit me like a sledgehammer.

When Jackal and his men had surrounded me, they had had something very dark on their minds. Something that might have broken me.

Jackal had sliced me open with a smile, just because I'd been there.

I looked at Wood, and couldn't reconcile those images with the man who was teaching me to fish.

"Do you believe that people can change?" I asked

slowly. My mind was screaming at me to get away.

But I'd been in the man's presence nonstop for more than three days. If he'd wanted to hurt me, he'd had ample opportunity. Didn't actions speak louder than words?

He laughed, and the sound held no mirth. "I believe that a man can spend a lifetime trying to atone for his sins. He will still get what he deserves in the end."

"Where I come from, that's called karma." I cocked my head up at him. Maybe I was batshit crazy, but I didn't fear him. I didn't fear him at all. "And charging into the middle of a group of assholes with knives to save a woman you've never met means that karma should smile kindly on you."

I believe that a man can spend a lifetime trying to atone for his sins.

Was that all I was to him? A way to repent?

I didn't care for the thought.

"Let's fish." My voice was tight. I felt his eyes on me, but he said nothing, instead giving me a curt nod.

The water gurgled at my feet. I focused on the gentle ripples, the little bubbles.

"Look," I said, and pointed to a speckled fish jumping from the water to catch a fly. I inched away, breaking the moment between us, but there was nothing I could do to erase the shiver of awareness trickling through my blood.

I'd experienced chemistry before but never like this.

Angling my head, I glanced at him over my shoulder. Despite what he'd just shared with me, the look on his face told me that I didn't imagine it.

With a nod, he grunted and lifted his spear.

I stilled, wanting nothing more than to admire his untamed beauty as he stood statue still. His size, the strength of his body as he held the spear, made me think of the king in the tomb, the ceremonial axe. The space for the long-dead king's queen.

The tiny hairs on the back of my neck stood up. For no reason at all, a shiver moved through me, right down to my toes.

Movement across the river caught my attention.

"Oh!" I clapped a hand to my mouth. Wood followed my gaze, stilling when he saw what I did—a white stag.

The creature stepped daintily down the embankment, dipping its head to lap at the flowing water of the river. I held my breath.

I'd taken several classes on religions of the world and mythology as part of my undergrad degree. The white stag had featured prominently across the beliefs of many religions and cultures, over the span of thousands of years. The symbolism varied.

In reality, I knew that a white stag was simply affected with albinism. Nothing symbolic about it.

Still, such a creature was rare. Very rare.

And yet I'd seen one by the cave, and here was another. It was hard not to assign meaning.

"Does the white stag hold meaning for the clan?" I whispered the words, not wanting to disturb it.

It heard me anyway. Lifting its head from the water, it looked across the river at where Wood and I stood. It looked at Wood and snorted. Then it looked at me and inclined its head.

I couldn't breathe.

"To the clan, the white stag symbolizes a new beginning." The stag snorted again. "And each leader is visited by their spirit guide before they take responsibility for their people. The animal differs depending on the person, but it is always white."

My hand dropped from my mouth, brushing against Wood's. Without thinking, I tangled my fingers in his.

He dropped his spear. As it clattered to the rock, the deer turned and took flight, running swiftly back up the embankment and out of sight.

I opened my mouth, feeling the need to say something about how strange the stag's appearance had just been, but Wood's eyes were fastened on the water. He slid his hand from mine, then bent to pick up his spear.

I was annoyed. What had just happened felt significant, though I wasn't yet sure how. I didn't like his lack of reaction.

I waited until he'd fixed his stare on the rippling water and lifted his arm, then deliberately jostled him. His spear came down, missing its target.

"Sorry." I couldn't quite hold back the smirk.

Wood grumbled and lifted his spear again. He was a patient man when it came to hunting—with me, not so much. A minute later, he speared something large and silver and pulled the wiggling fish from the river. The muscles of his arm strained under the weight. "Now it is your turn."

I turned my thoughts from the stag, still irritated. Was he just going to ignore this thing between us, then?

Isn't that what I wanted him to do?

Focus, London. Just fish.

Wood yanked the fish from the spear with a grunt, then handed me the weapon. I tried not to grimace at the blood that had been left behind.

"Like this." He set his catch down on the rock, then placed his fingers over my own, positioning my hands on the wooden shaft. His skin was warm against mine, as he lifted the spear, showing me where to hold it, how to handle it.

I held it upright like that, my arm quickly starting to tremble. A school of fish fluttered through the water in streaks of silver, but I held still.

"Exhale slowly," Wood said. I let loose air, and my body relaxed. "Aim for the head."

One of the fish broke from the school, and I fixed my stare on it. Willing my arm to listen to my mind, I brought the spear down.

It missed by a mile, the fish scuttling away, offended at having its swim interrupted.

"This is harder than it looks." I glanced at Wood over my shoulder, embarrassed. "You made it look easy."

"It takes much practice." He shook his head. "I have been doing this since I was a boy."

I couldn't imagine Wood as a boy. When I tried, I could only conjure up a miniature version of him as he was, plaid flannel, beard and all.

"Again." He placed his hands on my hips. "Breathe."

I was very aware of his hands on me. Struggling to

focus, I exhaled slowly, waiting for a clean shot.

Fourteen tries later, I stabbed a salmon, right in the belly. I pulled it out of the water, and the fish wiggled on the spear.

"I did it," I yelled triumphantly, and without thinking threw my arms around Wood's shoulders for a hug. My breasts brushed his torso, and his gaze dropped to my mouth.

Oh, boy.

I wet my lips without thinking. His stare tracked the movement. He didn't move, and neither did I.

"I…thanks for teaching me." I swallowed, hard. "Should I try for another?"

"That is a big fish, big enough for us both." His breath hitched, and the sound curled around me like an embrace. "Never take more than you need, or one day there won't be any."

"All right." I forced myself to step back, to put some space between us. My body instantly missed his heat, that overtly sensual moment.

I was in over my head.

Setting the spear down, I dropped to my knees to pull the fish from the shaft. Wood had made it look like it just slid right off, but that wasn't the case for me—it was stuck tightly.

The fish wiggled, its scales cold and rough beneath my fingers. I grimaced but continued tugging until I had it free. "Pass me your knife; I'll clean it."

So gross.

"You're a fast learner, London." He smiled, just a

faint one, but pride surged through me.

"You're a good teacher," I replied, and lifted my chin to meet his gaze.

After I'd cleaned the fish, tossing the guts to the shore for some lucky scavenger's dinner, Wood slid the fillets back on the spear, and we traced our path back to the shore. Beyond proud of myself, I followed Wood back to the cottage with a spring in my step. The sun was higher in the sky, the air a lot warmer as we walked, and I shed the big coat he'd given me, tossing it over my arm and wiping the moisture from my forehead.

"I think a dunk in the river might have been a good idea," I said.

Wood glanced at me over his shoulder and slowed his steps for me to catch up. I moved in beside him, and he matched my pace.

"This is not a good place to bathe. The current runs too fast." He gestured in front of him with the spear. "You can bathe in the river at home."

Home.

My stomach clenched at the word. No matter what I was feeling for Wood, this wasn't my home. Not yet, and it never would be if I could help it.

My brain hurt from trying to understand what had happened. By all the laws of science, it simply wasn't possible. I'd thought that the simplest explanation was that I'd traveled back in time. But what if the simplest explanation was actually that I'd gone a little mad and was making it all up?

"Wood?"

"Yes?" He glanced my way, and I noted the deep

color of his eyes. He seemed real. All of this did. "What is it?"

"Do you think I'm crazy?"

CHAPTER TWENTY-SEVEN

The Kiss

"I DO NOT think you are crazy." Wood nodded firmly. He might have been insane himself, but for some reason, his certainty reassured me.

"Do you…" asking the next question was hard. "Do you think I'll ever find my way home?"

His expression grew impassive. "I cannot answer that. I cannot even understand where you are from."

That made two of us.

I followed him in the direction of the cabin. I was beginning to recognize the surrounding vegetation, and I knew that we were still about ten minutes from the cabin when he began to push through some underbrush.

He disappeared into the middle of it. I sighed and followed, though of course, the plants that hadn't touched him scratched me, leaving stinging welts on my tender skin.

The bushes ended abruptly, and I found myself in a small clearing. Wood had stabbed the spear down into the dirt so that it stood upright, and was standing at the end of a neat row of plants.

"You have a garden!" I was charmed. "It's like the Secret Garden!"

"It is not a secret." Bending, he ran his hands over a leafy plant. "Not to the animals, at any rate. The deer eat half my harvest."

"No, The Secret Garden is a book…" I let my words trail off. Something told me that he wasn't familiar with the works of Frances Hodgson Burnett. "Did you plant all of this?"

"Yes." He dropped to his knees, and I imitated his stance. "Do you not have gardens where you come from?"

"Some people do." People who weren't away for months at a time. "I don't."

"Where do you get your vegetables from, then?" He was puzzled. "Do you trade for them? It is a far better use of your resources to simply plant your own."

"Not where I'm from." I pictured my local Whole Foods, the mountains of produce shining like jewels. My mouth watered—what I wouldn't give for a nice juicy orange right now.

"Explain."

"Someone else grows the vegetables, and sells them to a… trading post." I ran my finger over the leafy carrot greens. "I get what I need from there. I use… gold."

That was the best explanation I could come up with.

"Pull." Abruptly, Wood captured my hand and placed it over the greens he'd been stroking. Bracing myself on my knees, I gathered them in my fists and tugged. I expected resistance, but the carrot came out easily, and I ended up falling backward. My ass hit the dirt, and I flew back until I was sprawled out on the ground, spread eagle.

"You're not hurt?" Wood asked, coming into view as he stood over me.

I gave a slow shake of my head. "Just my pride."

He held his hand out, and I accepted it. He tugged me up, and as with the carrot, the amount of force applied wasn't the amount needed. I collided with his body. Air left my lungs with an oomph, and I wasn't so sure it was from our impact.

I backed away quickly, holding the carrot up like a shield. "Carrot survived."

His head dipped, and his lids lowered, hiding the hint of laughter there. "Perhaps you would like to move onto the potatoes. They don't fight back."

"You could have warned me." Breaking from his hold, I stepped around him, going back to my knees. "How many should I pull?

"Just what we need." I tugged another carrot free, examining it.

"Do you like apples?" he asked.

"You have apples?" I looked around, finally spotting the tree. It was pregnant with heavy red globes.

"It is why I decided to plant my garden here. I'll have to empty this tree soon, before the frost." He was tall enough that he didn't even need a ladder to grab us a couple. "Apples keep well."

The branches were weighted down with fruit, and my mouth watered for one. "Where will you keep them all?"

He moved to a small slope at one side of the garden, lifting a strip of sod. Following him, I looked over his shoulder.

The hill had been hollowed out, reinforced with wooden beams. "What is this for?"

"It is a root cellar. It prevents freezing in the winter and spoiling in the summer." He let the sod fall back with a thump. "I have two. One is for apples. The other for potatoes and carrots."

"Why can't you just put them together?"

"The apples will make the rest of the harvest rot." He furrowed his brow as if this was something I should have known. "Stored separately, everything will stay fresh until spring."

Would I still be here come spring?

"It's like a big refrigerator." He cocked his head. "We have something... similar at home."

The refrigerator running in my empty apartment back home held two half-eaten cartons of leftover Chinese food and some questionable yogurt. How long would the containers sit there before someone came to clean them out? Before my apartment was rented to someone new?

Wood pulled a turnip from the garden, and two potatoes. "We will cook these with the fish. It will be a good meal."

My stomach growled, thinking of the cinnamon braids on the table back in the cabin. At home, I could have sweets anytime I wanted. Here, they were obviously a luxury.

So much work went into simple survival. And this

was where I now lived.

My mouth suddenly watered for a KitKat bar.

"Do you stay out here in the winter?" I frowned. "By yourself?"

"Yes." He cast me that expression that said he didn't understand how I could ask the question. "The cabin is my home."

Survival was a lot of work now, in the fall. I couldn't imagine what it would take come snow.

"You must have a lot to do to get prepared."

"Enough." Weary of the subject, Wood slapped the apples into my hands. He juggled the potatoes and turnip while he pulled the spear back out of the earth.

When we again reached the cabin, I felt... heavy. As though something was weighing me down.

Wood was clearly accepted as part of the clan. Why, then, did he choose to live here instead of the village? Here, in a cabin, so desperately alone?

On the way through the door, I snagged a handful of wild mayflowers. Inside, I placed them in a cup and added a ladleful of water.

The man needed something bright and happy in his life.

Wood eyed the arrangement but didn't say a word. I wiped my hand over my brow again. It was damn hot inside, and I couldn't believe I'd worn a fur coat just hours ago.

"I think I'll take a swim." I stepped past Wood, aware that he was still eyeing the arrangement. I walked slowly back to the river we'd swum in the night before, cautiously confident that I knew my way there.

The sound of the current was the only thing to be heard. Taking a moment for myself, I closed my eyes, savoring the solitude.

With a quick glance over my shoulder to ensure that I was alone, I slipped out of my clothes, wading quickly into the water. I wish I'd thought to bring the chemise that Wood had gotten for me, a sort of makeshift bathing suit, but then I'd have to wash the river slime from it. More work. Not worth it.

The water was shockingly cold against my sweating skin. I waded out until it was at my waist, then dunked myself under the water.

When I surfaced, Wood was three feet away, the river lapping at his hips. I screamed.

"You scared me," I yelled. I kept one hand over my breasts as I splashed water at him with the other.

He flicked his long hair back and disappeared under the water.

I was naked under the water.

"What are you doing?" I asked, mostly to myself, and tiptoed around, looking for him under the rippling waves. He surfaced behind me, and I spun. "Stop that!"

I splashed more water on his face, to distract myself from the fact that he was once again close to me, and he was once again naked.

"I would not do that," he warned, capturing my wrist. My gaze met his, took in the fierce hunger of a wild animal, and my entire body came alive.

His big fingers closed over my arm, holding me still, and the sudden, inappropriate image of me under him, his body weight pinning me down, raced through my brain. I briefly shut my eyes, wanting to dispel the image, but instead found myself savoring it.

Not smart, London. Not smart at all.

His grip loosened, and I ducked under the water, self-conscious. I swam away, surfacing further from my clothes than I would have liked. I stole a glance over my shoulder.

Wood was still standing in the water. His hand shaded his eyes, and he was watching me.

"Shall I turn around?" There was an unspoken layer to his question.

I could say no.

"Please." My teeth started chattering. He didn't react, simply turning in the water, his back to me.

I bolted from the water and tugged my clothes on, battling with the friction created by my damp skin. I didn't wait for Wood, not sure I trusted myself to keep my eyes off him when he emerged from the river.

The swim had worked to cool me off, but by the time I got back to the cabin, I was freezing again. Inside, I stood over the stove for a moment, warming my hands.

I needed to do something.

Pulling out a knife, I sat at the table and started to peel and slice the vegetables for dinner, tossing them into the same pan I'd used the night before as they were cut. I set them and the fish on the stove, where they started to sizzle.

The brisk wind that entered with Wood made me shiver. I sank my teeth into my lip as I looked up, not sure what I would see.

His face was set in even lines, as though the tension

by the river hadn't happened. He'd also put his clothes back on.

I told myself that I wasn't disappointed.

"Why are you so often cold?" He shook his head as though it was something I could prevent. Striding to his shelves, he took down a bottle, handing it to me. "This will warm you up."

I opened my mouth, and he cut me off before I could ask. "It is not moon-shine."

I took the dark bottle from him, uncorking it for a sniff. I wasn't entirely sure, but the sweetness told me it might be brandy.

No matter what it was, it burned a pleasant trail down my throat and into my belly. I took a second sip, then passed it back to Wood.

He took a long swallow, passed it back to me, then pulled a chair close to the stove. He retrieved a basket I hadn't yet noticed, pulling out a ball of wool and…

Were those knitting needles?

"You knit?" My mouth fell open with shock. I couldn't help it.

He seemed taken aback by the shock in my voice. "Of course I knit. How else would I make socks?"

"They're two dollars a pair at Walmart," I joked, but I pulled the second chair over closer. I filled Wood's plate and served it to him right there, then got my own. He raised an eyebrow but didn't comment, inhaling his meal before again picking up his knitting. Leaning forward as I nibbled on my own dinner, I watched as he arranged the needles in his massive hands.

"Why are there four needles?" I frowned.

He arched an eyebrow. "Because that is how many you need to knit socks."

The wool started to fly through his fingers. I craned my neck to see. "What are you doing?"

He sighed, then gestured for me to pull my chair closer. Holding up the half-finished sock that dangled from three of the needles in his left hand, he wiggled the remaining needle in his right.

"See the stitch on the far right of this row?" He waved the hand holding the sock. I squinted, then nodded.

"To make a knit stitch, you take the needle in your right hand and slide the tip into that stitch so that it comes up in the back. Do you see?"

I watched as he did it. "I think so."

"Then you loop the yarn around that needle in the back." He moved slowly so that I could see. "Then you slip that needle to the front. And there is your new stitch."

One stitch now sat on the right-hand needle; the others were still on the left.

He showed me three more times, slowly, then handed me the knitting. I handed it right back.

"I don't want to wreck your socks." I knew I would. "I need to clean up dinner."

He shrugged and continued to work on the sock. The metal needles clicked softly, a pleasant noise against the crackle of the fire. We worked in silence for a while, but me being me, I couldn't stay that way.

"Do you get much snow here in the winter?" I wondered how isolated that must feel. "Where I live, we get heaps. Last winter after one storm, it was up to my chin."

"It can be like that here as well," he confirmed, and I winced inwardly. He would be cut off from everything in that case, trapped in the woods.

How could someone live like that?

"How long have you lived like this?" I was suddenly upset with him. Why did he cut himself off from the world? There had to be a reason. "Out here, all alone?"

"I have not always been alone." His breath hitched as soon as he realized what he'd said.

"You haven't always been alone." I searched his face, noted the anger, but barged right past it. "Were you married?"

He pinched the bridge of his nose. Standing, he took the bottle from my hand.

"I wasn't finished." I was. The alcohol was a fire in my veins, making me brave.

"You are finished."

"Don't tell me—" I stood.

"The spirits have loosened your tongue, girl."

"My tongue is not loose; I'm just—"

Wood growled. Before I even realized what was happening, he grabbed me by the waist. Yanking me against his chest, he angled his head down and pressed his lips to mine.

I made some sound against him, some cross between protest and pleasure. When he slid his hands firmly from his waist to glide over my back, I rose to my toes, my fingers digging into his shoulders.

His tongue ran along the seam of my lips. I opened,

tasted smoke.

Wanted more.

He tugged at the ends of my newly shorn hair, just hard enough to bring my nerves to life. Then he pulled away, staring down at me as the breath heaved in and out of my chest.

I opened my mouth to speak, but for once I had no words. He sucked in a breath through his nose.

"Go to bed."

CHAPTER TWENTY-EIGHT

A Fortnight

N EARLY TWENTY-FOUR HOURS had passed since Wood had kissed me silent, yet I could still taste him on my tongue.

After he'd ordered me to bed, he'd gone outside, shutting the door firmly behind him. Not knowing what else to do, I'd done as he'd ordered.

Sleep had been a long time coming, but when I finally drifted off, Wood still hadn't returned. Come morning, I found the bedding mussed, but Wood was up, tending to the fire. His behavior wasn't all that strange—not for him, at any rate—but something between us had changed.

We didn't talk about it.

Oh, but it had happened.

Now, here we were trekking through the woods to the village for a meal and the games. Wood had somehow procured a dress, laying it out on the bed.

I'd said that I would wear my trousers. He'd simply

shrugged, as though he couldn't have cared less.

I'd worn the dress. I was now regretting the decision. The fabric was heavy, uncomfortable, and it was slowing me down. How women managed to cook and clean in clothes like these was beyond me. Then again, they didn't know the comfort of a pair of well-worn jeans. They couldn't miss what they'd never had, right?

Wood glanced at me over his shoulder, and when he saw I was struggling, he slowed his pace considerably. I scurried to catch up. Now and then I'd look up to find him watching me, but as soon as I'd caught him at it, he'd looked away.

It was killing me. For several days, he'd seemed to be open to the idea of something between us. Something physical, at least.

But since something had happened, he'd backed right the hell off.

The scents of frying fish, bread, and smoke as we neared the village were welcome. I inhaled deeply as laughter burst from the village, letting the warmth wrap around me as the clan prepared for the night of food and fun.

At the edge of the trees, Wood stopped shortly and put a halting hand on my shoulder. His stare darted over my shoulders, around me but not at me. "Stay in the open tonight. Do not wander off alone."

"Why?" A measure of unease trickled through my blood. With the strangest sensation that someone or something was directly behind me, I shivered, moving closer to Wood.

His hand left my shoulder and slid slowly, hesitantly

down my arm. His palm found mine, and he gave a strange, comforting squeeze. The feel of his calloused scraping over my palm made my breath hitch.

"I will be busy with the games." He paused, tension tight in his body. I wasn't sure what to do with a Wood who was this edgy. "The clansmen are good folk, but they fear what they don't understand."

He started to move forward, but I squeezed his hand. "Wood?"

He looked back over a shoulder, eyebrows raised.

"Why are you helping me?"

"Restitution."

My heart sank, but he wasn't done speaking.

"At first, it was restitution. I could not let Jackal have you."

"And now?" I held my breath.

He flicked his gaze my way quickly before looking away again.

"Now it is something more."

WOMEN EYED ME suspiciously as Wood and I entered the village. They prepared food over fires, stealing glances my way, and I remembered the night I'd fled the hotel, the dig crew all talking about me over beers and bonfires.

"Stay here, and you will be safe." Wood dipped his head. "I need to speak with Guthrie."

Butterflies took flight in my stomach. This wasn't the first time I'd found myself surrounded by strangers who weren't necessarily friendly. This was the first time, however, that I had nowhere to run. I had no choice but to wade into the fray.

I glanced around, spotted the young mother with her colicky baby. Her smile was tentative when I waved to her, but when Wood left, she approached.

"Hello," I said. "I'm London. I never got your name."

"I am called Krissa." She rocked the baby in her arms. It was silent, swaddled tightly in tartan.

"And who is this?" I gestured to the baby.

Her expression warmed as she looked down at her baby. "This is my boy Deorn."

I peeked at the child and gave a tentative little tug on his wrap to get a better look at his face. He was sleeping soundly, and he looked healthy. I had to assume that the gripe water had continued to work.

"Deorn," I sounded it out the way Wood did every time I used a word he wasn't familiar with. "That's a nice name."

Her lips curled slightly at the compliment. "It was my father's name."

"The crying has stopped?"

She nodded, looking up at me sidelong through long, pale lashes. "How… how did you know what to do?"

I hesitated. This was murky water.

"I cried a lot like him when I was a baby," I finally said, deciding that was safe enough to reveal. "What I gave your baby was what my mother used to give me."

She seemed to accept it, though she continued to regard me out of startlingly pale eyes.

"Keltie says that you are one of Jackal's whores, sent here to spy on us."

I'd been inhaling the scent of the cooking; her words made me choke.

"No," I croaked, thumping myself on the chest. "I am not a whore."

She looked down, examined her boots like they held all the answers in the universe. "I suppose that Wood wouldn't have brought you here if he thought you were."

"I suppose not," I agreed, shaking my head inwardly. I'd never been called a whore in my life until I'd landed here in Bras d'Or.

"Krissa!" A stern-looking woman with iron-grey hair knotted tightly on the top of her head broke from the group of women cooking, glaring over at us. "Shouldn't you be working?"

With an apologetic glance at me, the young mother clutched Deorn tighter and scurried away.

The woman who'd scolded her strode over, making no attempt to hide her scrutiny. When I met her eyes, the hostility there sucked the breath from my lungs. "What was your business with Krissa?"

My spine stiffened. "I don't see how that's any of your business."

The woman's lips curled into a cruel smile. "One batch of herbs does not equal acceptance, lass."

"What does?" I lifted my chin.

She snorted with disgust, but when she moved away, I followed.

She led me through the village at a brisk pace, finally stopping outside a small stone building. The heat when we stepped inside took my breath away.

An entire wall was lined with stone ovens, fires roaring in each. Four young girls stood around a huge oak table, kneading the dough, and forming it into different shapes.

Is this where Keltie had made Wood's cinnamon braids? I couldn't picture the arrogant beauty getting her hands dirty.

"You will make bread." The older woman pointed me to the table. One of the young girls, a reed-thin waif with wildly curling hair, caught my eye and smiled at me in sympathy.

"You'll work with Anna." The girl who had smiled at me wiped her hands on her apron, gesturing me forward.

"Thank you, Margaret." Anna smiled at the older woman, who turned on her heel and exited the building quickly. I didn't blame her. It was unbearably hot, and I felt sweat start to pool at the small of my back.

Almond-shaped brown eyes narrowed as the girl looked me over. She shook her head. "You're not dressed for the kitchen."

I noted her lighter cotton dress—no heavy tartan for her.

I was going to get heatstroke.

She pulled a spare apron from a hook and handed it to me. Another layer. Oh, joy. Still, I tied it on, then watched as she sprinkled the wooden surface of the table with flour, then kneaded the dough.

She cut her dough in half and handed a wedge to me. "Make rolls, and place them on that sheet over there."

"All right." I pulled a piece of dough from the glob.

Make rolls. I could do this.

I placed the ball of dough between my hands and shaped it into a ball, concentrating on making a perfect sphere. When I set it on the tray, I noticed the other girls staring at me, bewildered.

"No, no." Anna pulled off a piece of dough to show me how to form it. "Like this."

"That doesn't look too hard," I said, and worked the dough through my fingers like she was. The dough was stiff, and I knew that my fingers would be sore tomorrow.

It seemed like some part of me or other had been sore since I'd landed here.

"It is hard on the fingers." She'd noticed my wince. "What did you do to Margaret to get sent here?"

"I existed, apparently." I concentrated on my dough. "How about you?"

She cast me a lopsided smile. "There was a boy."

"Ah," I said, quietly. I understood that only too well.

"I snuck out after dark."

I liked her.

"Was he worth this kind of punishment?" I asked and wiped my brow with the back of my arm. I wanted to drink a gallon of water.

A pink flush moved into her cheeks, as she nibbled on her lips like she remembered a kiss. I recognized the action because I'd been doing it all day, too.

"Yes, and I'd do it again."

I smiled at her, then focused on my rolls. When the dough grew sticky, I sprinkled the counter with an abundance of flour. I plopped the dough down, and a cloud of flour rose, directly into my face.

"Ack." I coughed, gagged, and blinked the flour from my eyelashes.

Anna laughed, then reached out and brushed her finger over my cheek. "You're a mess."

Bending forward, I wiped my eyes on my apron. I could only imagine the look on Wood's face when he saw me. I probably looked like a roll myself.

I sighed.

"I will watch Ewan at the games tonight, but I will not be able to go to him." Anna smiled at me sadly. "I sneak out because we cannot be together. Not yet."

"Why not?" I estimated her age to be around twenty, just a couple of years younger than me.

"He has not undergone his vision quest." She frowned down at her dough. "Guthrie says he is not ready, but it must be soon. He is only a little younger than me."

A vision quest? I wracked my brain, calling on my studies. A vision quest… right. That was when a boy entered a sweat lodge, which was basically a rustic sauna. The steam was meant to purify him as he meditated, and he would seek an animal spirit who would protect him in his manhood.

I thought of the white stag. Was it crazy to wonder if it was mine?

"Once he has gone through his vision quest, he will be a man. Then he can choose a wife." She grinned up at me. "He had best choose correctly."

I laughed with her as I continued to shape the dough and fill the tray with rolls. I wanted to ask her about

Wood, about who he had been before I'd met him. About what had made him who he was.

Asking someone other than him seemed like a betrayal of his trust.

I noticed Anna watching me curiously. It was obvious that she had a question.

"What is it?"

She cast a glance at the others before leaning in close to me. "Is it true that you came from the storm?"

My stomach lurched, and I darted a glance around to see if the others had heard our whispers. They were talking amongst themselves, paying us no mind, yet I lowered my voice even more. "I... what do you mean?"

"There is a story." She seemed to be choosing her words carefully. "A story of our people. That the first clansmen came from the storm."

My breath caught in my throat.

Surely...

No. Surely not.

And yet...

Was it possible that that first clansman had landed here from another time?

That meant that a passage had been opened more than once.

That meant that there was a chance, however slight, that I could find my way home.

"Are you all right?" Anna stared up at me with alarm. "It is just a story. It is not meant to be frightening."

"No, no." My voice was faint. I fanned a hand in front of my face. "It's just the heat."

"Of course." She smiled sympathetically. "We are

nearly done."

Still, I caught her eyeing me warily as I gulped for air. I needed to change the subject.

"Do you know Wood well?"

She shook her head. "He does not speak much."

That was the understatement of the century.

"Did he… has he always lived in the woods by himself?" I knew now, by Wood's admission, that he hadn't. The second I asked, I wished I could take it back. It wasn't my business unless Wood told me himself.

"No. Once he lived with Raquel. She—"

"Girls!" Margaret had returned. I cursed her mentally as Anna cut herself off. "It is time to bring out the bread."

Who on earth was Raquel?

CHAPTER TWENTY-NINE

Culture Shock

THE GIRLS HURRIEDLY piled bread and rolls into beautiful hand-woven baskets. I followed Anna as she removed the last rolls from the oven, tumbling them into a basket, hissing when the steam singed her fingers.

We followed Margaret like we were ducklings and she was our mother as she walked to a long stone building. Inside, the clansmen were seated around a single long table, metal goblets with what looked to be wine in each hand.

Guthrie sat at the head of the table. He looked directly at me when we entered, and his expression was not friendly. Next to him sat Wood, easily the largest man at the table.

"The women don't eat with the men?" I turned to Anna, my mother again squawking in my ear.

She shook her head, obviously bewildered by my question. "Of course not."

Shaking my head, I followed her lead, setting down

the bread I carried. I heated under the obvious scrutiny of every man in the room.

Hugely uncomfortably, I lifted my head, seeking Wood, and the intensity—the possession—I met when our gazes collided nearly sucked the air from my lungs. Honest to God, no man had ever looked at me like that before. A little gasp caught in my lungs, and Wood gave a slow shake of his head, broadcasting a warning.

I tore my stare away and followed the women outside, where large swathes of tartan had been spread out on the ground. "Do the women usually eat like this?"

"When the weather is good. In the winter, we eat in the kitchen where it's warm." I was off-put at first—why did the women sit on the ground while the men were at a table?—but as the fat orange sun sunk sleepily in the sky, and I seated myself on a blanket with a bowl of stew, I found that it was quite pleasant.

I noted Keltie watching me as she nibbled on a roll. After the heat of the kitchen, I didn't have the energy to deal with her, so I simply turned away.

I scooped a spoonful of stew and put it in my mouth. Flavor exploded on my tongue, and I made a sound of pleasure. "This is delicious. What is it?"

"Elk stew."

"I've never had elk before." The deer wandered into my thoughts. I pushed him right back out.

"What do you eat where you come from?" She cast me a furtive look, as though she was asking me to reveal a deep secret.

I opened my mouth to answer but hesitated. She would have no idea what I was talking about if I recited my typical grocery list—frozen pizza, Kraft Dinner, bagels, and K-cups. "Mostly beef, from a cow."

"We get beef from cow here too, and milk." She seemed satisfied with this answer.

I scooped up more of the rich, thick broth, savoring the food that wasn't fish. "What kind of games do the men play?"

I was still more than a little perturbed that the women were excluded.

"Foolish games."

I grinned at her. "Really?"

"Yes, they throw logs, or go down to the river and see who can ride the logs the longest. Most have already had too much ale and fall in, then need to be fished out before they drown. Idiots." When I chuckled, it drew the attention of Margaret, who was patrolling the perimeter of the blankets.

"I was just saying how delicious this was." I smiled brightly at the older woman. Her lips curled, but she nodded before continuing on her way.

"Shall we get warm?" Anna asked as she finished the last of her stew.

"I'd rather not go back to the kitchen." I shuddered. "This dress is as warm as a fur."

"That's not how we get warm around here." She stood, extending her hand to help me up.

I followed her as she edged away from the group of women.

"Where are we going?" I asked, remembering Wood's warning.

"The cellar." She smiled impishly. "It's where we

store the spirits."

She led me around the men's dining hall, to a series of steps that led down into the earth. I hesitated as I gazed down into the darkness.

But surely I was safe so long as I was with someone?

Anna led me down the steps. After pushing through a wooden door, she grabbed a lit torch, illuminating the room.

We stepped inside, and the dank smell of old socks hit me hard.

"Ugh," I said, and tried to breathe through my mouth.

"It's the hops they use for the ale," she explained. "I enjoy the smell."

"How can you?" I gagged. "It's like a men's locker room in here."

"What is a locker room?" She cocked her head at me questioningly.

"Never mind." I pinched my nose shut with my fingers.

She snorted as she handed me the torch. "Set this in the brazier."

I had no idea what a brazier was but concluded that it was the metal bracket on the wall. I took the torch from her and secured it the holder.

She uncorked the bottle, took a long pull from it, and handed it to me. "Try this."

I sniffed tentatively, thinking of Wood's moonshine.

"Drink!" Anna tipped the bottle. The liquid burned down my throat and I choked.

"Good, yes?" she asked, the fire lighting up her big

brown eyes.

"Strong." I coughed. "What is it?"

Anna took another swig. "Liquor. It's for the men."

She handed it back to me, and I took another drink, already feeling the effects.

"Why not for the women?" My mother would have been absolutely appalled at the gender disparity.

"Too strong. Apparently." She re-corked the bottle and put it back on the shelf. "These are for us."

From a rack, she grabbed numerous amber bottles, loading them into my arms. Once we were sufficiently weighted down, she retrieved the torch, put it back in its holder outside the building and we hurried back to the women.

We handed out the bottles as the men emerged, their raucous, drunken laughter shattering the tranquility outside. In the dimming light, my eyes sought Wood, holding a moment too long as the men swayed, lighting the torches that lined the entire perimeter of the village.

Margaret uncorked the bottles, and we all filled our goblets. My cheeks puckered at the tang of the spiced wine, but I drank it anyway, the alcohol easing the tension inside me. I sat back down next to Anna and watched the men line up.

I kept my eye on Wood, the biggest man in the group. He was obviously an outsider, his skin, hair, and size nothing like that of the clan. Still, he seemed more at ease than I'd seen him yet, engaging in banter with the other men.

This was his family, I realized. Why, then, did he not live here, among them?

A shorter, stockier man was the first to pick up a large piece of timber. His legs wobbled slightly as he walked. When he reached a red line painted in the dirt, he tossed the log. The men laughed and teased him as they took a measurement.

I sipped my wine, enjoying the flavor more and more with each drink, and watched the men all take their turns. When it was Wood's turn with the lumber, I sat a little straighter, and Anna noticed.

"You like him."

"Of course I like him." My face flamed, and I lifted my goblet to hide it. "He saved my life."

"Mmm-hmm." I angled my head to see her in the dark, a thread of vulnerability twining around my heart. She smiled reassuringly. "Don't worry; I won't tell him."

"Won't tell who what?" Keltie appeared as if from nowhere, lowering herself gracefully to a seated position beside us. Anna shifted close to me to make room for Keltie on the blanket.

"We were just enjoying the games," Anna said as she stood. "I am going to get more wine. Give me your cup."

I handed her my goblet, swaying slightly. My bladder suddenly whined. I needed to relieve myself.

"Father wants to see you now." Keltie eyed me impassively over the rim of her cup.

"What does he want?" I scanned the group of men but didn't see Guthrie among them.

"You're to meet him in the dining hall." She waved her hand at me as if to shoo me along. "Go now."

"I need a toilet first." I sighed at her blank stare. "I need to relieve myself."

She gestured again in the direction of the hall before turning her attention elsewhere. I assumed that meant that facilities of some sort were in the same direction.

The sounds of the games grew quiet at my back as I walked, and darkness enveloped me as I searched for and found the facilities. The outhouse was similar to Wood's, except with a little more privacy, which I enjoyed.

Lifting the hem of my heavy dress, I slid my underwear down to my knees. I'd been washing them almost every day since the bloomers left me feeling naked.

As I went about my business, I heard a scuffling outside, as though someone—a tipsy someone—was lurching toward me in the dark outside.

"I'm in here," I said, to alert whoever was coming my way. The rustling stopped at the sound of my voice, and unease rose.

Wood's warning slammed back into me. I'd only been thinking of the bathroom, but I'd done what he'd told me not to—I'd wandered off alone in the dark.

I hurriedly righted my clothing, anxiety rising. I slipped from the bathroom as silently as possible, arms outstretched so that I could feel the stone wall of the dining hall once I'd reached it.

I wished I'd thought to bring a torch.

The shuffling started up again, closer this time, and my pulse skittered. "Who's there?" I demanded.

There was no response.

Full-blown panic took hold, and I lifted my dress,

about to run. Rounding the corner, I collided with a solid body, a man with his weapon raised. I tried to scream, but the sound caught in my throat.

This wasn't good. This wasn't good at all.

CHAPTER THIRTY

Past Haunts

MY WORDS WERE frozen in my throat as moonlight glinted off the raised axe, but the familiar scent of Wood wrapped around me, cocooning me in an embrace of safety and comfort. I let out a small squeal, my voice no longer locked as I looked at the man who'd come to my rescue yet again.

"You wandered off." His face was furious. "I specifically told you—"

"I had to use the facilities." I wasn't in the mood to be scolded.

He growled softly, and pulled me to him for a quick squeeze. "You did not heed my warning."

I opened my mouth to speak, but he stilled. He put his hand over my mouth, muffling my words. He dipped his head, his lips near my ear. "Don't make a sound."

He straightened, and I slid my arm around his waist as he lifted his head to scour the area. One large hand gripped my arm, shifting me until I was hidden behind his body. Back against the hall's outer stone wall, a chill seeped into my skin, nipping at my bones.

I wanted to ask what was going on, what he saw in the dark that I couldn't but knew better than to open my mouth. We remained still for a long moment, then in a move that caught me off guard, he turned, slid an arm around me and ushered me away from whatever danger lurked in the surrounding forest. A moment later, I found myself inside the warm hall, but it did little to chase the chill from my body.

"Was…someone out there?" The thought that someone had been watching me, following me in the dark, brought on a hard shiver.

There was a new fierceness in his eyes when answered. "Someone or something."

I felt sick.

"You should have heeded my warning."

"Was it one of Guthrie's men?"

"I'm unsure." He scrubbed his chin, his nostrils flaring. Rage emanated from his every pore. "But if it was, he will be made aware of this treachery."

"Unless he set it up himself."

He squared shoulders that warned of power and strength and gave me a look I couldn't quite identify. "Why would he do such a thing?"

"I just… Keltie told me to meet Guthrie in the dining hall." Where we were standing right now. I looked around, but Guthrie wasn't here.

Wood's muscles flexed. "Keltie told you this?"

"Yes. She said her father had summoned me." Wood stiffened, and his dark pupils expanded in the darkness.

"Are you sure you heard her correctly?" His words were measured.

I thought for a moment, my heart still crashing against my chest, pounding in my ears as I came down from the adrenaline rush. I stepped away from Wood leaned against the long table for support, my knees still rubbery and blinked up at him. "Positive. Why?"

Instead of answering me, he stepped up to me, cupped my elbow and said, "It is time to leave."

"What's going on?"

"The night is over. It is time for us to go."

He hustled me from the hall. The sound of the games echoed, reminiscent of hearing the sound of children at play from a street over.

The night obviously wasn't over, but Wood wanted to be out of here as much as I did.

He guided me into the thick of the woods without saying goodbye to anyone, and we walked in silence. I jumped at every crack of a twig beneath my feet. Wood seemed to have a lot on his mind, so I left him with his thoughts as I considered my own.

Had Keltie been lying to me, or had her father summoned me? If he had, and I'd left with Wood, without seeing him… that wasn't good.

A light mist fell over us, and my heart leaped. The weather was changing. Perhaps lightning would strike.

"It's raining," I finally said.

"I'm aware."

Through the canopy of leaves overhead, I stopped to look at the dark sky, watched the clouds knit together. Water speckled my face, a new hope rising in me as the clouds broke open. "I need to get back to the cave," A new surge of adrenaline pumped through me.

When I looked back to Wood, he was gone, engulfed the forest. Alone, I swallowed against the sliver of fear moving through me.

"Wood," I said, my voice low, whispered, but bordering on hysteria.

"I'm here," he answered in the stillness of the forest.

I took a tentative step forward and listened. "Where are you?"

"Here," he said, and I followed his voice, stepping into a small clearing.

"What are you doing?"

He pointed upward, just as the rain started to come down harder. "There will be no storms tonight. Just rain."

"But what if—"

He put his hand on my shoulder. "There won't be."

"I need to try." I pushed away from him and started walking, determined to find my way to the cave, by myself. My life was in danger here, threatened by many, and I needed to get home.

"London," Wood said, his voice faint behind me as I started running. Damp tree branches smacked my face, and I stumbled on something. I fell, my knees hitting on a hard stump.

"Shit," I cried, but I climbed back to my feet, a few tears spilling as a new kind of desperation took hold.

"London," Wood said again, his voice closer.

"I have to try," I said, without bothering to turn around.

I kept running, with no idea where I was going. Wood knew the way. Why wasn't he helping me?

The rain fell harder, soaking my dress and boots and blurring my vision. Ignoring the discomfort, I kept pushing through the thick forest. Animals scurried in the underbrush as I disturbed them.

The trees all looked the same, and for all I knew, I was running in circles, doing nothing but exhausting myself. I pushed on, stopping once, only for a second to catch my breath as I placed a hand against a tree to keep myself from falling. Noise in the woods startled me, and I took off again.

I ran until I was breathless, until my lungs screamed at me to stop, then I when I couldn't run anymore, I sank down on the wet ground, so angry with Wood that I wanted to hit him with the twigs beneath my hands.

"Are you done?" he asked from behind me, his voice scaring the living hell out of me.

"I won't be done until I get out of this place."

He crouched down in front of me, his face close to mine. He cupped my cheeks, his hands warming my damp, muddy skin. "This isn't the way."

"Wood…"

He picked me up, and I pounded my fists against his chest.

"Take me to the cave!"

"There is nothing at the cave for you, little one." My fists stopped at the soft, intimate way he said *little one*. "I will take you when the skies open, but that is not tonight."

"How do you know for sure?"

"I am of the woods." His voice hitched.

Exhaustion crept over me, and the fight left my body. I nodded, accepting his answer. "You promise you'll take me when there's a storm."

"I will take you when there is a storm."

"Okay," I said, letting him carry me home. I could walk, but I was so damn exhausted, I just shut my mouth and let him take me back to the cabin.

Once there he deposited me in front of the fire, a wet, muddy mess. I glanced at the dress, one he'd obviously taken care to pick out for me. "I'm sorry about the dress."

"It's only fabric."

"Still, I'll wash it, try to get the stains out."

Wood handed me a clean pair of trousers and a long-sleeved shirt. As he put a few more logs into the fire and it flared to life, I turned my back to him and shimmied out of the dress. I carefully set it on the back of the chair and hurried into the warm clothes.

"Much better," I said, and when I turned, I found Wood watching me. His eyes were narrow, hungry.

I swallowed and picked the dress up. "I'll go down to the water and clean this."

He took the dress from me. "I don't want you outside alone."

"Don't worry. I'm not going to run." No, at the moment, running was futile in this foreign land.

"Stay here, keep warm," he said and disappeared out into the night.

Rain pelted against the cabin, and I had to admit it felt cozy and warm inside. Not knowing what to do with myself, I reached into the basket and pulled out the knitting needles and wool. I laughed quietly, despite my predicament. It was hard to fathom a man like Wood knitting, and yet he did.

I reached around in the basket and pulled out a few pairs of socks that he'd made, trying a pair on. They were huge, clearly made for his big feet and not mine. The door opened, and Wood came in, his clothes soaked. He paused for a moment, his gaze dropping to my feet.

"Oh, sorry," I said, and started to take the socks off, but he held his hand up to stop me.

"Keep them on."

I hold my feet out and examine the dangling socks. "Maybe now I should practice. I can make a smaller pair."

Wood tugged at his wet, flannel shirt, and slid it from his shoulders. Without a hint of modesty, he untied his trousers, and I averted my gaze. Completely naked, he turned his back to me and reached for clean clothes.

I couldn't help but look.

I lifted my gaze, let it roll down the length of him, a leisurely examination as he bent forward, to step into his pants. He tugged them up and turned my way, but I was far too slow to react.

His eyes narrowed, a hint of a smile on his mouth at having caught me staring.

"No tail," he said, and I couldn't help but laugh.

"What is it with you and tails?" I asked as I unwound the ball of yarn, only to wrap it around my fingers.

"What are you doing?" he asked, eyeing the wool.

"Not a clue."

He grabbed a chair, set it across from me. Our knees bumped, and a hot wave of awareness raced through me. He placed the half-done sock in my left hand, the spare needle in my right, then watched closely as I slowly, clumsily, imitated what he'd shown me earlier.

"Not many men knit where I'm from." I caught my tongue between my teeth as I struggled to slide the needle holding the new loop under the front needle. "How did you learn?"

The silence stretched as he watched me work painstakingly. I thought he was ignoring the question, but he finally answered.

"I learned from Jackal."

My gut tightened, bitterness coating my tongue.

"How do you... I mean..." I couldn't articulate the questions running through my head.

How had a man like Wood been lured by someone like Jackal to start?

What had happened to make Wood change?

A long moment later, he answered the words I couldn't say. "He... hurt... someone I cared very much about."

My heart pinched at the sadness in his eyes. I touched his hand, and he closed his fingers over mine. Everything about this was wrong.

"Raquel." The name Anna had mentioned slid from my lips, but the effect on Wood was electric.

His head snapped up, and rage-filled eyes latched on mine. "What do you know of Raquel?"

"Nothing," I said quickly, rearing back as anger emanated from him. "I just...Anna, the girl I met at the village, she mentioned Raquel's name. That's all."

"There is nothing more to be said."

His mood had shifted so quickly, just with the mention of one name. But the puzzle pieces now clicked together.

Wood had once been close to Jackal. Jackal had hurt someone Wood loved. Wood lived in solitude, trying to make up for something that he clearly blamed himself for.

And he clearly didn't want to talk about it.

I reached for him, but he pushed away from me. "Wood. I'm sorry. I didn't mean to upset you."

With his back to me, his shoulders sagged.

"It is not your fault." He tugged his shirt off and walked up to the bed. Big hands gripped the sheets and tugged. "Just know that so long as you are with me, Jackal will want you."

"Why?" I asked tentatively as I set the knitting back in the basket. I stood and swallowed against the thickness in my throat. Three steps took me to the bed, and I slid into the warm sheets beside him.

Wood didn't answer, so I asked another question. "Is there a way to stop him?"

Propping himself up on his elbows, he looked across the room. I followed his gaze to his axe, which was propped up beside the stove.

"Yes."

CHAPTER THIRTY-ONE

Life or Death

D AYS FLEW BY quickly in the forest. Tending to the garden, storing root vegetables, fruit, meat, and firewood took time. Everything here took longer than it did at home, but I wasn't unhappy about that.

At home, I checked my e-mail every twenty minutes and felt agitated if I couldn't read an incoming text right away. During a coffee date with a friend, it was normal for us both to check our phones four or five times over the course of an hour, our fingers always tapping, tapping, tapping on the screens, pulling up an endless stream of information to stuff into our already full brains.

It had been three long weeks since I'd lost my way, and I didn't miss my iPhone at all.

I did miss the sensation of Wood's lips against mine. He'd made no effort to kiss me again, and I certainly hadn't been brave enough to initiate.

Did I want him to kiss me again?

Of course I didn't. I needed to concentrate on finding my way home, not the closeness that was growing between us, the camaraderie, the level of trust. Yet, as much as I wanted to get home, I hadn't returned to the cave. The weather had been dry, no lightning storm in sight.

I hadn't been back to the village. Wood wouldn't allow me to return until he discovered who had been stalking me in the dark on games night.

Sitting by the river to wash clothes, I felt a shiver that had nothing to do with the frigid water. I'd been scared enough that night that I had no desire to return.

Wringing out one of Wood's flannel shirts, I lifted my head at the sound of leaves crunching. Wood was back. I smiled at that but didn't examine the little thrill that went through me too closely.

He'd gone to check on a few rabbit traps earlier. Now that he knew I wasn't going to run, he'd been leaving me alone more and more—he'd heard at the trading post that Jackal and his men were back on the mainland.

I ran my fingers over the raised scar from the man's sword. He would never be far enough away for my liking.

A gentle breeze blew over me, and my short hair brushed against my shoulders. It had grown enough that Wood was talking about cutting it again. I wasn't so sure it was necessary since Jackal hadn't been spotted in weeks.

I darted a glance around when the sound of boots crunching over leaves came closer. My heart slid into my throat when I saw a flash of black—an intruder—darting between two towering oak trees.

Abandoning the clothes, I picked up the fishing spear that I'd brought to the river. I quietly stood, sliding behind a thick tree, the trunk big enough to block me from their view.

Whistling broke the quiet, and my throat tightened. Another whistle pierced the vast emptiness, feeding my fear.

Panic tore through me, and I exhaled quietly, my breath hanging in the air like a cloud as my pulse thudded against my throat. I clutched the spear tightly in my sweaty palm.

Where was Wood?

I didn't know, but as footsteps grew closer, the crunching of the leaves inches from my ears, I had to react. As fight or flight tore through me, I pushed off the tree and ran. I ran as fast as I could, ignoring the sting of branches as they whipped across my face, slicing my cheeks and bare arms. Noise erupted behind me.

"*Où êtes-vous, cherie?*" The rumors of Jackal's men heading to the mainland were false. They were right here. "Come out and play."

Faster.

Mindful of the foliage, the rough ground beneath me, I picked up the pace, but the pounding of footsteps behind me told me I wasn't fast enough. My breath came harder, and as I fought to fill my lungs, the world spun around me.

I hopped over fallen logs, running in a direction I wasn't all that familiar with. My boots tangled with a gnarled tree root and I catapulted forward, my head slamming on the ground. The spear went flying.

Dizziness made seeing difficult, and my stomach rebelled. I gasped, fighting not to vomit, and climbed up onto wobbly legs. I held the tree for a moment, until my brain righted itself, then glanced up to choreograph my next steps.

A dark figure stood only a foot away.

"Where are you running, *putain?*" the man asked, blocking my way. He flashed rotten teeth and placed his hand on his sword, the gesture threatening.

"Oh, God," I croaked out and started backing up. I turned, but two men were closing in on me from behind. I darted a glance left, and then right. The river was one way, the forest the other. If I could get to the water, maybe I could swim away. I bolted, but the grassy embankment was damp from the morning dew, and my feet slid out from underneath me.

I landed hard, the men laughing as I tumbled, my head colliding with a rock as I splashed into the arctic water.

The laughter turned to curses as the current pulled me from the rough embankment, carrying me down the river.

Icicles formed in my veins. Panic gripped my throat as my arms flailed, looking for purchase, something, anything to grasp onto. Water filled my mouth, and I choked, only to dip under the waves and surface a few feet farther. My thoughts were scattered as I rode the angry rapids. But at that moment, I didn't care where I was going, as long as I was putting distance between the three men and myself.

I let the waves carry me, my teeth shivering and clacking so hard, I was sure they were going to break. Hypothermia would soon overtake me, putting an end to this nightmare. But I didn't want to die. Not here. Not like this. I gasped air, and struggled, catching a falling branch and hanging on for dear life. I tugged myself from the water, every inch of me soaked and shaking. I froze at the sound of a voice in the distance, but when I realized it was a woman's voice, relief washed through me. I struggled out of the river, went down on my hands and knees and crawled forward, keeping myself hidden as I climbed the embankment.

The trading post.

I picked myself up. I would head to the gate. I would see Freya. Perhaps she could guide me back to Wood.

"Grab her, Luc." I screamed as rough hands grabbed me under my arms, knocking me off my feet. The man named Luc reached out and gripped my wet shirt. It was the chemise, and soaking wet, it was completely see-through. He leered at my rigid nipples before curling the fabric in his fist and tugging me to him.

He leaned in and filled his lungs with my scent. Bile punched into my throat as I struggled to free myself.

"What shall I do with her, Henri?" Luc asked.

The bigger man reached for the string holding his trousers up. "Bend her over that barrel."

"With pleasure." Luc handled me roughly, and I bucked like an animal as Henri gripped the fabric on my pants, tugging them upward.

"*Qu'est-que c'est?*" he spit out like he was surprised to

find me in men's clothes. Thank God I was. Otherwise, my skirt would be over my head right now, and Henri would be…I couldn't even let my mind go there.

Anger and fear churned inside me. "Get your hands off me."

Before I could think better of it, I drew my hand back and slapped Luc in the face. Not stopping there, I kicked him, caught him in the shins, and he gripped my hair. He tugged hard, and I winced as his other hand dug cruelly into my elbow. "I ought to kill you right now."

The trading post loomed overhead, a fortress I couldn't breach. Safety was so close, and yet so far away.

Henri put his hand on Luc's shoulder. He smiled at me cruelly, his lips twisted as he stared at me lewdly. "Jackal wants her alive. But that doesn't mean we can't have some fun with her first."

My heart raced in my too-tight chest, and I was certain they could hear it. I struggled, but Henri's hands tightened on my waist as he pushed himself against me. I cried out as something warm, something that filled my mouth with the taste of pennies, trickled down my face.

Blood.

Rage, dark and dangerous pulsed in the air, and I fought against it, struggled to free myself, as they two men shoved me toward the barrel. I dug my heels in. Dirt kicked up beneath my dragging feet, caking on my skin and clothes.

"Wood will be here any second," I said, trying to stall, buy myself some time.

One of the men froze for a brief second, but then laughed. "Wood is nowhere near here," he said, and I knew he was right. He was back at the cabin checking his rabbit traps.

I pushed at them again, but their hold was too strong to break, and I was weak from my ride down the river. Still, I struggled, and kicked and bit their dirty flesh, until a slap came across my face so hard it nearly snapped my jaw out of place.

"Restrain her." Jackal's bellowing voice from behind made me jump, and I sucked in a sharp breath, failing miserably at showing no fear. Cheek stinging, I angled my head to see him, and a savagery I'd never met before seared his eyes as he circled me. My stomach plummeted. He wanted to hurt me in ways I couldn't even imagine. *Was* going to hurt me in ways I couldn't comprehend.

He stopped in front of me, stared at me for a long time, his alcohol-sour breath bringing water to my eyes. "You turn me down only to climb into Wood's bed?"

The calmness of his voice belied the hate in his eyes, the rage emanating from his body. His hand circled my neck, squeezed slightly. "And yet I saw you first, so by rights you should be mine."

My gaze left him, searching, hunting for escape, and that's when I saw a flash of flannel. My knees nearly gave way as a cry lodged in my throat.

I spat in his face.

"*Putain!*" As Jackal roared, I looked over his shoulder. Wood stepped from the shadows, breathing hard, sweat pouring down his face. I had no idea how he'd known to come, but I'd never been so happy to see him.

Our eyes locked, held tight. I gave him a pleading, apologetic look, knowing I was putting him and his clan in danger once again.

"I grow weary of this game, Jackal." Wood's body was so tightly strung, I feared his muscles would snap.

Jackal stilled, then twisted slowly, turning me with him, and his men flanked him. His hand around my neck tightened, his fingers biting into my skin. He gave a humorless laugh.

"Why don't you give this up and rejoin us," he said. "I'll let you have your whore back."

"Take your hands off her."

"Now you know that is not going to happen," he said, his accent so thick I could barely make out his words.

"She has nothing to do with us."

"She does now."

"Jackal."

"You came looking for her, just as I knew you would. You always protect what's yours, even though this *putain* rightfully belongs to me. I found her first."

Wood briefly met my eyes, hard, cold, murderous. I sucked in a breath and held it. Jackal laughed. "Ah, but no wonder you are weary. We've played this exact game before, though it has been so long."

Jackal ran a finger along my face, and when he pulled it away, it was stained with blood. He slowly licked it away, making my stomach turn.

"She is sweet." He smiled beatifically at Wood. "Though perhaps not as sweet as Raquel."

"*Chlanna nan con thigibh a' so 's gheibh sibh feòil!*"

This time I recognized the battle cry of the clan. I choked as Jackal's hand tightened around my throat.

Guthrie and more men than I could count flew from the woods, ululations piercing the sky. I focused in on their tartans, their swords, drawing from their strength.

None of them had runes painted on with clay. They must have hurried here, too.

Jackal cursed, his attention veering from me. I jabbed him in the stomach with an elbow, a hard sucker punch. His hold loosened as the air left his lungs, and I jerked away, running to hide behind the barrel that they had threatened to bend me over.

I wanted to taste Jackal's blood as he'd tasted mine, but I wasn't an idiot. I was unarmed, and I was weak. The best thing I could do was get the hell out of the way.

I peeked over the lid of the barrel, heart hammering in my chest, in time to see Wood charge his archenemy. Swords clashed, ringing in my ears. Warrior cries pierced the morning as birds took flight. I took in the battle. Everything in what I was witnessing felt too unreal, surreal, overwhelming.

I glanced around for a weapon. I needed to help, to fight. I found a rock, weighted it in my hand as swords broke the skin, and blood spilled, staining the dirt ground a deep coppery red.

I stole a glance at my bearded warrior, his features hard as his axe clashed against Jackal's sword. His eyes were a strange shade of iron as he focused his entire being on the battle.

A howl sounded, and I looked over my shoulder to see one of the clan members drop to the ground, crimson blood leaving his blood in short spurts.

All of the first-aid I'd ever learned raced through my

mind as I sprinted for the injured man. Flinging myself to the ground beside him, I scrabbled at my soaking chemise, ripping a strip from the fabric.

Spurting meant arterial. Arterial meant death.

"London, get back!" Wood broke from the fight long enough to shout my way. I shook my head, trying to wrap my pitiful tourniquet around the fallen warrior's leg.

With Wood's attention momentarily diverted, Jackal jogged backward, a piercing whistle leaving his lips. He retreated with his men, running for the river, ready to finish this battle another day.

I crawled over the wounded warrior. "You're going to be okay," I said, a bold-faced lie. I could see his life leaving him, one spurt at a time.

More voices sounded—more people arriving. The gate of the trading post was open, and people rushed to see what had happened.

"Where is your healer?" My voice was hysterical. I'd never seen anyone die. I didn't know how to handle this. "Please, where is Freya?"

I found her face in the crowd. She looked from the man to me and slowly shook her head.

The man below me gasped, one deep breath, and as he let it out, his body relaxed. Tears poured down my face, my chest too tight to breathe.

"London," Wood said after a long moment.

I couldn't look at him. I couldn't take the anger on his face, the disappointment. What had happened here was my fault. This man would be alive if it weren't for me. I shouldn't be here. I needed to go home. Now.

"Bring him home," Guthrie said.

Wood captured my elbow and helped me to his feet. I sagged against him. The clan gathered around the dead man, lifting him onto their shoulders before retreating into the woods, leaving me alone with Guthrie and Wood.

"I'm so sorry," I croaked out. "I didn't mean for any of this to happen. I was washing clothes in the river when the men attacked. I got carried here in the rapids."

Guthrie's stare was chilling. When I looked into his eyes, I saw grief over his fallen clansmen. "Punishment for putting the clan in danger, and for the loss of a good warrior, is exile or fifty lashes."

A strange stillness settled over me. Wood's hand around my waist tightened.

Guthrie held his spear up to cut Wood off. The air changed, charged, grew thick as he turned his glare on me "Choose."

I straightened. This was my fault. I would make it right.

"I will take the lashes." I felt Wood sag against me.

"London, no." His grip on me tightening, he faced Guthrie, spine again straight. "There is another way."

Guthrie's mouth fell open with shock. He slammed the tip of his sword into the earth as he shook his head.

"Wood. No!"

*Loved Wood? Find out how to connect with us in our bios and get an alert for the release of **Bound**, the next full-length novel in the Wood saga!*

Confessions of a Bay Boy Professor

Excerpt

Copyright 2017 Cathyrn Fox

Justin

ANOTHER WEEKEND. ANOTHER party.

I need to give this shit up.

I swirl the amber liquid in my glass and glance around the bar to take in the group of loud girls partying around me. I try to find the one I'd just danced for in a private party room off the main bar. I'm not really sure why I'm looking for her. She's just another girl in a sea of women I dance for once in a while.

My gaze lands on her, sitting at the other end of the bar, uncomfortable, nervous and so goddamn beautiful my dick swells.

Okay, maybe I do know why I'm looking for her. I've been doing this gig for a long fucking time, and none of the girls I danced for were ever like her. The guys and I started dancing at parties to for cash when we were in college, and well, maybe my reasons had more to do with rebellion than money. The business flourished and spread to other states, and even though none of us need the money, we now dance when we have to fill in, or for kicks. But I'm tired of flying around, putting on a mask and shaking my cock in some drunk girl's face. But this girl, well, she's been nursing a drink for the last hour, and doesn't seem at all like the kind who would enjoy a half naked guy shaking his junk at her.

I catch her gaze, and hold it for a minute. She quickly turns away and my cock swells at her shyness. Shit. She's way too young and innocent for me. I have no idea what her story is or why her friends would hire me to dance for her twenty-first birthday, and I should leave it at that. If I knew what would good for me, I would.

But, fuck it. I rarely go with what's good for me, which is why I'm sitting on a goddamn bar stool in Virginia sipping on a scotch when I should be back at Penn State, grading papers. I'm bored with that job, too. But dear old dad is the dean, and while I had different career aspirations, both he and mom pushed me into education—hence my rebellious stage.

I swallow the rest of the liquid, let it burn its way down my throat. I don't normally stay for a drink after a gig, but tonight, I don't know, there's something about the birthday girl that's throwing me off. I pick up the backpack at my feet, the one stuffed with my dance clothes and mask, a necessity for me now. I'm a fucking psych professor, for Christ's sakes. Ever hear of a code of conduct? Yeah, well, I'm violating every rule I promised to uphold.

I really need to give this shit up.

I toss the bag over one shoulder and stand. The heat in the room, as well as the mixed scent of alcohol and perfume, washes over me. I'm anxious to get the hell out of here. Looks like the recipient of my dance is, too.

I push through the lively crowd, and slide in beside her at the bar. Her body goes stiff, and shit, I'm pretty sure I'd do anything to help her relax.

"Hey," I say.

She nibbles her bottom lip. Sexy as hell.

Fuck me.

I shift, and lean on the bar so she can't see my swelling cock.

"Hi," she says.

"Not really your scene, is it?"

She crinkles her nose. "Am I that obvious?"

"Yeah, a little bit." I take a glance around. "Want to get out of here? Walk the beach?"

Her back stiffens, and her chest juts out, her lovely nipples pressing against the silk of her blouse. "I don't even know you."

It's true. She doesn't. I was in costume when I danced for her, so no way can she know I'm the guy her friends hired to shake it in her face. I take in her wide blue eyes. So fucking innocent she's killing me.

Desperate to put her at ease, I shrug. "I don't know you either. How do I know once we're outside you won't try to get me out of my clothes and have your way with me?"

She smiles, and it rocks my fucking world. "I really could use some fresh air…"

I pick up on her hesitation. "Pass me your phone."

What the fuck am I doing?

Breaking all kinds of rules tonight, that's what I'm fucking doing.

"Why do you want my phone?" she asks as she slides it across the sticky bar top.

I hold it up, and take a selfie. "There, now you have my picture. If I try anything you don't like, you'll have my mug shot for the police."

She looks at me like I'm a bit insane. Maybe I am, because I should really leave this alone. She reaches for her purse, and I say, "Do you need to tell a friend?"

Her gaze flickers to the dance floor, but none of her friends are paying any attention to her. Girls are supposed to look out for one another when partying—come together and go together. But it doesn't look like she's made that pact with any of these drunk party girls. She frowns, a hint of loneliness ghosting her eyes, and my heart squeezes. At least she's in good hands with me. She's sweet and innocent and I don't—okay I do, but won't—want anything more from her than a conversation.

"Yeah, let's get out of here," she says.

"Wait." I pull out my phone and take a picture of her. "There, now if you try anything I don't like, I'll have your mug shot."

She blinks, surprised and I put my hand on the small of her back and guide her out the door. The night air is warm, sticky, but it's a break from the heat and bodies inside. I breathe deeply as the waves laps against the sand in the distance.

"I'm Justin, by the way."

"Violet."

Pretty, just like her.

The music becomes faint as we remove our shoes

and step onto the sand. She exhales and runs the warm grains between her painted toes. *Painted toes.* Fuck, that's sexy, too.

Don't go there, dude.

"Can I ask a question?"

Her long curls bounce around her face and she purses her pouty, heart-shaped mouth as her big blue eyes meet mine. "You can ask, but it doesn't mean I'll answer."

Beautiful and funny.

A dangerous combination.

She doesn't know I'm the guy who danced for her, so I need to word my question carefully. "What were you doing at the bar? It doesn't seem like it's your kind of scene."

"It's not really. I work with those girls. We're not close, so I guess that's how they thought I should celebrate my twenty-first birthday."

"I've only known you for five minutes and I would never throw you a party like that."

"No? Then what would you do?" she asks.

I take in her skirt, the sleeveless silk blouse she has tucked into the hem, and say, "Quiet dinner, walk on the beach."

"You can tell all that from looking at me."

"Gut feeling." I'm not about to tell her I'm a psychology professor and study behavior and mind. Her behavior tonight told me everything I needed to know. She's a good girl, and I need to stay away.

She arches a brow. "You're pretty intuitive."

"You're beautiful." Shit. I hadn't meant to say that.

Fucking just slipped out. I don't want her to think I'm coming on to her. She turns from me, and looks at the water. I'm pretty sure she's about to run the other way. I'm a stranger, eight years older than her, and I'm probably coming off like a stalker.

"Race you to the water," she says, and takes off. "Last one there has to go skinny dipping."

Skinny dipping?

I stand still for a moment, processing that as her skirt flies around her backside and she darts to the waves. She's not the kind of girl to go skinny-dipping, of that I'm certain. My brain kicks in and I chase after her. When I catch her, she's laughing and breathless.

Jesus fuck, the sound goes straight through me, and zaps what little control I seem to have around her. I touch her face, my thumb sweeping across her cheek. Her laugh dies and her eyes go wide as they latch onto mine.

"Violet."

"Yeah?"

"I really want to kiss you."

A moment of hesitation, then, "Okay."

I step into her, meshing my hardness with her softness. Sweet fuck, my cock grows another inch, and she gives a little gasp when she feels it. "Sorry," I say, but somehow I'm not. I actually want her to know she's beautiful, see what she does to me. I dip my head, and softly, lightly brush my lips over hers, not wanting to hurry the moment I might never have again.

A moan escapes her throat and I slide my hand to the back of her neck as I increase the pressure. I push my tongue in and we tangle. I catch the taste of the syrupy drink she'd been nursing, but it's not nearly as sweet as her. I close my eyes, savor, enjoy, drown in her flowery scent and taste. I'm only half aware as her hands snake around my back, her questing fingers splaying, touching, exploring my body.

I want to do the same.

Using slow movements so as not to scare her, I sweep my hands lower, run my fingers along her vertebrae until I'm at the small of her back. The sweet curve of her ass calls out to me. I dare to go lower and cup her roundness, and massage lightly as I pull her against my cock.

A sound lodges in her throat as she breaks from the kiss. I pull my hands away, and take in the flush on her cheeks as wide eyes stare up at me. Okay, now I've gone to far. She's going to run.

"You lost," she says on a breathless whisper.

Her words are a jumbled mess in my lust-filled brain. "Lost?"

"The race."

It only takes a second for my thoughts to catch up. Holy fuck. Is she serious?

Here I thought she was going to bolt, only for her to be staring at me, waiting for me to shed my clothes.

Fine, I'll play it her way. For now.

Christmas Sanctuary

Excerpt by Lauren Hawkeye

Copyright 2017 by James Patterson

FROM ABOVE, SALT Spring Island resembled three chunks of land that some unseen hand had smooshed together, a solid-looking mass furred by pine trees covered in snow.

So much snow.

Thanks to the modern wonder that was social media, Emma had quickly tracked her father to the tiny Canadian island off the coast of Vancouver. There had been no denying that the man in the Facebook photos was the right Michael Nagorski. In fact, she'd gotten quite a jolt when she'd first clicked on his profile.

Emma looked nothing like her mother, who was of average height with curves that she controlled carefully through strict diet and rigorous exercise. She had sleek dark hair that always looked like she'd come straight from the beauty salon.

Emma, on the other hand? Emma was tall and slender, like she'd never quite gotten over the gawky phase of adolescence. Her hair was so blonde it was nearly white, like corn silk, and her eyes, set in a pale ivory face, were the light blue of ice. Next to her mother, she'd always felt washed out, a photocopy that didn't quite capture the detail of the original.

Looking at the photo of Michael Nagorski, Emma finally understood where her unusual coloring had come from. The man didn't have many pictures uploaded, and those he did were all candid, preventing her from getting a clear look at his face, but there were things that leapt right off the screen—the sunshine-colored hair, the ghost-white skin, often reddened with a sunburn since he clearly didn't share Emma's affection for SPF 50.

Yes, she believed that he was her father. And that was why, two and a half weeks before Christmas, she was one of five passengers seated in a tiny Cessna 208 seaplane, clutching her stomach to keep it from rolling as the pilot landed on the rollicking waves and maneuvered them into the dock.

When she set foot on the wooden planks, she gulped in the brisk air, and her stomach settled slightly. Once the nervous sweat dried from her brow, though, she quickly decided that *brisk* wasn't quite the right descriptor.

"Wow." Wrapping one arm around her waist against the cold, she grabbed for the handle of her practical brown suitcase and hurried toward the two taxis that waited by the small building at the end of the dock. Goosebumps prickled her arms as the light wind bit through her thick sweater.

She'd read up on local weather before she'd left Georgia. The temperatures had been about half of what they were back home, but all of her research said that the Vancouver area was mild compared to some regions of

Canada. Being here now, with dampness hanging over the frigid air, heavy as wet wool, she was pretty sure she wasn't going to be touring anywhere else in the large country anytime soon.

The driver of the taxi shoved Emma's suitcase into the trunk and she sighed with relief as she scrabbled to get into the backseat, where the dry blast of warmth from the heater chased the chill from her skin. A faded Santa Claus ornament hung from the rear-view mirror, making her grin. Pulling out her phone, she read off an address, then settled back in the seat to catch her breath.

She was really here. She'd really done it. She'd called off the wedding, and she'd gone against her mother's orders to leave well enough alone.

She was going to meet her birth father.

Outside the window, the greenery was a snow-laden blur as the taxi headed inland from the dock. Emma couldn't focus on it with the nerves that were suddenly doing a tap dance in her belly.

What would this man who had supplied half of her genetic code be like?

It was a curious thing, discovering that what she'd believed all her life had been a lie. She'd never known Sawyer Kelly, the man her mother had created as her father figure, so she'd never loved him, not exactly. Still, the loss of that ideal had hurt, or maybe it was more that it had turned her life upside down when she thought her path was finally set.

She knew half of her story, but the rest was unwritten. Or rather, it was written, she just couldn't read the pages. She knew that she looked like him… Michael…

her father... what was she supposed to call him? Yes, she looked like him, but she didn't know anything else. His Facebook profile had helped her track him to an art gallery in Vancouver, and, from there, his studio on this small island. So she knew her father was an artist who focused in sculpture, but until she met him, what meaning did a fact like that have?

"This is it." The cabdriver, a man with his plaid sleeves rolled up like it was the middle of summer, stopped the taxi in front of what appeared to be a shabby double garage, the cornflower blue paint faded and even peeling in some places. One of the doors was open, and Emma could see sparks emitting from inside.

Was her father in there right now, working on one of his pieces? Would he be happy to see her? Angry? Shocked? How would she feel in return—what would replace this gnawing anxiety that she couldn't seem to shake?

She paid the driver, having to look closely at the change he gave her in return, certain he was shorting her because it was all coins, but apparently in Canada there were no one or two dollar bills. It only enhanced the sensation that she was Alice, and she was steps away from falling down the rabbit hole.

The snow in the driveway was a milky blanket, untouched until she stepped gingerly forward, wary of ice beneath her ankle boots, which she was becoming increasingly more aware were inappropriate for the weather. Behind her she tugged her suitcase, which left stripes from the wheel tracks in the snow.

This was it. She'd literally left prints here—there was

no leaving and pretending that none of this had ever happened. Sucking in a deep breath, she looked up, studying the string of Christmas lights draped crookedly from the roof. The string alternated red and green, except for a swatch by the open door, where two reds stood beside each other. The change in sequence caught her eye, held it, and her fingers twitched with the need to pull the string of lights down and fix it.

Get a grip, Emma. They're Christmas lights. Not a big deal. They don't have to be perfect.

Except, up until a few days ago, she'd lived with the notion that that was exactly how her life was supposed to be—perfect. Anything that marred that image was cause for upset.

She didn't want to be the person who had to fix the pattern in a string of stupid Christmas lights to feel comfortable or even happy. It spurred her forward, the sound of her steps marred by the white carpet underfoot.

The sound started as a quiet discordant buzz, and by the time she stood in the open door it had intensified, similar to sizzling bacon in a frying pan. The garage was of an average size, but crowded with what at first glance was junk and at second was scrap metal and tools. There was so much clutter that it almost blocked any sign of life, but from the corner emitted those sparks that Emma had first seen from the end of the driveway.

Was that her father?

"Hello?" The crackling noise drowned her out, so she slowly skirted a pile of jagged metal. On the other side, bent over a work bench, was a tall, sweaty man. Dressed in ripped jeans and a filthy white undershirt, his face was obscured by a visor, but even if she hadn't been able to see a shock of chestnut hair, she would have known that this wasn't her father.

Have mercy. Setting aside his—was that a welding torch?—the man straightened, lacing his fingers together and stretching his arms out over his head as he studied the thing he'd been working on—a sculpture. The movement caused the fitted cotton of his shirt to rise up, giving Emma a glimpse of rock solid abdomen, and she was pretty sure that her mouth actually watered.

Have mercy was right. Just looking at him, she had to stomp down the urge to go run her hands over the exposed skin. The need shocked her, because she'd never felt that kind of raw attraction for Matthew—Matthew, the man she'd been about to marry.

This man was a stranger—one whose face she still hadn't seen—and he was in her father's studio. Her father didn't seem to be anywhere around.

So who the heck *was* this guy?

NICK WASN'T SURE how he knew someone was there, but something made him look away from his work. Standing not five feet away from his worktable was a leggy blonde dressed in fitted black pants and a thick, pale pink sweater. Her hair, a startling shade of white blonde, was pulled back neatly in a ponytail, and her arms were tightly crossed in an obvious attempt to ward off the cold that Nick didn't feel when he was working.

Annoyed at the interruption, he shoved his visor up

off of his face. The woman's lips formed a soft 'o' as she made a breathy little sound that caught his attention.

"Like what you see?" He grinned as his sudden desire shoved away any irritation he felt at the disruption. "I've got more I can show you if you're interested."

This time when she inhaled sharply, the sound carried insult.

"I'm looking for Michael Nagorski." Her voice—wow. If he'd been intrigued by her just because of the way her sweater hugged her curves, he was downright turned on by the slow drawl in her voice, sweet as a ripe peach. "I was told I could find him here."

"Just you and me here." Tugging off his protective mask and elbow-length gloves, he tossed them on the table and picked up his bottle of water, chugging half of it down in big, messy gulps. "And much as I like being all up close with you, you're going to want to step back a bit. Be a shame for these sparks to hit that pretty face of yours."

She frowned, her eyes narrowing, and he felt—almost—like he should bite his tongue. He'd perfected his flirtatious patter, and on the island here, even back on the mainland, it worked just fine.

This woman clearly wasn't impressed. Nor was she moving to do what he said—instead she stayed exactly where she was. "You're wearing far less than I am. That can't be safe."

He shrugged the comment off. Yeah, he should be fully covered when he worked. No, he wasn't going to change his work uniform, now or ever. When he wore too much clothing, his creativity was stifled. He'd rather risk the scars.

Not that the piece he was working on was going all that well, anyway. Furrowing his brow, he glared over at the shelf that held Michael's most recent creations. His mentor had never been blocked. Probably because he did his best work when he was depressed, a pretty habitual state of being for him.

That sweet Southern drawl melted into his consciousness again, drawing his attention back to the woman standing in his garage.

"What was that?" He set his now empty water bottle back on the table.

"I said, when do you reckon he'll be back?" The look in her pale blue eyes was full of exasperation, and something about the way she compressed her lips tugged at his mind.

She looked like… no. No way.

"Who are you, exactly?" Stepping closer, he watched her spine straighten as he looked her up and down. The *Game of Thrones* dragon-lady hair color… the tall, slender frame. The same crinkle of frustration that Nick had seen on Mike's face a million times, usually directed at him.

"My name is Emma Kelly." Her words floated in honey, sweet and heavy. So different from Mike's clearly enunciated voice.

She wasn't old enough to be a sibling, yet the resemblance was undeniable. The next logical relation would be a daughter.

"I'm his… it seems that Mr. Nagorski would be… my father." Well. That confirmed it.

Mike had never mentioned a daughter to Nick. Not that it was any of his business, but he was surprised. Shocked, actually. He'd met Mike ten years ago when he'd signed with the same agent as the older man. Mike hadn't been too happy when Hannah had pushed him into mentoring her new client, and Nick hadn't been overly thrilled to be receiving advice from someone who was so sure he was right all the time. Somehow they'd pushed through their differences, and Nick was pretty sure he was the closest friend that Mike had. Hell, the whole reason that he was on Salt Spring Island in the first place was to keep an eye on his friend, who was prone to slip into deep depressive episodes without someone nudging him along.

Okay, that was about half the reason. But it was a generous half. Mike was an anti-social creature, happier when he was alone in the studio or camping in the woods, and Nick knew he was pretty much the only confidante that the other man had. Which was why he was startled that he'd never heard even a whisper of a daughter from his friend.

The woman—Emma—cleared her throat, and Nick realized that she was waiting for more information. Where she could find Mike, probably, or when he would be back.

His attention was caught on her lips again as she ran a delicate pink tongue over them, leaving a sheen of moisture behind. His instinct once again was to hit on her, to let deliberately cocky words and his usual arrogant charm draw her into his bed. Or onto his worktable—that would work, too.

It occurred to him that the reason Mike had never mentioned her might be because he didn't know she existed. As his friend, the best thing Nick could do was get her out of the way long enough for him to give his friend some warning.

Pulling his attention away from those full lips again, he felt a strangely strong surge of disappointment. Nick usually used sex to help him achieve that blankness of mind that he needed to chase away his grief, but he suspected that if he had this Southern treat beneath him, it would be more than that.

She was Mike's daughter. And there was no way he would hurt his closest friend by sleeping with his kid. Especially if Mike didn't know he had one. So, she had to go. And he'd learned the best way to chase women off was just to be himself—after all, there was a thin line between arrogant charm and asshole.

"Well, baby, I'm afraid Mike isn't going to be coming back anytime soon," he said as he turned back to his torch, reaching for his gloves. "So unless you want to stick around and *entertain* me until he is, I'm going to have to ask you to go."

About Cathryn Fox

New York Times and *USA today* Bestselling author, Cathryn is a wife, mom, sister, daughter, and friend. She loves dogs, sunny weather, anything chocolate (she never says no to a brownie) pizza and red wine. She has two teenagers who keep her busy with their never ending activities, and a husband who is convinced he can turn her into a mixed martial arts fan. Cathryn can never find balance in her life, is always trying to find time to go to the gym, can never keep up with emails, Facebook or Twitter and tries to write page-turning books that her readers will love.

Connect with Cathryn

Newsletter:
app.mailerlite.com/webforms/landing/c1f8n1

Twitter:
twitter.com/writercatfox

Facebook:
facebook.com/AuthorCathrynFox

Blog:
cathrynfox.com/blog

Goodreads:
goodreads.com/author/show/91799.Cathryn_Fox

Pinterest:
pinterest.com/catkalen

About Lauren Hawkeye

New York Time and USA Today bestselling author Lauren Hawkeye never imagined that she'd wind up telling stories for a living… though when she looks back, it's easy to see that she's the only one who is surprised. Always "the kid who read all the time", Lauren made up stories about her favorite characters once she'd finished a book… and once spent an entire year narrating her own life internally. No, really. But where she was just plain odd before publication, now she can at least claim to have an artistic temperament.

Lauren lives in the Rocky Mountains of Alberta, Canada with her husband, two young sons, pit bull and two idiot cats, though they do not live in an igloo, nor do they drive a dogsled. In her nonexistent spare time Lauren can be found knitting, reading anything she can get her hands on, or sweating her way through spin class. She loves to hear from her readers!

Connect with Lauren

Newsletter:
eepurl.com/OeF7r

Facebook:
facebook.com/LaurenHawkeye

Instagram:
instagram.com/laurenhawkeyeauthor

www.ingramcontent.com/pod-product-compliance
Lightning Source LLC
Chambersburg PA
CBHW051640180726
48284CB00006B/1799